HOSPITAL ANGEL

Jess Levins

Published by Jess Levins aka Omega Writings, 2023.

HOSPITAL ANGEL

First edition. February 27, 2023.

Copyright © 2023 Jess Levins.

ISBN: 979-8986773209

Written by Jess Levins.

COPYRIGHT & DISCLAIMER

Library of Congress Cataloging-in-Publication Data
ISBN 979-8-9867-7320-9 Paperback
ISBN 979-8-9867-7321-6 eBook
Created in the United States of America

THE HEALER

"I am not a God, and I cannot perform miracles. I am simply a person who has been given the rights and responsibilities to be a healer. I pledge to myself and all who can hear me that this is what I shall become."

Excerpt from *The Oath of the Healer* 1991
by Louis Weinstein, M.D., Ph.D.

ACKNOWLEDGMENT

A special thanks to Adena Pavkov for proofing the initial draft and providing excellent feedback.

FOR MY DAUGHTER
JILL A. LEVINS

CHAPTER 1 SELECTING WHO WILL LIVE

Doctor Angel Carpenter was happy working at the Christian Health Hospital in Miami. The faith-based non-profit hospital treated over two hundred thousand cancer patients each year, and Angel was now one of over two hundred physicians providing care to these patients. He had just implemented a controversial holistic approach for treating selected cancer patients while testing a new cancer drug. Most of the doctors and staff were supportive or neutral, but one doctor went out of his way to be inimical toward him. Angel was not overly concerned with these attitudes since he had the support of the hospital's Board of Directors. He hoped such support would give him time to win over the neutral doctors and hospital staff he would interact with on a daily basis.

The hospital administrative support was based upon the sizeable medical grant he had received from a pharmaceutical corporation. The corporation wanted to see if Angel could improve the cure rate of a new semi-universal cancer drug recently approved by the FDA for expanded human testing. A private foundation provided a secondary grant. These two grants would provide significant revenue to the hospital to offset the continued reduction in payments by the healthcare organizations and Medicare. Besides handling patients assigned by the hospital, Angel would select fifty patients initially to be the first group in a Phase Three Clinical Trial using this new cancer drug. He would add twenty-five additional patients each week until he reached one hundred. There were over twenty-five hundred active cancer patients being cared for by doctors at the hospital and around five hundred were terminal. The terminal group is where he would get his initial patients. Many in the terminal group were inpatients, while others were cared for on an outpatient basis.

He was dreading the selection process. Those selected would have the possibility of living while the ones not chosen would die. Also, he would have to be severely strict with some potential candidates to ensure they were committed to following a holistic lifestyle, which was an essential part of the trial. He required them to be one hundred percent committed. He believed in the drug trial and had staked his reputation on the approach he was taking.

Angel had only recently received his Doctor of Osteopathic Medical Degree. Many considered the MD Degree to be more prestigious than a DO Degree. However, Angel preferred the more holistic approach to medicine, since he had used it to prolong his father's life.

Angel enthusiastically explained this holistic approach to the hospital directors during his presentation, which was his second presentation at a hospital. Ten of the twelve directors attended his presentation, and all the directors were physicians. It surprised him the discussion following the presentation was significantly more rigorous, primarily due to one director who wanted control over the grants.

Angel, in his presentation, stated: "The Tyzugmod Corporation cancer drug is effective in curing specific types of cancers. These curable cancers represent approximately half of all the various types of cancers. Unfortunately, the cancer drug is only about forty percent effective. This means we can reduce the fatality rate of cancer by twenty percent worldwide. However, while working at the Tyzugmod Cancer Research Center, I used a holistic approach to analyze the transgenic mouse models used to develop the cancer drug. The results conclusively showed that mice with a better diet had a slightly higher survival rate. Mice in larger pens had a slightly higher survival rate, which could be associated with less stress. Also, mice with a more normalized weight had a slightly higher survival rate. After much data analysis and computer simulations, I postulated two theories. My first hypothesis is that mice with a single item of improved physical or mental health had a slightly higher survival rate from cancer. My second hypothesis is that mice with multiple improvements in physical and mental health will have a significantly higher survival rate from cancer. The simulation projects the cure rate using the cancer drug could exceed eighty percent if we implement all health items simultaneously."

Angel looked around and saw his audience was still with him. "The medical community has been telling the world that smoking is bad for your health, reduces your life expectancy, and causes cancer, but twenty percent of the people in the world still smoke. Obesity is a leading cause of health problems, including an increase in cancer, but over forty percent of the adult population in the United States is obese. Everyone knows exercise improves your health and increases your life expectancy, but only a little over twenty percent get the minimum level of exercise for good health. People want to be healthy but do not have the discipline to live a healthy lifestyle in their current environment. The holistic approach associated with this drug trial places the patient in a controlled environment where they have no choice concerning diet, exercise, and proper mental health."

Angel paused and took a drink of water. He scanned his audience. They were still paying attention, and several nodded in agreement. "Human trials with small sample sizes were approved and conducted, but as I have already mentioned, the cure rate was only forty percent. At the Tyzugmod Corporation, I showed my supervisor the computer projections of the proposed holistic approach coupled with their new cancer drug. The supervisor arranged for me to present my proposal to their corporate directors.

At the Tyzugmod director's meeting, I explained how I would like them to sponsor a trial at a hospital with terminal cancer patients, and they approved the funding for my proposed drug trial. They also planned to use my proposal to conduct other human trials with a less robust, holistic approach. Patients are cured in twelve weeks when the cancer drug works. As approved by the FDA, the drug trial will start with one hundred patients, and if everything works as planned, a replacement group will enter the drug trial every twelve weeks. Are there any questions?"

The hospital directors were quiet for only a few seconds. "Doctor Carpenter, I commend you on obtaining these rather large grants," Director Andrew said. "However, you do not have the administrative and medical experience to be in charge of these grants. To accept you and these grants, the hospital needs to appoint a senior doctor to oversee this project."

"That would not be acceptable," Angel responded. "As far as experience, while earning my medical degree, I spent the summers working full time with the researchers at the pharmaceutical corporation that developed the cancer drug. Also, I continued to work at Tyzugmod on a part-time basis while completing my medical degree. Plus, I have direct access to the doctors and scientists at Tyzugmod. These same individuals will review my reports for this Phase Three Clinical Trial. If the trial results for the initial two years are positive, then the FDA should fully approve the drug. Upon FDA approval, the dollar amount of the grants will be increased and extended for four additional years. During the extension, the hospital will continue to send data to Tyzugmod and serve as a model for other cancer centers. For this project to be successful, I need complete control."

Director Andrew did not even try to control his anger. "And if we do not agree with your demand for control?"

"Then I will conduct the trial at a hospital that has already agreed to my proposal."

Director Andrew's face flushed with anger. He was too mad to make an additional retort. Other directors asked medical questions concerning the actual treatment of the patients. These conversations were entirely positive. Director Jenkins, the Treasurer, asked for additional details on the applications of the funds.

"Tyzugmod will provide the cancer drug free for each patient accepted into the trial," Angel said. "Plus, funds from the second grant will cover all the hospital's associated administrative expenses. The funds from the grants will reimburse the hospital for its actual costs."

Now, all the directors were smiling except for Director Andrew. Angel answered two more questions regarding the selection of patients. Then, Chairperson Stanford asked Angel to wait outside the conference room while they discussed his proposal. Twenty minutes later, they asked Angel to return to the meeting room.

"Congratulations," Chairperson Stanford said with a pleased look. "We have unanimously accepted your proposal."

All the directors were smiling and nodding their approval except for Director Andrew. Director Andrew had reluctantly voted with the other directors for political reasons when he realized it was going to be approved.

Angel spent the weekend relaxing since he knew it might be a long while before he would have free time again. He had reviewed the files of all the terminally ill cancer patients and was ready to start the selection process.

It was Monday morning and time to meet his first potential patient, Robert Hill. Doctor Stanford assigned a member of the administrative staff to assist Angel. She had filled out a detailed questionnaire based on Mr. Hill's answers to various questions and her observations. The information was much more inclusive since they needed a complete profile to address each patient's mental, emotional, and physical needs. Angel pulled up the patient's file on his computer tablet. He reviewed the file again. Angel shook his head. Mr. Hill was 63 years old, weighed 190 pounds, and stood five feet nine inches in height. He grew up in a Christian home but had not attended church in a long time. Mr. Hill owned a large, highly profitable company and was a workaholic before being diagnosed with cancer. He was divorced and estranged from his daughter. However, he was close to his son, who was currently running his company. Mr. Hill had a health club membership he never used, regularly complained about back pain, and ate antacid tablets like they were mints. Mr. Hill's cancer was the type that fit within the protocol of the drug. This made him a prime candidate for the drug trial. However, he was disrespectful to the hospital staff, used foul language, had a poor diet, complained about the hospital not serving beer with his meals, and seemed to be in a continuous foul mood.

"Good morning Mr. Hill. How are you today?" Angel asked with a compassionate voice.

"Hell, I am dying of cancer, and the treatment I am receiving at this damn hospital is awful," Robert Hill said with a scowl. "How do you think I feel?"

Angel paused and gave the patient a stern look. "I was considering the possibility of treating you with a new drug that could cure your cancer, but I cannot accept you as a patient."

"Why in the hell not?" Robert said with indignation. "I have got nothing to lose at this point." Robert knew he was dying and did not feel like being nice to anyone, but now he wanted to hear about this cure.

Angel closed the file and looked Robert straight in the eyes. "Well, besides taking the drug, you have to be on a strict diet, be nice to the hospital staff, adhere to a customized exercise program, practice meditation, and use appropriate language. Swearing is not acceptable. Also, prayer is recommended as an additional form of meditation, as it helps calm the soul, to put the body in a better frame for healing. It is obvious you could not follow such a program. Therefore, I will leave you so you can die in peace."

Robert was piqued. "Now wait a damn minute." He noticed Angel's frown and immediately changed his tactics.

"I apologize, but just wait a minute. What are my chances if I use this new drug and do everything you mentioned?" Robert saw the serious expression on the doctor's face and knew he needed to listen attentively.

"Currently, the cure rate is around forty percent, but I believe the rate can be doubled, and that is the purpose of the trial."

"Doctor Carpenter." Doctor Angel Carpenter interrupted him. "Just call me Angel."

"Fine, call me Rob. Doctor Angel, I am a rich man. I will pay whatever it costs to receive the new cancer drug."

Angel started to tell him it was just Angel and not Doctor Angel, but he would address it later.

"Rob, your wealth is immaterial. The only way you can become a patient and be part of this trial is if you can convince me that you will follow the program exactly as required." Angel waited for a response.

"Doctor Angel, I regret some things I have done over the years, but I have always kept my word. I give my word. If you accept me as a patient, I will do whatever you ask me to do." Rob was dead serious with his response since, without the drug, his condition was terminal.

Angel wanted to make sure Rob was committed. "Okay, I will accept you on a trial basis, but if you cannot follow the program one hundred percent, I will remove you from the trial."

Angel took a box from his mobile cart, removed a computer tablet, and handed it to Rob.

"Here is a fully charged tablet and a charger. I have already installed the apps for this trial." Angel positioned the tablet in front of Rob.

"Press your finger here for the touch ID and enter your password twice. Good. Tap the icon in the upper left-hand corner." A contract popped up on the screen.

"I expect you to read this entire document prior to my visit tomorrow. There is a space for an electronic signature on the last page of the contract if you want to be my patient and be part of the trial. Do not even think about signing the contract unless you are fully committed."

Angel took the tablet and entered some additional data. He reached into his case and pulled out a watch health monitor. After making a few adjustments to the monitor, he placed it on Rob's arm. Angel checked to verify the watch was active and remotely connected to the tablet. Then, he handed the tablet back to Rob and briefly explained how to view the results from the health monitor. Angel pointed to a separate icon that provided a detailed explanation of how to use both devices. He opened another icon with the activity Rob was to follow each day. Angel told Rob the tablet and watch would have to be returned if he failed to follow all the procedures or decided he did not want to continue as a patient in the drug trial. Angel explained he would return the next day and left the room to meet with his next patient.

After Angel left, Randy, the patient in the bed next to Rob, pulled the curtain back and looked at him. Rob was pissed he was in a semiprivate room and not a private one. The hospital said they would switch him to a private room when one became available.

"Is your doctor really an angel?" Randy asked.

"Yes, he is an angel. That is why I am going to be cured of this cancer. Now shut up so I can read about this trial."

Rob had finished reading most of the document when breakfast was delivered to his room. Abigail was on the name tag.

"Thank you for bringing my breakfast, Abigail. I want to apologize for anything I said in the past that may have offended you."

"Apology accepted, but can I ask why you suddenly decided to be nice?" Abigail asked with raised eyebrows and a questioning look.

"This tablet says I have to be nice to everyone if I want Doctor Angel as my doctor."

Abigail was unaware of a Doctor Angel, and after giving the patient his meal, she stopped by the nurse's station and asked who the doctor was for Robert Hill. The duty nurse, Michelle, pulled the file.

"Doctor Carpenter is his doctor. He is new here," Michelle said.

Abigail was slightly puzzled. "I thought it was funny when the patient said Doctor Angel was his doctor."

"Angel is Doctor Carpenter's first name," Michelle replied as she laughed.

Michelle smiled mischievously. "I think I will start calling him Doctor Angel as a joke and see if he has a sense of humor."

Abigail shook her head. "I have not met a doctor with a sense of humor. Tell me, what does he look like?"

"Well, his looks match his first name," Michelle said. "He is young, extremely handsome, has blond hair, and has the bluest pellucid eyes I have ever seen. He actually looks like an angel, and he is single. However, before you make any comments, I am not interested since I am happily married, and who has time for an affair?" Michelle and Abigail laughed. Abigail knew Michelle was joking. She had met Michelle's husband several times, and they were perfect for each other.

"How did you find such a wonderful husband?" Abigail asked.

"I got the military to pay for my Bachelor of Nursing Degree," Michelle replied. "I spent eight years as a commissioned officer where the men outnumber the women ten to one. I took my time and picked a winner. We think alike on the things that matter. My husband and I saved our signing bonuses and most of our regular pay when on deployment. We have no mortgage and two adorable sons. We love spending time together when we are not working."

"I am so jealous of you," Abigail said as she went to check on a patient.

The rumor mill quickly accelerated and was running at high speed. It spread throughout the hospital that an angel was working at their facility, and Doctor Angel may have divine healing powers. A humorous story helps when you have a stressful or tedious shift.

Angel was happy with his progress as he arrived at the entrance to the room for Mary Baker. Mary Baker had advanced metastatic breast cancer, and it had spread to her lungs. He knew he would not accept Mary as a trial patient. Without a miracle, she was unlikely to live much longer, and her death would reflect negatively on the drug trial. However, the hospital had assigned Ms. Baker to his care as a regular patient. He knocked on the door frame even though the door was open.

"Hello, Ms. Baker. I am Doctor Angel Carpenter."

She looked up from reading a book with a captivating smile. "Come in. They informed me a Doctor Carpenter was interviewing patients to find volunteers for a new cancer drug. Are you that doctor?"

"Who told you about the drug trial?" Angel said with a frown.

"It was Doctor Andrew."

Angel was qualifying patients and only selecting those who met specific requirements. He was upset Doctor Andrew would tell any patient he was seeking volunteers when it was simply incorrect. It would give false hope to people who could not benefit from the drug. Also, it could unnecessarily upset people if they thought he was withholding a cancer medication that could heal their cancer.

"Ms. Baker, I am sorry Doctor Andrew misled you. I am interviewing numerous cancer patients, but I am only allowed to select a few patients for the initial part of the drug trial. Prior research shows your cancer is unlikely to be treatable using the cancer drug. However, you are one of my regular patients, and I will provide you with traditional treatment." Angel had carefully tried to choose the correct words. He did not want to leave Ms. Baker with no hope.

"Doctor Carpenter," Ms. Baker said with a pitiful look.

"You can call me Angel."

"Then you can call me Mary. Angel, I want to be part of the trial. I have read the entirety of your notebook, and I am happy to adhere to all the requirements."

She picked up a notebook off the nightstand and showed him.

"Where did you get the notebook?" He was upset since the notebook should not be in the hands of a patient.

"I received the notebook from Doctor Andrew."

Angel reached out and gently took it out of her hand. He opened the cover and confirmed it was one of the original notebooks given to the directors who attended his presentation. Fortunately, the financials and other confidential pages had been removed.

"Mary, please excuse me. I will be back in a minute." Angel had kept a straight face, even though he was justifiably upset.

Angel called the front desk and asked for Doctor Andrew's cellphone number. He dialed the number, and Doctor Andrew answered on the third ring.

"Doctor Andrew, this is Doctor Carpenter, and I want to know what you were thinking when you gave your copy of the Drug Trial Notebook to patient Mary Baker?"

"I am just trying to help since she is an excellent candidate for your drug trial," Doctor Andrew said in a smug voice.

Even though Angel was angry, he tempered his voice. "You know she is not a candidate for this drug. I made it quite clear I would manage this trial with no interference from you or anyone else."

"How dare you speak to me in such a manner," Doctor Andrew shouted. "I am a senior physician at this hospital, and you will show me the respect I deserve. Furthermore, I do not have to listen to you." Doctor Andrew prevented any additional response from Angel by abruptly hanging up.

Angel was furious and could barely control himself. He was unsure how to handle the situation and called Doctor Stanford, who had provided his cellphone number shortly after Angel's presentation. Doctor Stanford had instructed him to call if he needed help with anything. Doctor Stanford answered the phone, and Angel explained what had taken place.

"I am sorry this happened," Doctor Stanford said. "I will have a talk with Doctor Andrew."

Angel thanked him. However, Angel knew he would need to be careful in all future dealings with Doctor Andrew.

Angel returned to Mary's room. He looked at her pleading face and knew she had been crying. "Angel, I have been praying you would help me."

There was no way Angel could ignore her prayer. "Okay, Mary, I will add you to the trial," Angel responded with a gentle voice.

He then repeated the same explanation he had given to other patients he had selected. He provided Mary with a tablet and a health watch.

Angel worked a double shift each day since he planned to select the initial fifty trial patients during the first week by adding at least ten patients each day. Half of the patients he interviewed were happy with their existing doctor and did not wish to try an experimental drug. He selected about half of the patients he interviewed.

Angel was pleased with the progress he had made during the week. He had intentionally stopped interviewing Doctor Andrew's patients, which helped speed up the process. After their altercation, Doctor Andrew told his patients Doctor Carpenter was an inexperienced doctor. He further stated the trial involved a dangerous experimental drug. As a result, none of Doctor Andrew's patients wanted to become subjects in the trial. Therefore, Angel stopped wasting his time talking to those patients.

It was Friday, and Angel was about two hours into the second shift. He only needed three more patients. Although Angel was tired, he felt good about the selected patients, except for Mary Baker. He was looking forward to finishing the day and going home. Angel had the weekend off. He planned to get a good night's sleep with the alarm clock turned off.

Angel read the notes on his next patient, Paulina Wilkerson, a young eighteen-year-old girl. His assistant had called the child's mother. The mother had consented to Angel discussing the trial with her daughter. However, the mother would make the final decision under a healthcare proxy. Paulina Wilkerson had leukemia. She had undergone both chemotherapy and radiation therapy, but the treatments were unsuccessful. Paulina appeared very thin, but her hair was starting to grow back from the radiation treatment. She had inclined her bed and was playing a game on her cellphone. Her mother was to meet them at 6:00 PM, but she was running late. Angel walked up to the bed. After a few seconds, Paulina looked up.

"Hi, you must be Doctor Angel," Paulina said. "Everyone is talking about you." Paulina put her phone down and saw Angel's puzzled face.

"Who is everyone?" Angel figured 'everyone' was a reference to people talking about the cancer drug.

"All the nurses and most of the patients. They say you are an angel."

Paulina's mother had arrived and heard her daughter talking with the doctor. She waited outside the room and listened to the conversation. She wanted to see how the doctor treated her daughter when he thought they were alone. She had a recent unpleasant experience where a doctor showed a complete lack of compassion when talking to her daughter about her condition. Afterward, Paulina cried intermittently for three days, and she did not want to see a repeat. She had filed a complaint with the hospital and threaten legal action. Doctor Stanford met with her and apologized on behalf of Doctor Andrew. He assigned Doctor Mark Seneca as a replacement doctor for her daughter. However, she was now cautious of all doctors. If her daughter got upset, she would enter the room and stop the discussion.

"Doctor Angel, how old are you?" Angel had taken college-level courses while in high school and had skipped his senior year. He had attended college year-round and completed his undergraduate degree at nineteen. Three years later, he graduated from medical school.

"I am 23 and way too old for you." They both laughed.

"I didn't mean it like that. You just seem so much younger than the other doctors. However, in five years, I will be 23, and you will be 28, and then it would work." They both laughed again.

"Do you think I will make it to 23?" Paulina asked and then frowned as she looked at him.

"I do not know. You could get killed in a car accident or have a skydiving accident if your parachute fails to open or die in a wide variety of ways. However, if you drive safely and stay away from the extreme sports, then I think you may live a long time. The purpose of the drug trial is to see if my theory is correct. If it is correct, over eighty percent of the cancer patients in the drug trial will be cured using a holistic approach. However, there are no guarantees. Also, to be part of the drug test trial, you must follow a rigorous plan."

Angel paused. "For example, no alcohol," he said with a straight face.

She burst out laughing again. "I am only eighteen. I am too young to drink, but I promise, no alcohol."

"While I am here, let me give you a quick exam."

He checked her eyes, ears, throat, blood pressure, and heart rate.

"Doctor Angel, your hands are warm."

She then reached over and took one of his hands in hers. "I have never felt such warm hands."

"I have an active hypothalamus, which causes me to have a higher skin temperature, but it is normal for me. My skin temperature is considered an outlier on the right side of a bell distribution curve, whereas some people have a temperature below the norm and are on the low side of the same bell distribution curve."

"What's a bell distribution curve?" Paulina asked, as she scrunched her eyebrows with a questioning look.

"I am sorry. You will learn about the bell distribution curve when you take a statistics course in college. While we are on the subject, you should think about what college you wish to attend."

"I will do that," Paulina said with enthusiasm.

"You have an excellent doctor," Angel said. "Doctor Seneca knows I am talking to you, and he highly recommended you for the trial. However, both you and your mother will have to make the final decision. Your mother is supposed to be here."

Paulina's mother decided it was time to make her entrance. "Doctor Angel, I am Susan Wilkerson, Paulina's mother. I apologize for being late, but the traffic was terrible. Doctor Seneca is Paulina's current doctor. He recommended I consider having Paulina participate in your drug trial. So, other than taking the drug, what else is involved?"

"Your daughter must follow a restrictive organic diet. Paulina will have a high protein shake each day specifically designed for her, which provides a daily regimen of vitamins and minerals. She will see a chiropractor once a week, attend an exercise class every morning, and a meditation class every afternoon. Each day she will spend an hour on a hobby. I will assign her a psychologist who will meet with her once a week. She will attend a Yoga or a Tai Chi class once a day. My younger patients mostly sign up for the Yoga class, whereas my older patients select Tai Chi, but she can take either. She will maintain a written list of things she is thankful for, wherein she will add an item to the list each day. I highly recommend prayer for both of you as an additional form of meditation. Meditation has been shown to assist the body in healing. The plan is for your body to become physically fit through a healthy diet and exercise, to create a positive mental outlook with little to no stress through meditation, and put your soul at peace through faith. The goal is for your body to heal itself with the drug's help. Also, unlike most treatments conducted on an outpatient basis, your daughter will remain hospitalized for three months. According to your application, you are Baptist. You may wish to have your preacher visit with you to help with your faith. If he visits, you need to explain how the meetings are to be no longer than thirty minutes and are to be positive. There is to be no talking about death or dying. However, he can discuss going to heaven in the far distant future. In your tablet, you will see the drug trial has a three-pronged approach by supporting the cancer drug with a healthy body and a healthy mind. A fourth part is faith, but I included it as part of the healthy mind to get the funding."

Angel then proceeded with the explanation and demonstration of the computer tablet and the health watch. Angel turned to the mother.

"Mrs. Wilkerson, you need to discuss this with your daughter, and you can email me when you decide. I will keep a space open for twenty-four hours."

"Doctor Angel, if you could give my daughter and me a couple of minutes, we will give you a decision now."

"Take your time. I will be down the hallway reviewing the next patient's file."

They waited a minute for the doctor to move down the hall. Susan looked at her daughter. "Well, what do you think?" Paulina looked at her mother like she was from another planet.

"Are you out of your mind? With him as my doctor, I know I will get well, and besides, he is so hot!"

They both laughed. Susan agreed with her daughter. The doctor was handsome. Susan grinned as she left to get the Doctor. It had been a long time since her daughter was happy. Susan got Angel's attention, and they returned to her daughter's room.

"We have decided we want Paulina to be part of the trial," Susan said.

"Good," Angel replied. He was pleased since he felt Paulina was an extremely promising candidate for the drug trial, and he had an overwhelming feeling they would cure her.

Angel took the computer tablet, pulled up the signature page, and held the tablet in front of Susan for her signature. After her signature, he took the tablet and forwarded the document to his computer. He then handed Paulina the tablet and explained how to download her schedule.

It only took Paulina a few seconds to complete the setup and the download. She quickly scanned her schedule.

"It does not look like I will have much free time."

She saw a line item on Monday and Wednesday from 5:00 PM to 6:00 PM with the word Cube. Paulina looked up at Angel.

"Doctor Angel, what does this Cube item mean?" Angel had added an extra item to her schedule in anticipation of Paulina becoming part of the selected group.

"You are going to learn how to solve the Rubik's Cube. Two nights a week, a young boy your age, Rick Grant, will teach you how to solve the Rubik's Cube after school is out."

Angel did not say how he was personally paying Rick, and the money was not from the grant. Rick was an ambitious high school student. He lived in Angel's apartment complex with his mother and always asked everyone if they needed any work done. Rick impressed Angel when he solved the Rubik's Cube with one hand in less than twenty seconds. Angel thought it would be good for Paulina to see someone her age, since she was the youngest patient in the drug trial. The FDA had approved the test for adults who were eighteen or older.

"Isn't solving the Cube hard?" Paulina asked.

"Try it for a few weeks, and if you don't want to continue, I will fire your trainer."

"I noticed you allotted time for my high school classes," Paulina said with sadness. "I have access to my classes online, but I have been falling behind." Then she stared at him with a determined look. "I will work extra hard to catch up."

"On your schedule, you will have over thirty hours a week for class time and homework. Plus, you have free time every night after seven o'clock, but lights out at ten o'clock. Let me know if you need more study time, and I will work with you to adjust your schedule."

Paulina did not say how she had stopped studying since she figured it was a waste of time if she was going to die.

"A nurse will see you on Monday morning and start you on the program. She can probably answer whatever additional questions you may have. However, you can send me an email if you have questions she cannot answer. You need to understand, I only answer my emails at night after I go home. You will need to contact a duty nurse if you have an emergency. I will see you at least once a week. Welcome to the trial."

"Would you mind taking a selfie with me?" Paulina asked.

Angel rolled his eyes but nodded his head. He leaned in next to her, and she used her phone to take the picture.

"See you next week," Angel said as he left the room to go to the next patient.

"I need to leave, but tomorrow is Saturday," Susan said. "I will see you in the morning." Susan hugged Paulina and picked up her purse to leave.

"Mom, would you mind if I used your credit card to make some online purchases? Also, can you bring me my school tablet and backpack?"

"Of course, to both questions." Susan was happy her daughter was finally thinking about a future. Even if the trial failed, at least her daughter would have some happy days. Then she stopped herself. For this to work, she needed to have faith. She decided she would start praying for her daughter each night. After all, it could not hurt.

Paulina thought for a moment. "Also, bring me my cosmetics when you come tomorrow."

Susan smiled again and nodded her head. When they packed for the hospital, Paulina had intentionally left her cosmetics at home and said the mortuary could apply the makeup after she died.

As soon as her mother left the room, Paulina prepared a message, attached the picture she had just taken, and sent it to Brenda, her best friend. They had applied to the same universities, but she stopped communicating after being told she was going to die. She had been so depressed that she had not sent or answered her emails or talked with any of her friends. It was only a few minutes before she received a call from Brenda. They talked for several hours about her gorgeous doctor, school, who was dating who, fashions, and everything else.

Angel entered the room of the next patient, Martin Moore. According to his chart, he was six foot four and weighed two hundred twenty pounds, but the prison medical record did not reflect the patient's current condition. Martin was skinny and frail.

Martin looked up and watched as the doctor entered his room. His mother had told him about a Doctor Angel with blond hair who would cure him. She had asked him to be extra nice to the doctor. His mother's request was more of an absolute command, which no one in their right mind would ignore.

"You must be Doctor Angel," Martin said in a hoarse voice.

"Yes, I am. Your file shows you were a guest at a correctional hospital before coming here."

Martin smirked at the description of being a guest. "I was serving three years in the local Miami prison for drug possession. I had just turned eighteen when I was convicted. When my mother found out I was dying of cancer, she started stirring things up and insisted the prison provide me with proper care. The prison did not want the medical expenses and did not want to deal with my mother, so they paroled me for good behavior. Me, good behavior? I have never been good at anything. I am not sure if the warden got me released because he felt sorry for me or was just scared of my mother. Regardless, my mother is like a force of nature. She continued working to get me proper care, which is how I ended up in this non-profit church hospital. Angel, can you help me?"

"Probably not," Angel said with a frown. "The drug trial requires a mental discipline to follow a specified program. I do not believe you would follow such a program. Also, it requires faith, based on some form of religion."

Martin avoided eye contact as he looked down. "I have not lived a good life, but I believe in God and grew up in a Christian home. Until I was older, my mother dragged me to church every week. Now, I am not going to sing kumbaya, but I am a Christian. Yes, I stole a few cars, broke into a few empty homes, and roughed up some people. Luckily, I never got caught for those crimes. Also, I cannot see the tattoo on your arm since your shirt covers it up, but I am sure you have a gang tattoo. A friend of mine in prison is in a gang, and we talked a lot. He told me about the Angel Gang and how he wished he had been a member of that gang. The leader of the Angel Gang was called Angel. He had blond hair and blue eyes. Tell me, are you the angel he talked about?"

"Yes, I was the gang leader of the Angels." Angel answered honestly since he was not ashamed of his former affiliation with the gang. Martin pulled up his sleeve and showed a gang tattoo on his arm.

"Angel, you understand what it is like being in a gang. Being a gang leader did not stop you from being a good person, and you are now a respectable doctor. Come on, give me a break. I am only twenty years old and do not want to die. Also, I will find some way to help you if I ever get the chance. I have never begged before, but I am begging now. Please help me with this cancer."

"I only have a limited number of slots available. If you are healed and do not change your lifestyle, then you will be back in prison. I will have wasted an opportunity to cure someone else."

"I promise you and more importantly, I promised my mother that I will stay out of trouble."

Angel was thoughtful, knowing he should decline the patient's request, but he nodded his head. "You must follow all of my instructions if you wish to be cured." Angel proceeded to explain the tablet and health watch monitor.

"Good, now I will not have to sic my mother on you," Martin said in jest. Martin coughed and wiped the blood off his mouth with a towel. "Angel, all kidding aside, I will not let you down. I have one wish in life. I want my mother to be proud of me and that is my new goal in life."

Angel continued to see patients. He only needed one more person to complete the initial group. The next patient on his list was Holden Sorenson. Holden was sixty-two years old, a Mormon, previously treated for Thyroid Cancer, and currently diagnosed with Lymphoma. As Angel entered the room, he noticed a lady sitting in a chair beside the bed. Holden was sleeping.

"Good afternoon, I am Doctor Angel Carpenter."

"Doctor, I am Nephi Sorenson, and this is my husband, Holden," she said. "He is a sound sleeper. My husband has the dubious honor of being a member of the Downwinders, which is why he is ill. Are you familiar with the Downwinders?"

"No, I am not familiar with the term. Would you care to explain?"

"We are from Utah. From 1951 through 1992, the United States detonated over a thousand nuclear warheads at the Nevada Test Site. Over a hundred blasts took place above ground. The radioactive clouds from the above ground tests were carried by the wind directly through southern Utah, where my husband was born. No one informed the people. Radioactive fallout settled on the children playing outside. Cows ate the contaminated grass, and the people drank the radioactive milk. People ate the contaminated vegetables and breathed the radioactive air. Thousands of children and adults died from the resulting increase in cancer. Many of the children who died were under the age of 14. The victims tested positive for Radioactive Iodine 131, which is traceable solely to the nuclear bombs detonated at the Nevada Test Site. Various individuals in the military and government agencies told everyone there were no safety concerns regarding the nuclear bombs being detonated a few miles away. Many Downwinders have died. My husband is lucky to have survived this long. That is our story." Angel was appalled by the explanation.

"Mrs. Sorenson, there is nothing I can do about the past, but I believe I can help your husband."

Mrs. Sorenson woke up her husband. Angel was troubled by what he had heard but tried not to think about it while explaining the cancer drug trial. Holden was very calm and asked thoughtful articulated questions. Holden and Nephi told Angel the suggested daily prayer was something they had been doing for a long time. They liked the holistic approach and fully supported the program as described by Angel. After a brief conversation with each other, they readily agreed to be part of the cancer drug trial.

Angel had his first fifty patients and finished inputting the data. He arrived home late, but he got a good night's sleep. He had planned to spend the weekend resting, but instead, he reviewed patient files. He was excited to start the drug trial.

Angel was extremely busy the following two weeks as he added fifty more patients and worked sixteen-hour days to ensure the patients adhered to the rigid schedule. Now he faced the beginning of the fourth week in a more relaxed state. He decided to shorten his days to a more reasonable twelve hours as he proceeded to his office. At the beginning of each day, he liked to spend an hour reviewing the electronic files before visiting his patients.

As Angel approached his office, he saw a young lady sitting on the floor next to the door. A child was sitting in a wheelchair next to her. The mother saw him approaching and stood up.

"Doctor Carpenter, I am Carol Brittle, and this is Cathi, my daughter. May we talk to you?" Angel unlocked his office.

"Ms. Brittle, only hospital staff are allowed in this area. How did you get past security?"

"I am a registered nurse and came here before the end of the night shift. A maintenance worker let me in when I showed him my identification card. Please, I need to talk to you about my daughter."

Angel shrugged. "Come in and take a seat." She pushed the wheelchair in and sat down. Cathi stared at him with a child's expression of hope.

"My daughter is five years old and has cancer. As a nurse, I learned about the cancer trial you are conducting, and I would like my daughter to become part of the trial. Here is a summary of her medical history."

Angel took a few minutes reviewing the file, and Cathi fit the profile of the patients who could benefit from the cancer drug.

"I am afraid you have been misinformed. People do not just show up and become part of the trial. We receive thousands of applications, but we can only accept a hundred patients at a time. Also, we are conducting a Phase Three Clinical Trial for adults. No clinical trials have been approved for children. We are at least a year away from getting the drug approved for adults. Getting it approved for children is probably going to take three or more years. The safe dosage for children will most likely be considerably smaller than the amount used for adults. Eighteen is the youngest age the FDA has approved for testing the drug."

"My mom said you would heal me, and I would not have to die," Cathi said in a soft voice.

Angel did not know what to say. "I am truly sorry." He could see the desperation in the mother.

"My daughter needs to start taking the drug immediately. You say three years, but she will not be alive in three months. Surely you can make an exception for my daughter. You are our last hope. Even though I am broke, I can pay you a large sum for saving my daughter's life."

Carol pulled a slip of paper from a file she had been holding and handed it to him. Angel read the message and saw the willingness of the mother to risk her own life for her child. A sizable amount of money was written on the sheet to purchase a kidney and part of a liver.

"Ms. Brittle, we do not accept money for admitting someone into the drug trial, and selling your organs is against the law."

"I will do whatever I can to save my daughter's life. Organs are sold regularly to the rich, who are not subject to the same laws as the poor. I do not know if you are naive or intentionally lying. If you do a little research, you will find how two of your current patients paid a large sum to be part of the drug trial."

Angel could not help but be appalled at the accusation, but Carol seemed sure of her statements, and he believed her. He wondered if the two patients approved by Doctor Stanford had paid by making a present or past donation to the hospital? He planned to determine if she spoke the truth.

"I will check out your accusation, but I still cannot help your daughter."

"Please, tell me what I can do to save my daughter, and I will do it."

Angel sighed and shook his head. "I want to help you, but I am sorry. To save your daughter, I would have to violate the FDA restrictions, and I would have to take an existing patient off the drug trial, and they would die. We have an outstanding cancer center. If you fill out the admission forms, we will care for your daughter using traditional methods, plus I will let her take part in the holistic part of the drug trial."

Tears started forming in Carol's eyes as she realized she had just failed in her last chance to save her daughter.

"I will submit the forms to you and pray for a miracle, but her organs are starting to fail," she said with despair. "Her doctor said she has at most two to three months. They say you are an angel, but it seems you are playing god as you decide who will live and who will die."

Cathi tried to console her mother. "Please don't cry."

Carol hugged her daughter. Angel watched as the mother left the office and pushed the wheelchair down the hallway. When Carol arrived, she had been full of hope, but now she was just an empty shell filled with hopelessness. Still, she would do everything possible to ensure her daughter's final days were comfortable. She would have her daughter admitted to the hospital and pray for a miracle.

Angel was distraught over his inability to help the young child. The child's files were very detailed. He felt Cathi's doctor was optimistic about the length of time remaining. Angel would remember her for a very long time. He prayed for a time when he would not have to turn down such a request. He remembered one of his professors lecturing how a doctor needed to stay detached from his patients, but how do you ignore the pleadings of a mother for her dying child?

Angel continued to wonder if the accusations of the mother were correct. The mother was quite convincing. Angel decided he would not ask Doctor Stanford why he approved the two older men for the trial. He was hesitant to listen to a response when he already knew the answer. Angel hoped there would be no such approvals in the future. He decided to take a subtle approach and tell Doctor Stanford about the girl and her mother. He would say it was unfortunate no spaces remained for the young girl. Doctor Stanford fully supported him, and he did not wish to lose his support, but where should he draw the line when the line decided who should live? He wondered if he knew enough to judge Doctor Stanford.

CHAPTER 2 ANGELS HAVE WARM HANDS

Angel met with Robert Hill and reviewed his charts. Rob was trying to follow the drug program, but he was not at 100 percent.

"Rob, you are close, but you are not adhering to the daily requirements."

"Doctor Angel, I really am trying. It is a lot harder than I thought. I know the incentive is to beat this cancer, but in all my accomplishments, I always had a lot of short-term incentives to keep me focused."

As Angel continued reviewing the file, Rob's meal arrived. Rob gloomily looked at his lunch. "I would look forward to this meal if it came with a cold beer." Angel had an epiphany.

"Rob, I work half days on Saturday. If you achieve one hundred percent for the week, I will bring you a beer on Saturday, but it must be one hundred percent. Ninety-nine percent does not count."

"For a beer, I will give you two hundred percent," Rob stated with enthusiasm.

Angel found the exaggeration humorous but did not correct him. He also thought about rewarding some of his other patients. Angel checked the files each day for the rest of the week, and Rob achieved a perfect score.

On Saturday, Angel entered Rob's hospital room with a small Styrofoam ice chest. He sat the ice chest on the floor, pulled out a cold can of beer inside a koozie, and handed it to Rob.

"I had to cover it with a koozie since the hospital does not allow patients to drink beer," Angel whispered. Rob responded with a conspiratorial grin.

Angel had placed the beer in a koozie to keep Rob from seeing the label. Rob opened the beer using the ring tab and took a swig. The beer was ice cold, and Rob savored each sip. He moaned as he let the cold liquid slide down his throat. Angel did not tell him he was drinking Upside Dawn Golden Ale which was a non-alcoholic beer made by the Athletic Brewing Company. In blind taste tests, everyone thought it had a superior taste, and the vast majority of people could not distinguish their non-alcoholic beer from regular beer. Besides being non-alcoholic, it only had fifty calories.

"This is so good!" Rob exclaimed. After Rob finished the beer, Angel took the empty can and put it back in the ice chest.

"Do you think they have beer in heaven?" Rob asked.

"Of course, they have beer, but you need to know where to look," Angel responded thoughtfully. "Once you are in heaven, you need to take the gold paved Heavenly Parkway south until you reach Paradise Boulevard, then head east on Paradise to Rapture Road, turn right on Rapture Road and go all the way to the end. At the end of the street, you will see a building. The building does not look too inviting from the outside, but they have the best beer in heaven. You simply must try the Heavenly Brew."

Rob and Angel both laughed. However, Rob could not tell if Angel was joking or telling the truth. If they serve beer in heaven, maybe he needed to work harder to get there.

Angel sighed and breached the doctor-patient confidentiality. "My next patient is Ms. Green," Angel said with concern. "Like you, she is improving each day, but when she leaves here, she has no place to go. She is behind on the rent for her apartment and just received an eviction notice."

"Rob, I will see you next Saturday with another beer if you get another perfect score." Angel left to see his next patient.

The guy sharing the room with Rob had been watching in disbelief. "I cannot believe your doctor brought you a beer. Do you think he could bring a beer for me?" Randy asked.

"Randy, he is not bringing you a beer. He is not your doctor. Angel is my Doctor, and he is the best doctor I have ever had."

"Doctor Andrew is my doctor," Randy said. "He told me not to participate in the experimental drug trial. He said Doctor Carpenter did not have the experience to conduct a drug trial. Also, Doctor Andrew said I should continue with the standard treatment since it was safer. Now, I regret following his advice."

Rob thought more about the bar in heaven Angel had described. Angel sounded so believable when giving the directions, and he knew all the streets. Only an actual angel would know the names of the roads in heaven. After hearing about Ms. Green's trouble, he decided to pay the back rent. He had more money than he could spend in several lifetimes. Facing death had changed his outlook. He would see who else he could help, and he would start right here at the hospital.

After visiting with Ms. Green, Angel met with Holden Sorenson. Nephi Sorenson was sitting at her husband's bedside reading. She looked up and gave a half-smile when Angel entered the room. Holden was awake, and Angel walked over next to the bed.

"Your evaluations are looking better each day. I can give you some good news. We did not see any cancer nodules in your last blood test. However, due to your surgery, you will need to stay a week longer than we originally discussed. Also, I want to see several more blood tests without cancer cells before saying you are cured."

"I am feeling better," Holden said with confidence. "Initially, even with help, I struggled to get out of bed, and now I can get out of bed unassisted. I have less trouble breathing. The instructor in the exercise class complimented me even though I am the slowest student. I have lost twenty pounds and plan to lose more."

"Great, keep up the good work. The scar from your surgery is healing nicely."

Angel, with Doctor Seneca assisting, had removed Holden's appendix. The appendix had a malignant tumor, and the cancer was too far along to be treated with the cancer drug. Fortunately, his other organs were in better shape, and Holden was getting well.

Next, Angel checked on Martin Moore. Martin turned off the television when Angel entered the room.

"Martin, there are no cancer cells in your most recent test results. Also, we need this room, so we are going to check you out of the hospital."

"I was afraid you might want to get rid of me. My mother has already told me about all the work I have to do when I go home."

"Your cancer is in complete remission. You can check out of the hospital at the end of the week. I want you to continue the nutrition and exercise program. Also, I would recommend you continue your prayers. I want to see you for a follow-up visit in three months and then once a year."

"I will see you in three months unless my mother works me to death. Angel, please tell my mother I need to rest and how I am too weak to do a lot of physical work."

"You are strong as a horse. Your mother scares me, and I am not about to lie to her. Besides, I should tell your mother how work is good for you and will keep you healthy."

"You are supposed to be an angel, but you have the heart of a demon," Martin bemoaned. Angel chuckled as he left the room.

Angel visited Mary Baker, his last patient for the day. She looked up from her tablet when Angel entered her room. Mary always broke out with a big radiant smile whenever she saw Angel. She thoroughly enjoyed his visits. Mary noticed Angel seldom mentioned her condition and never discussed her cancer.

"Hi Mary, how are you doing today?"

"I am fine. It seems to me you are working way too much. Do you even have a social life?"

"I have plenty of time to develop a social life in the future."

"Doctor Angel, you are a cancer specialist, and you know that is not true."

She locked eyes with him. "Please review my file with me," she said sternly, leaving no room for dissent.

As a doctor, he was obligated to be truthful and answer her medical questions. He pulled up her file on his tablet. "Your blood pressure and heart rate have improved."

"Angel, level with me. I am not getting any better, am I? Please be truthful with me."

"No, you are not getting any better. I am sorry. The rate of spread of the cancer has slowed, but it is still progressing. The holistic part of the drug trial has helped. You are feeling better, and you have outlived the time your prior doctor gave you."

Mary nodded her head. "You told me what I expected to hear. Regardless, I have lived longer than expected, and I am not dead yet. So, I will enjoy each day I have remaining. My family and friends have visited me, and I feel better than I have in years. Your plan makes your patients eat right, exercise right, and embrace the right mental outlook. Thank you for letting me be part of the cancer drug trial. I am sorry if I am messing up your trial results."

"Mary, you are not messing up the trial. Your results show how even a failure is successful if it extends a person's life and improves their quality of life. I am sorry we did not get the miracle you were hoping for in your prayers."

"We got a miracle," she said with a look of contentment and an acceptance of her fate. "I feel blessed to have been given the additional time to spend with my children, grandchildren, and siblings. The extra time allowed me to reflect and realize I had a wonderful life. My faith has been restored, and I am no longer afraid of dying. I am at peace. You are truly one of God's angels. Please do not be sad when I pass away."

The days passed, and Angel continued to meet with his patients while providing the results to the Tyzugmod Corporation.

As usual, Angel awoke a little before the alarm and proceeded with his morning routine at his apartment. Today he was looking forward to going to the hospital and meeting with previously discharged patients. He had prepared a detailed interim report for the drug corporation and a presentation for the hospital Board. An assistant scheduled checkups with forty-eight of his former patients over the next three days. These were patients from his initial group, and they were here for their three-month checkup. Two of his patients from the first fifty had moved out of town, but he received blood test results showing they were cancer-free. He was optimistically cautious after he examined each of the test results.

His first appointment was with Paulina Wilkerson. Paulina and her mother were sitting in the examination room when he entered. A nurse had taken Paulina's blood pressure, weight, and height measurements. Angel used his digital ultrasound stethoscope to check her internal organs and reviewed her blood test results.

"I am happy to say you are cancer-free, and all your vital signs are excellent. Also, you have put on some much-needed weight and look healthy. How are you feeling?"

"I feel great, and I just had a birthday. I am nineteen."

"Happy birthday!"

Paulina grinned. "Thanks. I am a freshman at Florida International University. I decided to go to FIU because they have a medical school, and some of my friends are going there. Also, I commute from home which keeps my student loans to a minimum."

"That is outstanding. I think you will make an excellent doctor. You should set an example for your future patients by continuing the meal plan and the exercise routine."

"I will. Angel, thank you for healing me!"

"To make it easy for Paulina, our whole family is on your diet and exercise plan," Susan said. "My husband has lost thirty pounds. I have lost twenty pounds, but the main thing is how good we all feel."

"My husband and I cannot thank you enough for saving our daughter."

"You are welcome. It was a team effort. The Tyzugmod Corporation developed the amazing cancer drug. We just ensured it had the environment to get the best results."

"Paulina, I want to see you again in a year."

As they got up to leave, Paulina hugged Angel before she and her mother left. Rick Grant, his neighbor, had also thanked him since he and Paulina were dating. They were both excellent kids with big hearts. Rick had enjoyed telling Angel how he got a part-time job at a burger restaurant. He got free food while working and fifty percent off when he was off the clock. His mother bragged about all the money they were saving on food.

Angel had helped Grant fill out scholarship applications. His grades and his mother's low income qualified him for a need-based academic scholarship. Grant called Angel immediately upon receiving the scholarship which paid for tuition and books. Grant confirmed he would continue working part time since he would need money for food, gas, and other miscellaneous expenses.

Angel felt good as he prepared to meet with his next patient. His next appointment was with Robert Hill, and he was pleased with the results. Rob looked like a poster for a health magazine.

As soon as Rob saw Angel, he jumped out of his seat. "Good morning, Doctor Angel."

"Rob, you look great!"

Rob responded with enthusiasm. "I feel great. I am still on your diet plan and work out at the gym every day. Last month, I took all my children and grandchildren on a vacation. We had an excellent time, and my daughter is actually talking to me again. Also, my oldest granddaughter graduated from college and had trouble finding a job. She is now working for me, or I should say she is working for my son. My son took over while I was sick. I left him in charge since he did such a good job. I am just a figurehead now and loving my free time. Also, my son is smarter than I thought since he gets me involved with the big decisions. Doctor Angel, I have not been this happy in a long time. Now, give me some good news."

"All your tests came back negative. You are one hundred percent free of cancer and healthier than men half your age. I want to see you again in a year. Also, I would like you to continue with the diet and the exercise."

"I will. Thanks again for saving my life. My outlook on life has changed, and I am thankful for each day. I continue to say my prayers in the morning to start the day and at night when the day is over. I just might make it to heaven."

Angel chuckled. "There is no doubt in my mind."

Angel continued to have similar meetings with his patients. As expected, some patients were no longer on the diet or exercise program. However, except for Mary Baker, they were all free of cancer.

Now, all of his current patients were on the same floor. He maintained the one hundred bed count by adding a new cancer patient for each patient discharged.

Angel presented his second quarterly report to the hospital's Board of Directors and concentrated on the results of the first fifty patients. He mentioned at the beginning that he would provide an analysis of the first two hundred patients at his next presentation in three months. At the end, the directors asked meaningful questions.

Doctor Andrew spoke up and commented sarcastically. "Would you like to tell us about the special treatment you provided to Robert Hill?"

"Robert Hill is completely cured of his cancer and is healthy," Angel replied. "He received the same treatment as everyone else."

"Are you giving alcoholic drinks to all of your patients?" Doctor Andrew asked. "You have turned the hospital into a bar."

"I have never given an alcoholic beverage to any of my patients. During his time at the hospital, I gave non-alcoholic beer to Mr. Hill each Saturday if he fully complied with his assigned tasks. The beer served as an incentive, and it worked."

Doctor Stanford stopped the discussion. "I was aware of Robert Hill's incentive since Doctor Carpenter mentioned it in his weekly reports. While such motivation for a patient is unusual, it achieved the desired results."

Doctor Andrew was shocked into silence. He felt Doctor Stanford had lost his mind and needed to be replaced.

"Can you tell us about the one patient in the first group of fifty who is not responding?" Doctor Stanford asked as he leaned forward with a thoughtful look.

"The patient you are referring to is Mary Baker," Angel replied in a sad voice. "The holistic lifestyle has improved her physical and mental health. She has lived longer than expected. However, her cancer is still progressing, but at a slow rate." Mary Baker was still alive, but Angel regretted he could not cure her.

Doctor Stanford put his hand on his chin. "Is she the former patient of Doctor Andrew?"

"Yes, you are correct."

Doctor Stanford turned his head toward Doctor Andrew and gave him a malevolent look before turning back to Angel. "We will look forward to your next presentation."

When Angel arrived home that night, he searched online through the medical journals and relentlessly searched for any recent medical advances that might help Mary Baker. Angel was so involved in the search efforts he failed to notice it was two o'clock in the morning. He was exhausted and grabbed a couple of hours of sleep before reporting to the hospital for his daily rounds.

Angel was contacted late in the afternoon and asked to report to radiology. An x-ray technician greeted him when he arrived and showed him three mammograms.

"All three x-rays are identical in showing what appears to be breast cancer," said the technician. "It is not just similar. It is exactly the same on each chart."

"This cannot be correct," Angel exclaimed.

The technician was at a loss and shook his head. "I took the x-rays on the same day using the older Computed Radiography X-ray machine. The new Digital Radiography X-ray machine transfers the image directly to the computer and saves time, but the machine costs five times as much. We did not perform any maintenance on the older machine or replace the old plate since we were replacing the entire machine. The older plate must have picked up image noise, or a residual signal. Either scenario would create a false positive result. These ladies were told they had breast cancer. The ladies need to return for a new mammogram, and I need a doctor to explain the results. Unfortunately, the radiologist is on a two-week vacation. I checked and found you are a trained radiologist and are qualified to review the results with patients. These three ladies are not your patients, but I contacted their doctor. He gave approval for these patients to meet with another doctor during his absence. Would you be willing to meet with these ladies when they return for a new mammogram?"

"Yes, I will meet with them. See if you can get all of them to come in tomorrow afternoon at around three o'clock."

Angel returned to his rounds and left at the beginning of the second shift. He turned in early and slept for twelve hours. The next day went well. At three o'clock, he proceeded to radiology and saw the three ladies sitting in the waiting room outside the lab. Angel had reviewed their files earlier in the day. He asked the first patient, Marie Fletcher, to come into the examining room. He checked each of her breasts and detected the small lumps noted in her files.

Marie had been cold when she removed her blouse and bra, but now she felt the heat from Angel's hands as he examined her breasts, and she suddenly felt warm all over.

Marie saw his name tag. "You are the angel who is healing all the cancer patients. A friend told me about you when she found out I had cancer. A friend of hers had a friend who is a recent patient of yours. She has been telling everyone how you cured her."

"I am not an angel, but my name is Angel Carpenter. I want to retake your mammogram. It will just take a minute, and then I will meet with you again."

Angel examined the other patients. The x-ray technician took mammograms of the ladies using the new equipment. As Angel suspected, none of them had cancer.

Angel met with Marie again and showed her the new x-ray. "I am happy to report that you do not have breast cancer. We unknowingly received a bad x-ray on the plate of an older machine we were replacing. I am sorry we put you through the fear of thinking you had cancer. I apologize on behalf of the hospital. We contacted you immediately upon finding the error."

She had tears in her eyes as she thanked him. Angel met with the other two patients and gave them the same explanation. They were all relieved as they left.

Marie had used the bathroom and stood waiting at the elevator. One of the ladies she met in the waiting room ambled over and stood next to her.

"The angel cured me of my cancer," Marie stated. "Did he also cure you?"

"The doctor said there was just an error with the prior x-ray."

"Did you not feel the heat of his healing power when he placed his hands on you?" Marie said with a pious demeanor.

"His hands were very warm," the lady replied.

Marie looked at the lady with complete confidence. "When I came here the first time, I had a friend who told me about Doctor Angel. All his patients get well, and his patients must pray each day. He has never lost a patient. All the patients who come to him are terminal, but none of them die. He heals them. If you do not believe me, ask any of the nurses. He is the archangel Raphael, the angel who heals. His last name is Carpenter. Jesus was a carpenter. Doctor Carpenter healed me with his touch, and I know he is an angel."

The third lady from the waiting room joined them and listened to part of the conversation. She had also noticed the hot hands and how pleasant they felt against her skin. She was a devout Christian with a vivid imagination and felt a need to comment.

"His hands were extra warm, and my breast did not hurt the way they normally do after an examination."

Two patients leaving the hospital felt Angel had healed them. The other patient was skeptical but did not completely discount the possibility of being healed. Regardless, they were all relieved and happy. Marie told her family, relatives, and everyone she met how an angel had healed her cancer. She posted a video on social media. It went viral with followers wanting to learn more about her miracle and her encounter with a real-life angel.

Angel sat in his office reviewing recent blood and urine results before starting his rounds when two men approached. They entered his office, shut the door, and sat in the two chairs facing his desk.

"We are with the State Attorney's office," the older man said. "We have an individual with cancer who needs to be in your cancer drug trial program. Here is his medical file showing his condition." Angel took the file and reviewed it. Someone had redacted the name of the individual.

"I am sorry, but I cannot help you. All of our beds for the drug trial are taken. The current group is in its fifth week of a twelve-week cycle. The next group of patients has already been selected. Also, the drug we are evaluating cannot cure his type of cancer."

"You do not understand," the younger man said. "We are not making a request. You will accept this patient. He has agreed to testify against a mafia family if he is placed in your cancer drug trial."

"I thought the mafia was no longer in existence," Angel replied.

The younger man shook his head with a scowl. "In other areas in the United States, a mafia family controls a given area. Miami is an open market with seven mafia groups operating in Dade and Broward counties, including the five original mafia families. The five families keep a low profile, but not the other groups. The Russian mafia is the most violent, followed by the smallest group. You doctors are clueless and know nothing about the real world."

"I still cannot accept him since I do not have a spare bed. The trial only allows for a hundred patients. I would have to remove one of my existing patients from the trial, and I will not decide which of my current patients should die."

The older man decided to resolve the doctor's dilemma. "We have already selected the patient to be removed. Judith Stephono is her name. Before she married, her last name was Gambezze. Her family is one of the five original mafia families. Her father took over as head of the family sixteen years ago. The family is wealthy with huge real estate holdings and a wide range of businesses. Taking his daughter off the cancer drug will put more pressure on him. Maybe he will confess to his criminal dealings to save his daughter's life by getting her back on the drug trial. That is our backup plan if the witness dies from his cancer, before we can use his testimony to send Gambezze to prison."

Angel did not have a choice. "Today is Thursday. Bring your witness in on Monday morning at eight o'clock. I will meet with him and start him on the program."

The two men stood up. "We will see you on Monday," the younger man said with a superior demeanor. The older man felt his younger partner could have been more diplomatic.

After they left his office, Angel sat there for a while, trying to decide what to do. There was no way he would remove Judith Stephono from the program. Her blood and urine samples showed a continuing reduction in cancer cells. He decided to discuss the matter with Judith as he walked down the hallway. Angel entered her room and shut the door.

Judith saw the troubled look on Angel's face. "Are you okay?" She asked.

Angel grimaced. "No, I am not okay. Two gentlemen from the state attorney's office just told me that your father is the boss of a mafia family. Tell me, are you in the mafia?"

Judith sounded earnest as she tried to explain. "My ancestors were part of the mafia in the distant past. Father runs legitimate businesses, and people just make wrong assumptions because of our last name. My father is an exceptional businessperson and has a

Bachelor of Science Degree in Finance. My husband and I are accountants. All of my siblings have degrees. My family knows there is more money to be made legitimately. We own hotels, apartment buildings, restaurants, and other business ventures. We are not involved in organized crime, and I am not in the mafia." Angel thought Judith's explanation sounded plausible.

"I have been ordered to remove you from the program. However, your cancer is improving, and I wish to continue treating you. I will need to move you to another room and temporarily reschedule your activities, but you need to change your appearance."

"What is the name of the person they are adding to the cancer trial?" Judith asked.

"I am sorry, but I have already said too much. I could lose my job or possibly face criminal charges if they find out I am keeping you in the program."

"When do you plan to move me to another room?"

"Sunday morning near the end of the third shift since there is less activity and fewer employees."

"Then, I will change my appearance Saturday night. I will need to tell my husband and brother since they regularly visit me. I will make up a story for my two children."

After Angel left, Judith called her father. "We have a problem," Judith said as she informed her father of the discussion she had with Angel.

Angel met his new patient Monday morning. John Smith was the name they put on the patient chart. John Smith was short, overweight with a beer belly, and mostly bald with gray hair around his ears. Angel could tell the man was a heavy smoker from his yellow-stained teeth and from examining the man's lungs using his digital ultrasound stethoscope. He attempted to go through the complete program, but John Smith kept interrupting and said he just wanted the drug. Angel knew the cancer drug would be ineffective.

However, if John followed the holistic part of the drug trial, he could probably live for several years. Angel gave John a placebo instead of the cancer drug. Tyzugmod rigidly controlled the quantity of the drug they shipped to the hospital. They could not risk the drug being sold at a high price on the underground market. Therefore, they kept the drugs in a secure area. Access required a key and a code.

An armed police officer stayed with John Smith at all times. John ate the holistic food but complained continuously. After attending one exercise class, he decided to stay in his room. He got some exercise since he insisted on going outside four or five times a day for a cigarette break. Smoking inside the hospital was strictly forbidden.

John had been a patient for several weeks and had settled into a routine of watching television and taking his smoking breaks outside.

John decided it was time for another smoke on a cloudy Saturday afternoon. It was late in the day and getting dark, but the outdoor lighting kept the hospital brightly illuminated. John and his guard meandered aimlessly along the side of the hospital. John was on his third cigarette.

"I am feeling better," John said. "It seems the cancer drug is working. I even lost a few pounds. Doctor Carpenter continues to insist I quit smoking. Also, he keeps trying to get me to attend the exercise and other classes. The doctor means well, but I wish he would stop harassing me."

The police officer was tired of listening to John. "Finish your cigarette so we can return to your room."

John threw his third cigarette on the ground and stepped on it when his head exploded, causing him to fall over backward to the ground. The officer looked around and ran toward a trash dumpster about ten yards away. He jumped behind the dumpster and crouched down. He immediately started screaming into his small police radio. Within a few minutes, half a dozen patrol cars arrived at the scene.

After several hours with no more gunshots, a medical examiner performed a cursory examination of the body. They took photos of the body and then transported it to the coroner's office for a forensic autopsy. The following day, the detectives found a 50-caliber bullet and knew the shooter used a high-power sniper rifle. They put in their report that the weapon probably had a silencer since the officer did not hear a gunshot. After the autopsy, they were told what they already knew.

Except for Judith, all the adults of the Gambezze family were attending a formal event with hundreds of witnesses. The police detectives first thought it might be Judith Stephono since she would have a motive for being kicked out of the cancer drug program. However, an attorney for the Gambezze family informed the police that Judith was in her hospital room at the time of the murder. Several friends from her office were visiting with her at the time of the shooting. Also, at the time of the shooting, a nurse came to her room when she complained of chest pains.

The police took Angel to the police station and interrogated him for three hours until his attorney, George Martinez, arrived and stopped the questioning. Angel and George had been close friends since high school.

The Assistant State Attorney arrived toward the end of the questioning and accused Angel of violating the law, but they did not arrest him. They had just lost their key witness and wanted to blame someone.

"You should rethink your accusation against my client," George said with his attorney demeanor. "The real question is why you were parading your witness outside the hospital several times a day. He would be alive if he had been in his assigned room. The culpability for his death is with the police and not with my client."

George and Angel left the station. "This whole matter is ridiculous," George said when they were alone in the parking lot. "If this witness had any credible evidence, they would have placed him in the witness protection program, and the United States Marshals would have provided total security. The word on the street is that your former patient used the local State Attorney's office to get accepted into your cancer drug trial. He was too far down in the organization to have useful information. He may have helped get a few individuals at the bottom arrested. There is no way he would have been able to bring down a mafia boss. The Gambezze family killed him, just to send a message."

The next day Angel went to Judith and was blunt. "Did your family have any involvement with the patient killed outside the hospital?" Judith appeared offended and hurt by his accusation.

"No, I heard about a patient who was shot, but why would you think my family would kill some stranger smoking outside the hospital? What are you not telling me?" She was quite sincere with her statement.

"The patient planned to testify against your family," Angel said.

"I only know a few individuals who work for my father, but my father would never kill a person."

"Judith, how did you know the patient was smoking outside the hospital?" While news agencies reported the shooting, none of the reports mentioned smoking. Judith knew she had made a mistake. "I know your family is responsible for his death. Because of his murder, the police and State Attorney have threatened me. Your family put our entire cancer test at risk. A hospital transporter will be by later to return you to your former room." Angel was visibly upset.

Judith watched Angel leave. "It seems my doctor is not as naive as I thought," she whispered to herself.

However, she liked Angel and was indebted to him since he was curing her, and her family honored their debts. Also, they might have need of his talents in the future since he is willing to bend the rules.

A few days later, Angel approached his car in the parking garage and noticed his taillight was broken. Someone had smashed it with a club of some type since there was no other damage to the car. Angel's gang experience made him street smart. He knew driving a vehicle with a broken taillight would give the police probable cause to pull his car over on his way home.

Angel called for transportation. While he was being driven home, he called George and explained what had taken place. George said he would have a car tech call him.

The following morning Angel paid for a ride to the hospital. On the way, he contacted a mobile vehicle repair shop. Later in the day, the auto tech called and asked Angel where he parked the vehicle and said he would be by shortly to get the keys.

By the middle of the afternoon, an auto repair person had replaced the entire taillight assembly. The repair labor only took a few minutes since the complete unit was removable by unbolting four screws and unplugging a cable. However, the cost of the car's taillight assembly was expensive. The tech guy was even more costly, but Angel did not mind paying the invoice when he saw the equipment.

On the way home from the hospital, Angel saw a flashing light behind him. He pulled over to the side of the road and turned his cellphone to record. Angel reached into the glove compartment, pulled out the vehicle's registration, and set it on the dash. He put his wallet next to the vehicle registration. He let down the car window and waited. Two officers approached his car, one on either side of the vehicle. Angel kept both hands on the steering wheel.

Angel started talking when the officer approached. "Good afternoon, officer. How may I help you?"

"You ran a stop sign and were speeding."

"There must be some mistake," Angel said calmly. "I came to a complete stop at the stop sign. I carefully watched my speedometer and drove under the speed limit."

"Are you calling me a liar?"

"No," Angel answered demurely.

"Give me your license, registration, and proof of insurance."

"I am going to take my hands off the steering wheel to reach for my registration and wallet sitting on the dash."

Angel handed the officer the registration. Then, he carefully removed the driver's license and insurance card from his wallet and handed the items to the officer.

"May we search your car?"

"No, you may not search my car," Angel responded with extreme politeness.

"Then, you will have to wait until a K-9 unit is brought to the scene. While we are waiting, you need to step out of your car so that I can conduct a sobriety test."

Angel eased out of the car and locked it after shutting the door. He breathed into the breathalyzer and then walked in a straight line as directed.

Angel noticed another car had pulled off the road a short distance away. One man stood outside the vehicle's passenger door while a second man continued sitting inside on the driver side. The police ignored the second vehicle.

A K-9 unit arrived, and the drug dog circled the vehicle. The dog failed to detect the presence of drugs. Therefore, no probable cause existed to search the car. The officer gave Angel a ticket for failing to stop at a stop sign and a speeding ticket.

The same patrol car stopped Angel the following night and repeated the routine, including the K-9 unit, before issuing two more tickets. Angel saw the same second car again, but no one got out of the vehicle. After that, Angel started using paid transportation.

The hearing date for the traffic violations finally arrived. Most people simply paid the fine. However, Angel did not have such an option since he received four tickets in two days, and the state would suspend his driver's license. They entered the courtroom and found a seat near the front. George and Angel stood up when their case was called.

"Your Honor, my client pleads not guilty to all four traffic violations," George said.

The judge set a trial date, which gave them four weeks to plan their defense. George told Angel not to worry, but he was still worried. George told Angel it would be a bench trial before a judge without a jury.

The judicial clerk announced the case on the day of the hearing, and the trial started. The first officer took the stand. "Your Honor, on the night designated, Angel Carpenter was speeding over twenty miles per hour above the speed limit. We watched him dangerously weave from one lane to the next as he passed other vehicles. His high rate of speed created a danger to himself and other drivers. Also, he failed to come to a complete stop at a stop sign. After being pulled over, he refused to allow us to search his car. He exhibited the same dangerous driving habits the following night."

"Do you wish to question this officer?" the Judge asked George.

"Yes, Your Honor, but I would like to defer questioning the first officer until after the second officer testifies."

The testimony given by the second officer was nearly identical to the first officer. This time, George questioned the witness.

"I visited the police station and filed a request to view the dash camera on your police car only to be told there were no videos,"

George said. "I made the same request to view the videos from you and your partner's body cameras with the same results. Is there a reason all three of the cameras were turned off?"

"I guess we just forgot," the officer said and grinned.

"Are you aware it is against your department's policies for your car video or body camera to be turned off when pulling over a vehicle for a traffic violation?" The officer no longer thought it was funny and had a worried expression.

"Yes," he replied.

"Well, we are in luck because I have videos of both incidents." George positioned his computer tablet so the officer and the judge could see the screen and started a video. He displayed several videos from different angles. The videos clearly showed what had actually occurred. One video was focused on the speedometer with a split video showing Angel stopping at the stop sign before continuing. The next-to-last video from outside Angel's car was the most damaging to the police since Angel's vehicle remained in the right lane as it traveled down the highway, closely followed by the police car. George finished with a final video of the parking garage showing a third officer breaking the taillight of Angel's car.

After George finished showing the various videos, he looked at the officer. "Please confirm with a yes or no if the videos clearly show what occurred during both incidents."

"Yes," the officer said in a subdued voice.

George looked straight at him with a determined look. "I have one more question. Were you acting on orders when you stopped my client?"

The officer looked trapped, and it was apparent from his body language that he lied when he said: "No, I was not acting under orders."

"Your Honor, I have no more questions for this officer. I would like to recall the first officer."

"That will not be necessary," the Judge said. "All charges will be dropped. Do you wish to file charges against these officers?"

"I will not file criminal or civil charges if they cease harassing my client."

The Judge looked at Angel. "Doctor Carpenter, you are free to go. The police will not harass you in the future."

"Thank you, Your Honor."

The Judge motioned for the first officer to approach the bench. The second officer was still sitting in the witness chair.

She lowered her voice so only the two officers could hear. "Both of you committed perjury in my courtroom. You are a disgrace to your uniform. You can be thankful Doctor Carpenter is not pressing charges. The penalty for perjury is up to five years in prison plus up to a five thousand dollar fine. You are to go back to whoever ordered you to harass Doctor Carpenter and tell them to stop. The last thing the police department needs is a lawsuit with such damaging video evidence. Also, I plan to talk to the Police Chief later today about this incident. Now, get out of my courtroom before I change my mind about having you brought up on perjury charges."

Once George and Angel were outside the building, George said: "Hopefully, you will not suffer any further problems with the police but be extra careful."

"Several of the videos you showed in court did not come from the cameras in my car," Angel said with a puzzled expression.

George shrugged his shoulders. "The flash drive for the videos outside your car showed up at my office in a sealed envelope with no identification on who sent it."

Angel thought he knew who sent the flash drive, but he remained quiet. "Thanks for your help. You are a good attorney." Angel knew his comment would get a response from George.

"How many times must I tell you? I am not a good attorney. I am a great attorney!"

Angel chuckled. "I stand corrected. You are a great attorney! Thanks again."

"Angel Code," George said.

"Angel Code," Angel replied.

They were referring to their gang code, where all gang members looked out for each other. George and Angel walked to the parking garage and separated to go to their separate vehicles. It was midday, and Angel still had patients to see.

As Angel drove to the hospital, he felt a little guilty about the officers. They had lied, but there was some justification for their actions since it was partially his fault the witness, John Smith, had been murdered. Also, it was apparent they were following orders. He had made additional enemies and knew he would need to be extra careful in the future. Plus, he wondered if the mafia had provided the videos taken from outside his car. The officers could be wondering the same thing. They would assume he was working for the mafia or on their payroll. However, with his small bank account, it would be apparent he was not receiving money from the mafia or anyone else.

CHAPTER 3 NO ONE DIES

The holistic cancer drug trial at Christian Health Hospital exceeded all expectations. The prior non-holistic trials had ranged from thirty-six to forty-four percent. After nine months, no one accepted into the holistic cancer drug trial had died. The directors at Tyzugmod assigned additional researchers to analyze the results being achieved at Christian Health Hospital.

Angel prepared his presentation for the Hospital Board and sent a written report to the Tyzugmod Corporation. He arrived at the conference room and waited outside while the Hospital Board discussed finances and other administrative issues.

Angel had arrived early and anxiously reviewed his notes several more times before being called into the meeting. He then started his presentation.

"I will provide you with a handout at the end, or you can download the test results after my presentation. It has been over nine months since we started the cancer drug trial, and I am happy to say we have not had a single death."

Angel projected his first chart on the screen. "We are in our tenth month of the cancer drug trial. We treated patients in groups of one hundred, with each test group lasting twelve weeks. Therefore, I will present the results for the first three hundred patients. I have broken the analysis into groups of one hundred, except I will divide the first group into two groups of fifty patients each. As you can see, forty-nine of the initial fifty patients are cancer-free and have been discharged. One patient is getting gradually worse but is still alive."

Angel put up the second chart. "In the second group of fifty, forty-four patients are cancer-free and have been discharged. Four are getting gradually worse, and two are stable without any improvement. Therefore, we still have seven patients from the initial one hundred who are not cured. These uncured patients were moved to another section of the hospital so we would have 100 beds available for the next group."

Angel continued with the third chart. "In the second group, ninety-one patients are cancer-free, five have been getting gradually worse, two are slightly better, and two show no improvement but are stable. As with the first group, we moved these nine non-cured patients to the same section of the hospital as the previous non-healed group."

Angel put up the fourth chart. "In the third group, ninety-two patients are cured and discharged. Of the remaining eight patients, two are getting better, three are gradually worsening, and three show no improvement but are stable."

Angel put up the fifth and final chart. "Out of the first three hundred patients, two hundred and seventy-six are cured while four patients are better but not cured. Unfortunately, twenty of the first three hundred patients are not responding to the drug. Thus, ninety-two percent of the patients who took part in the holistic cancer drug trial were cured. We do not know if any of the remaining twenty-four patients will survive. Prior trials show there are adverse reactions from the cancer drug if taken for more than twelve weeks. I still hope some of the twenty-four non-cured patients will survive."

Angel turned off the computer presentation. "We are maintaining the bed count at one hundred patients. The fourth group started two weeks ago."

Angel's face showed remorse as he sadly said: "Tyzugmod is reviewing our medical results and doing additional research to see if there is anything we can do for the patients who are not responding."

"The results are fantastic and are greater than we could ever have envisioned," Doctor Stanford said enthusiastically.

There were only a few questions. However, there were many positive comments as the directors showered him with their compliments. They were nearly universal as they expressed admiration for what had been accomplished. Once again, Doctor Andrew took exception to several of Angel's statements. He did not hide his contempt or animosity toward Angel. Doctor Andrew truly believed he should be managing and getting credit for the drug trial because of his seniority in the cancer ward. In his opinion, the pharmaceutical company was primarily responsible for the results. He believed all of Angel's propaganda about the healthy mind, healthy body campaign was a deliberate fabrication and had nothing to do with the patients' recovery. He had already collected a lot of evidence he could use once Angel was discredited. Doctor Andrew decided to wait patiently for the right moment to spring a trap to show Angel was nothing but a charlatan who should not be allowed to practice medicine.

Angel continued to be concerned about the patients who were not responding to the drug trial. He spent time each night reviewing the urine and blood tests. Angel believed something in the data would provide the key to curing the non-responsive patients. He expanded the blood analysis to include several non-routine tests in an attempt to ascertain why these patients were not getting well.

Angel reexamined Mary Baker's file. He knew the drug was ineffective for her type of cancer, but why was she still alive? Empirical studies determined the drug was ineffective against bone cancer, myeloproliferative neoplasms, or cancers in the brain or spinal column. Also, prior studies showed the drug would not work for progressive Stage IV cancer. The problem was determining when the treatment would be effective. It would be cruel to give false hope to individual patients who were past the point where the drug would be effective.

Unfortunately, curing cancer was costly, so there was a financial consideration. It was essential to have a high survival percentage to get coverage under the various health insurance policies, including Medicare and Medicaid. If the survival rate were low, the health insurance companies would classify the drug as experimental and exclude it from coverage. The results of the drug test trial would determine if the company had a blockbuster drug or a massive bust. It would rank as a blockbuster if it generated over a billion dollars in sales.

Tyzugmod supported Angel due to the results of his research and his ability to convince them that his approach would work. The corporation had been willing to take a chance on Angel and had appointed their top scientist to manage the research for the cancer drug. She did not believe prayer and religion had anything to do with the success of the test trial. However, she had supported the test proposed by Angel, and the religious angle gave the drug unprecedented support from the hospital. Science supported how patients with a positive outlook did statistically better in drug test trials. Therefore, she considered it possible that prayer contributed to a positive outlook. Plus, it was a scientific fact that diet and exercise improved health.

Angel was at his apartment and in the middle of a late dinner when his cellphone rang.

"Hello," Angel said as he tapped the speaker button.

"Is this Angel?" A person in a strained voice asked.

"Yes, how may I help you?"

"This is Joseph Adler, leader of the South Bay Warlocks. It has been a long time since we entered into our agreement. I have been shot, and I need your help."

"Give me your address." Angel did not try to get out of the agreement or say how the agreement no longer applied

Angel received the address and realized he was familiar with the area. "I will be there in twenty minutes."

Angel arrived at the address of an old single-story home with peeling beige paint and a carport instead of a garage. There were two cars parked in the driveway and three other cars parked on what was left of the lawn. He saw four guys standing outside the door to the home, and they were armed. Angel was still dressed in hospital scrubs, and they waved him through the front door. A guy met him just inside the door and directed him to the second bedroom. Angel immediately went to Joseph and examined his wounds. Joseph had been shot in his upper chest and in his thigh. Both wounds were bandaged.

"Who bandaged the wounds?" Angel asked.

"I did," said a guy standing in the corner. "I served in the military and received basic field training in first aid,"

"You did a good job," Angel said as he nodded to the speaker.

Angel turned back to Joseph. "I need to get you to a hospital."

"No hospitals, there is a warrant out for my arrest. Just remove the bullets and patch me up." Joseph grunted in pain and gritted his teeth.

"You have been watching too much television or seen too many movies. If I operate on you here, you will die. If you do not go to a hospital, you will die."

Angel thought for a moment. "Is there anyone here similar to you in looks, height, weight, and age? Someone who does not have a warrant out for their arrest."

"Get Phillip," Joseph said.

A minute later, a guy entered the room, and Angel looked at him. "You will do. Change wallets with Joseph."

Angel took the wallet and looked at the driver's license. He held it up next to Joseph.

"Close enough. I am calling an ambulance. Two of you can stay, but the rest of you need to clear out."

Angel handed Joseph the wallet. "Remember, you are now Phillip Grainger. Memorize the information on the driver's license. If anyone asks, say you were shot by a drive-by and do not remember what happened."

Joseph chuckled. "It was a drive-by shooting! It is okay. I recognized the guy driving the car and the shooter in the backseat."

Angel heard the siren of the ambulance and went out to the street. The ambulance pulled in, and Angel directed them into the house. The paramedics put Joseph on a stretcher and transported him to the ambulance.

"What hospital are you taking him to?" Angel asked.

"Mercy Memorial," a paramedic replied.

Angel threw his keys to the closest gang member. "Take my car to Mercy Memorial hospital."

Angel got in the ambulance. A paramedic had already started an IV. Angel identified himself again when they arrived at the hospital and volunteered to assist with the surgery. The emergency room was shorthanded, and he was ready by the time the x-rays were completed. After becoming aware of Angel's surgical expertise, the trauma doctor scheduled successive surgeries. He would operate on the chest, and after completion of his surgery, Angel would operate on the thigh.

The trauma doctor completed his surgery in a little less than an hour. Then Angel, assisted by two ER nurses, removed the bullet fragments in the thigh. It was a straightforward procedure, but the bullet had splintered. It took about twenty minutes for Angel to remove all the bullet fragments. Sutures were applied where needed, and the nurses finished bandaging the wounds. Angel complemented the nurses as an orderly entered to take Joseph to the recovery room. Angel was getting ready to leave when multiple stretchers arrived at the emergency room. A domestic disturbance during a party had resulted in eight people being shot, including two police officers. One victim was pronounced dead on arrival. The emergency room was at capacity before the new arrivals. A nurse who had assisted Angel accosted one of the doctors. During the discussion, she pointed at Angel.

The doctor approached Angel. "I am the second shift Physician Director, and if you are willing, I would like to assign you to a surgical room. The nurse manager will assign you the same nurses who previously assisted you, if you have no objections."

"I would be happy to help, and the two nurses who assisted me earlier were excellent."

It was a busy night. As soon as Angel finished with one patient, another was waiting. He operated on one of the police officers with a bullet wound to the arm and other victims with less serious injuries. Two trauma surgeons were kept busy with the severe chest and stomach wounds. Angel, with the surgical assistants, continued to take whatever patients were wheeled into their operating room. Ambulances continued to bring in patients who needed emergency care. The ER became calmer at about three in the morning, and Angel decided they no longer needed him. He learned the trauma surgeons had operated on twelve critical patients. Two patients died, but the other victims would live, barring infections or other complications. The Physician Director thanked him for his help.

Angel decided to check on Joseph before he left. Joseph handled the anesthesia well, and after he regained consciousness, a nurse moved him from the recovery room to an inpatient room.

Angel saw Joseph was weak but in good spirits. "When will I be released?" Joseph asked.

"If there are no complications, three to four days. You were lucky the bullets did not hit a vital organ."

"Thank you," Joseph said. "I owe you one."

"Forget it. We honor the code."

Angel proceeded to the admittance area and saw the person to whom he had given his car keys. "Joseph is going to be okay," he said as he approached the gang member.

The gang member gave Angel the car keys and walked him to his car. He thanked Angel before heading back to the waiting room. He had already called most of the gang and informed them Joseph was going to be all right. He was second in charge and told them to prepare for revenge. They knew their leader would hit back and hit hard. It would not be a minor hit. The goal would be to kill every member of the rival group. No one attacked the Warlocks unless they were prepared for war.

Angel looked at the time and figured he might get two hours of sleep before starting his rounds. The Warlocks kept their end of the agreement over the years. Now, he had honored his part of the pact. He knew it was late, but he called his friend George. George answered on the fifth ring and noted the caller ID.

"Angel, it is mighty early for a social call."

"Joseph Adler, the leader of the Warlocks, was shot. The bullets have been removed, and he is recuperating at Mercy Memorial Hospital under the name of Phillip Grainger since there is an outstanding warrant for his arrest. You know our agreement. He needs a great attorney."

"Mercy Memorial, Phillip Grainger, got it. I will take care of it. Be careful, Angel."

"I will. Good night, George."

"Good night, Angel."

George was thoughtful and no longer sleepy. He decided to get an early start and stop by the hospital on the way to the office. After taking a shower and getting dressed, he checked the court files online to determine the reason for the outstanding warrant.

After arriving at the hospital, he was given the room number for Phillip Grainger. The door was open, so he went in and looked around. George saw they were alone.

"I am attorney George Martinez. An angel told me a friend of yours named Joseph Adler might need an attorney."

"The angel is correct," Joseph said with a snicker. They discussed the warrant, and he answered George's questions concerning the allegations.

"Do you have an alibi and witnesses who can attest to your whereabouts on the night in question?" George asked.

"Yes, to both questions. How many witnesses do I need?"

"At least two, but three would be nice."

"It just so happens there were three witnesses with me on the night in question, and they can attest I was nowhere near where the crime occurred."

George handed him a business card. "Here is my card. It has my email address. Send me the names and contact information of your alibi witnesses. Once I talk to the detective handling the case, I am confident they will no longer consider you a suspect. I will file a motion with the court to get the arrest warrant withdrawn because of mistaken identity. Good luck in your war with this other gang. The Angels will be open for attack if the Warlocks are destroyed."

"They caught us off guard," Joseph snapped. "It will not happen again. They made a big mistake attacking the Warlocks. Thank you for your help. Angel honored our agreement, and I am indebted to him. I was young when Angel helped me maintain my leadership of the gang. If I had shot Owen, I would have lost standing with my gang since everyone would think I was afraid of him. However, when Angel beat him in a fistfight, he appeared weak since Angel was smaller. After losing the fight, he pulled a gun and shot Angel. At that point, my entire gang was disgusted with him, and no one was ready to accept him over me since it was a cowardly response. They all fully supported me killing him at that point. They still talk about that day, and how you cannot kill an angel with a bullet. I hope one day I can repay Angel for his help then and now."

George remembered the day Angel walked into their gang meeting after a drive-by shooter had gunned down their leader. Angel stated his name and said he was their new leader. Three of the members objected, and the next thing anyone remembered was seeing all three objectors on the ground nursing their injuries while Angel had not even broken a sweat.

"You may be an angel, but you fight like the devil," George said.

"We should call ourselves the Angels," another member shouted.

Everyone joined in, and the group became the Angels. Angel asked George to become second in command, and George supported him completely. Angel explained his plan for their gang, and they established their brotherhood on that day. From the beginning, Angel started teaching martial arts to the gang members. It was years ago, but the gang continued its existence with successive leaders who followed the same code.

A representative of the Tyzugmod Corporation contacted Angel and arranged for him to fly to the corporate headquarters for a meeting with the Board of Directors. Angel boarded a private corporate jet at the Miami Executive Airport. It was a two-hour flight, and he was the only passenger on board. The flight attendant prepared a full course meal for Angel. He had dressed in a suit for the trip and had prepared a presentation as requested. A limousine picked him up as soon as the jet touched down, and he was sitting in a conference room thirty minutes later. After his presentation, the entire Board was vocal in expressing their satisfaction with the test trial results, which had exceeded all of their expectations. They then asked Angel for his recommendations. They wanted to see if he thought like a corporate person or just a physician.

"You should continue to offer the treatment to future candidates who benefit from this drug," Angel instructed. "If you stick to those cancer patients and use the holistic approach, the cure rate should be above ninety percent. I recommend you do additional research to examine possible modifications of the drug for the patients showing slower or no improvements. I would further recommend you set up separate cancer treatment centers which can better utilize the holistic approach. Traditional hospitals are not the best facility for fully implementing this drug. We can save over five hundred thousand lives annually in the United States. Due to the difficulties manufacturing the drug, you should spend the next two years expanding its use in the United States. You must find a way to mass-produce the drug if you wish to meet the worldwide demand."

"When do you think we should go public with our findings?" the Chairperson asked.

"Our initial trial will end in six months," Angel said. "I recommend you have all the results available to present to the FDA at that time. You could provide an interim report, but I believe it would have the greatest impact to have one major presentation to the public when the initial test is complete, and the FDA application is submitted. The announcement might encourage the FDA to speed up their approval."

The Chairperson was thoughtful. "Angel, would you mind waiting in the break room down the hall? I need to meet privately with the directors for a few minutes."

Angel nodded, stood up, and left the room. He walked down the hall and took a seat in the break room, which was quite extravagant. While waiting, Angel had a cup of coffee.

The directors became more impressed with Doctor Carpenter with each visit. Much of what Angel said was intuitively apparent from examining the drug test results. It was only a brief wait before an administrative assistant found Angel and escorted him back to the conference room.

The Chairperson looked up as Angel reentered the room. "Angel, I speak on behalf of the entire Board when I say we are extremely pleased with your results. When the drug trial is completed, we want you to join the Board as one of our outside directors. You would only need to meet with us once per quarter. Your expertise and knowledge would allow us to make more informed decisions. We also voted to give you stock options for one hundred thousand shares of common stock in the corporation based on today's price. The options are exercisable over five years from the date the Phase Three Clinical Trial is completed, and the New Drug Application is submitted to the FDA for final approval. We have included an extra incentive for each one percent increase in the percent cure rate above eighty percent, which is double our previous rate."

The Chairperson motioned to the person sitting to his left. "Our attorney has already prepared the documents for the stock options. We will follow his recommendation to make sure there are no legal issues. Also, we would like you to be a spoke person for the corporation when the FDA has fully approved the drug."

Angel had only minimum knowledge regarding financial matters and did not know the worth of a stock option but figured he could look it up later. Angel thanked them, and they asked him to join them at the next quarterly board meeting in three months. They met monthly, but the quarterly meetings involved review of the financials for filing with the SEC and impacted their stock price. They added the data from the drug test to the financial reports.

After Angel exited the conference room for his trip home, the directors continued their meeting. They discussed the best way to maximize the profit for the cancer drug once it received FDA approval. Following Angel's recommendation, they decided to open private cancer centers without the high costs associated with running a full-service hospital. However, they voted to go upscale to maximize their profits.

"There are large hotels available for sale at discount prices," the Treasurer said. "This is because many businesses eliminated or significantly reduced their travel budget in favor of telecommunications. Even though travel rebounded after the coronavirus, hotel occupancy is still low. A hotel would be ideal for treating cancer patients. There would be restaurants for food preparations using holistic menus. Plus, a hotel would have the space for all the other parts of the holistic program. I propose we set aside funds immediately and arrange banking to purchase several sufficiently large hotels to provide us with at least a thousand rooms. If the average treatment takes three months, we could treat up to four thousand cancer patients per year. These hotels would be for wealthy individuals who could pay for premium care. If we charge a base fee of two hundred fifty thousand dollars per patient, the annual revenue would be over a billion dollars per year. We could probably charge up to a million dollars for VIP suites. Statistically, out of the five million people dying from cancer each year, three hundred thousand are millionaires. This premium income would be in addition to the traditional sales of the drug. In the traditional market, the non-wealthy cancer patients will use their healthcare insurance and Medicare for treatment at hospitals and clinics."

"What is the downside if the drug does not meet our expectations?" Another director asked.

"We could convert the hotels into premium assisted living facilities as a fallback plan in a worst-case scenario or we could simply resale them," the Treasurer replied.

"What about political fallout," the Chairperson asked.

"Not a problem," the attorney replied. "We donate heavily to the campaign funds for both parties. Also, most of the politicians are rich and we continue to receive requests from numerous politicians asking for access to the cancer drug. They want preferential treatment, and this will allow us to give it to them while enhancing our profits."

"We can gain public support by saying we are milking the rich in an effort to keep the drug costs lower for the poor," the Marketing Director interjected.

"You are not suggesting we lower price, are you?" The Treasurer asked.

"No, of course not," the Marketing Director replied.

After further discussions, they passed a motion to have their executives proceed with a search for the hotels.

"We are going after two completely different markets for the drug," exclaimed the Marketing Director. "Therefore, I propose we develop a unique drug name for each market." They passed a motion to provide marketing funds to select the two names for the drug.

"Doctor Angel Carpenter will soon become a director," the Finance Director said. "Was there a reason for not involving him in our discussions about our proposed expansion into cancer treatment centers?"

"I believe it would be a mistake to provide such information to Doctor Carpenter at this time," said the Chairperson. "He is currently too idealistic. Did you notice how he did not seem excited about the stock options or ask how much a director earns for being on the Board? I think our doctor will be less idealistic when he is a millionaire and begins enjoying the higher lifestyle associated with wealth. Until then, we will keep him in the dark so he can concentrate on getting us the best test results."

"We have a patent for the drug, but what about the holistic approach used by Doctor Carpenter?" The Research & Development Director asked. "Is there a legal way to maintain our advantage by limiting or preventing our competitors from using the holistic approach?"

All eyes turned to their attorney. "Good point. I will have several of our best patent attorneys research the matter to see what options might give us the best protection. While it is probably not patentable, it may be possible to protect it as being proprietary. You should do additional trials with some of your other drugs to see if the holistic approach used by Doctor Carpenter could improve the efficacy of those drugs. Also, you need to determine what parts of the holistic approach can be eliminated without reducing the effectiveness of the drug. For example, we need to change, reduce, or eliminate the religious parts of the holistic approach. That is another item we should not discuss with Doctor Carpenter." They agreed to follow the advice of their attorney.

The Treasurer pointed out the obvious. "This drug will generate more profit than all our other drugs combined." Everyone in the room was thinking the same thing.

"I suggest you give Doctor Carpenter whatever he wants," the attorney advised. "Once the FDA approves this drug, it will not be long until our competitors offer Doctor Carpenter incentives to work for them. We primarily offered him the stock options to give him a huge financial reason to stay committed to our corporation. Again, you need to do whatever it takes to maintain his loyalty to you and only to you. The primary contact for Doctor Carpenter should have the authority to provide Doctor Carpenter whatever he needs without waiting for Board approval."

Everyone nodded in agreement. A motion was made, seconded, and unanimously approved to grant the recommended authority to their representative. The authorization also allowed the representative to spend up to a million dollars without additional Board approval. After setting a date for their next meeting, a motion was made and unanimously approved to adjourn the meeting.

Angel returned to Miami and resumed his regular work schedule. Angel was finishing up another day and chose to have dinner at the hospital cafeteria. He ordered from the same menu used by his patients. A female employee attempted a casual conversation by saying that being a doctor must be exciting. Angel was oblivious to the flirtatious attempt. He said his job was routine and somewhat dull, but he liked it. He would remember his comment later. His life was about to become anything but routine and dull.

CHAPTER 4 INTERROGATION

Doctor Angel Carpenter was sitting in an interrogation room at the police headquarters on Second Avenue in downtown Miami. A SWAT team had broken down the door to his apartment during the night, handcuffed him, and destroyed his apartment using a search warrant. When the police busted into his apartment, Angel had been reviewing his patients' medical records on the kitchen table and was still wearing his hospital scrubs. He was shocked and confused to see multiple guns pointed at him as they screamed for him to get face down on the floor. Out of fear, he promptly complied with their orders.

One officer had a knee pressed against the back of Angel's shoulders, while another had a knee against the lower part of his back. They roughly twisted his arms behind him and placed handcuffs on his wrists. His cellphone and keys were on the kitchen countertop. An officer examined his cellphone but could not access it because the security required a fingerprint and a code. The warrant had covered both his apartment and car. Two officers took his car keys and went to the parking lot to search his vehicle.

Four officers escorted Angel out of his apartment. They marched Angel down the stairs and outside to a waiting police car. A crowd of onlookers formed and started taking videos using their phones. The officers put Angel in the backseat of the police car. After a short wait, two officers got into the car and brought him to the police station.

Upon arrival, Angel was booked and fingerprinted electronically. Judy, the lady booking Angel took longer than expected since she kept staring at him with his blond hair and deep blue eyes. She processed hundreds of criminals each year but never booked a person who looked less like a criminal. Judy felt she was a good judge of character, and he did not look like a murderer. However, she knew they were almost always guilty. She confiscated Angel's wallet, comb, health watch, and pen. She placed the items inside a plastic sealable bag and gave him a receipt.

Then, Angel was locked in an interrogation room. The room had no clock, but Angel figured it was around ten PM. There was nothing to do as he relaxed into yoga meditation. He could only sit in a half yoga position since they had again handcuffed his hands behind his back after the fingerprinting. Once Angel achieved the proper state of mind and body, time no longer existed. He relaxed and mentally escaped to a pleasant place.

Five officers at Angel's one-bedroom apartment conducted a thorough search. The mattress was removed from the bed and ripped apart. The closets and the clothes therein were searched. They removed the drawers from the dresser and dumped the contents on the floor. An officer checked inside the refrigerator and behind it. They removed everything from the kitchen cabinets and examined each item. No hidden areas were found in any of the cabinets or closets. They removed all the air conditioning vents and looked in the ducts. Their forensic expert used ultraviolet light to check for blood and other bodily fluids, but it came up empty. After several hours they gave up. Nothing incriminating turned up from the search.

A personal computer was being used by Angel when they entered the apartment, so they did not need a password. A tech officer immediately searched the emails, and the documents stored on the computer. The search showed the computer contained nothing other than patient files and work-related emails. The only personal emails were to his mother, and all searches performed by Angel Carpenter were medically related. Regardless, they confiscated the computer and cellphone. A search of the car proved to be a further waste of time.

Detective Stone and Detective Avery had been waiting in Stone's office for the search results. They were on their second pot of coffee.

The officer in charge of the search came into the office, shaking his head at Stone. "The search of his apartment turned up nothing. His computer only contained patient files, and we could not search his phone since it requires a password and a thumbprint. We found nothing incriminating in his car. In summary, no blood, no guns, no ammunition, and no gun powder residue on any of his clothing. Also, even if we had found blood, he is a doctor, and it would not be unusual to find blood on a doctor's clothing."

Stone looked at Avery. "Let's get on with it," Stone said aggressively like a predator ready to pounce on a defenseless prey.

The detectives used the Reid interrogation technique. The technique is an accusatory process. One detective tells the suspect the results of the investigation proved he committed the crime in question. The goal is to make the suspect gradually more comfortable telling the truth. The department recognized Stone and Avery as being their best interrogation team.

They entered the interrogation room and were immediately upset since it looked like Angel was sitting in the chair asleep. Stone slammed the door, but Angel slowly opened his eyes and did not appear startled by the noise. Angel uncrossed his legs and put both feet on the floor. This was a first for them. They had never encountered a suspect who seemed so calm. However, they did not see any reason to change their approach since it worked successfully in most cases.

Stone took a seat facing Angel while Avery stood next to Angel. "Let me take off those cuffs," Avery said.

After taking the handcuffs off, Avery took a seat next to Angel. "Angel, an officer previously stated your Miranda Rights. Would you like me to repeat those rights?"

Stone and Avery had been working together for several years. Avery always played the role of the good cop since it fit his personality along with his appearance. Whereas Stone just looked intimidating with a taller and heavier physique. They had switched roles at times when they first started working together, but it did not work as well.

Angel looked toward Avery. "No, I understand my rights."

"Do you understand why you are here?" Avery asked.

"I do not have a clue," Angel said with a questioning look. "I am a doctor and need to resolve this misunderstanding so I can report to the hospital at the start of my shift. If you had called me, I would have come to the station voluntarily."

Angel continued to be perplexed. He did not know why they had broken into his apartment and taken him into custody. He was willing to answer their questions and continued to believe this was just a big mistake by the police.

"If you answer our questions truthfully, I am sure we can take care of this misunderstanding," said Avery as he displayed a friendly smile and an open posture. "Answer truthfully, and we will let you leave so you can take care of your patients." Lying to get a confession was part of their technique and was considered an acceptable interrogation technique.

"Where were you on the twenty-first of April?" Stone asked as he continued to examine his notes.

"What day of the week was that?" Angel asked.

"It was a Friday," Stone bellowed.

Angel was thoughtful and knew from giving presentations, you should always make sure you understand the question. Then, you take a moment to consider an appropriate answer before responding to the question in a slow controlled voice. The approach had served him well in medical school and as an intern. Avery sounded like a nice person, so he would do his best to answer the questions so he could go home or to work, depending on when they released him.

"My alarm goes off at five o'clock every morning," Angel said as he proceeded with a detailed response. "I brush my teeth, shave with an electric razor, shower, get dressed, and leave my apartment at around 5:45 AM. Depending on traffic, I arrive at Christian Health Hospital between 6:15 and 6:30 AM. My shift officially starts at 7:00 AM, so I always like to arrive a little early. I have a full schedule each day. I meet with patients until noon and then take a thirty-minute lunch. In the afternoon, I meet with patients until around 4:00 PM. I review patient test results until around 7:00 PM. Then I normally go home unless there is an emergency. If there is an emergency, I stay as long as it takes. When I arrive home, I exercise in the gym at my apartment complex for approximately an hour. After working out, I eat a healthy dinner, work on patient files, and generally go to bed at around 10:00 PM. I would have to check my notes for the exact date to be more accurate, but what I provided is my typical workday. On a hectic day, I may skip lunch or take five minutes to wolf down a sandwich."

Stone leaned forward. "Is there anyone who can verify your whereabouts on April 21 after you left the hospital?"

Angel thought for a minute. "No, I live alone, and the gym is normally empty when I work out." Angel did not know where the questions were leading, but he was becoming concerned.

"So, you have no alibi for the night of April 21 after seven o'clock?" Stone said with a menacing look.

Angel shrugged his shoulders. "No, I guess not."

Stone looked Angel in the eye. "Could you have visited a house on Pratt Avenue in South Beach on the night of April 21?"

"No," Angel said warily, and now he was genuinely concerned.

"Angel, I cannot help you unless you tell the truth," Avery said. "We have several witnesses who say they saw you there. You need to tell us what happened. Tell the truth, and we can probably straighten everything out."

Avery was very convincing as he lied about the witnesses, but he would say whatever it took to get a confession. This was usually when the suspect would confess to being there and try to pin the murder on someone else or explain how he acted in self-defense.

"I am telling the truth. I was not there. Your witnesses are mistaken if they think the person they saw was me."

Stone then opened a file folder and placed four pictures in front of Angel. The pictures were of a Glock 38-caliber pistol and three different dead bodies.

"Do you recognize this gun and these victims," Stone said with a brassy voice as he leaned toward Angel with a disgusted expression. "Before you decide to lie, we have your fingerprints on the gun. Also, as Avery pointed out, we have several witnesses who identified you."

"Angel, if you confess, we will cut you a good deal," Avery said with a compassionate gentler voice. "Let me help you. If you confess, you will feel better, and if you were provoked or felt threatened, you can enter a plea of self-defense. The three people you killed with this gun were bad individuals, and you did the city a big favor. Tell me what happened, and I will do what I can to get the state attorney to go easy on you. We can probably get him to drop the charges. If you do not confess, we have to assume the killings were premeditated, and you could face the death penalty for a triple homicide. So, let me help you."

Unfortunately, Angel could not control his facial expressions as he recognized the gun and one of the victims. He knew they were not lying about his fingerprints being on the gun. This had just turned into a nightmare.

"I want an attorney," Angel whispered as he leaned back in the chair with a sigh.

Both detectives looked angry and disappointed. Avery stood up, told Angel to turn around, and handcuffed him again. They took him down a hallway and through several doors before coming to a row of cells. They removed the handcuffs and placed him in a cell.

Detective Stone and Detective Avery returned to Stone's office. They were disappointed with the results of the interrogation. Their approach had worked well over the years. They had hoped for and expected a confession.

Detective Stone hit his desk with his fist. "He recognized the pictures, so we know he is guilty. He did not even say he was innocent before asking for an attorney."

Avery was shaking his head. "We probably should have softened our questions before showing the pictures and mentioning the fingerprints, but we cannot undo it now. However, the State Attorney will have a straightforward case with the suspect's fingerprints all over the gun. Once he talks to his attorney, he will agree to a plea deal, and we get to clear up three outstanding homicides. A confession would have resulted in three First-Degree Murder charges, but a plea to three counts of Second-Degree Murder will result in life in prison without a possibility for parole. Either way, he will spend the rest of his life behind bars, and there will be one less criminal on the streets or, in this case, in a hospital."

"All we can do now is write a preliminary report and call it a night," Stone said.

They finished around one o'clock in the morning. Stone filed the report electronically with the Criminal Investigations Division. However, they left a hard copy of the report in the Captain's inbox. Being older, the Captain still preferred paper. Everyone else would read the electronic file. They would not be involved in the case again except to serve as witnesses for the prosecution if it went to trial. These type cases seldom made it to trial since most criminals accepted a plea deal. For all practical purposes, they felt this was already a closed case.

Angel sat in a holding cell with three individuals, and now he was worried. The other detainees noticed Angel's medical attire. Once he confirmed he was a doctor, they took turns asking for medical advice. None of them had seen a doctor in years, and each had multiple ailments.

One prisoner was a heavy smoker with difficulty breathing, and it was apparent he had a respiratory problem. He had been arrested for assault and battery. He told Angel he would plead guilty to assault to get them to drop the battery charge. For assault, he would get a maximum of sixty days in jail, less time served. Whereas you can get up to five years for a battery. Angel advised him to see a doctor when he got out and gave him the location of a free medical clinic.

A short, overweight individual told Angel a plain clothes detective had arrested him for drug possession. It was the first time he had been caught, and he planned to plea bargain for probation.

The third person was slim and lanky with tattoos covering his arms and neck. "What crime did you commit?" He asked.

"I am innocent," Angel answered. Everyone burst out laughing.

"We are all innocent. What crime are they alleging against you?" The tattooed detainee asked. Angel was hesitant to answer and felt like he was in a bad dream.

"I am wrongfully accused of a triple homicide." The jail cell became quiet.

"Wow, you do not seem like a murderer, but you can never tell," the short, overweight detainee said. "Do they have any witnesses who saw you?"

"They say there are two witnesses."

"That is not good. Do they have any physical evidence?" The smoker asked in a raspy voice.

"They have my fingerprints on the murder weapon."

"That is bad," said the tattooed detainee. "In fact, it is very bad. Any chance you have an alibi?"

"No, I am normally alone when I am not working."

The other guys were shaking their heads. They felt pretty good compared to what Angel was facing.

"Your best option is a plea agreement," said the smoker. "That is what I plan to do." Angel did not answer, and the cell became quiet since there was nothing left to discuss.

The detainee with the tattoos knew he was in trouble since this was his third arrest. Under Florida's three-strike law, he was looking at possibly getting a life sentence without parole. Also, he had a nine-millimeter pistol in his possession when the police arrested him, which violated his parole. He knew how the system worked and smiled as he realized Doctor Angel Carpenter could be his get out of jail option. He hoped the doctor would plead not guilty. If so, he would ask his court-appointed attorney to contact the District Attorney. He would be a witness for the prosecution since he heard Doctor Carpenter bragging about getting away with murder. He was still smiling when he laid on the bed to take a nap. The one rule among common criminals was to look out for yourself. Honor among criminals was a Hollywood creation and had nothing to do with reality unless there was an association with a gang or organized crime.

A little while later, a uniformed officer came to their jail cell and allowed Angel to make his call. Angel called George Martinez.

Midmorning of the following day, two officers removed Angel from his cell and escorted him to the courthouse. Angel was happy to see George when he arrived in the assigned courtroom. He explained to George what had happened during the interrogation. Angel acknowledged he had never been in a courtroom, so George explained the procedure.

"Today, the judge will ask you how you wish to plea, and you will say not guilty. Then the judge will decide on the bail amount. How much cash do you have?"

"Less than five thousand dollars. I have been using all my excess funds to repay my student loans."

"What about your mother?" George asked.

Angel was visibly upset. There was no way he would ask his mother for money. "My mother has some savings, but I will not borrow money from my mother. Since my father died, she is barely taking care of herself. My father had a small life insurance policy, but there was little left after the funeral costs."

"If you cannot make bail, you will stay in jail for the entire length of the trial, and it could take several years. Do you know anyone who will loan you the money or post bail for you? You have to come up with ten percent of the bail amount if you use a bail bondsman."

"There is a person who may be willing to provide me with a loan. First, let us see if a loan will be necessary."

The court was packed, and it was several hours before the judge's judicial assistant called their case. At the hearing, Angel was charged with three counts of First-Degree Murder. He entered a plea of not guilty. The prosecution asked that bail be denied because of the heinous nature of the crimes.

Attorney Martinez approached the Judge and handed him a summary of the cancer drug trial. "Your Honor, my client is innocent. He is a medical doctor currently conducting an FDA approved cancer drug trial. If successful, millions of lives will be saved. My client is critical to the success of this drug trial since it is based on his research. Doctor Angel Carpenter is a respected member of the medical community and is not a flight risk."

The Judge reviewed the summary of the cancer test results and was impressed. He would normally have denied bail, but he could not ignore a cure for cancer. He set bail at one million dollars and required that Angel wear an ankle monitor.

Angel called Robert Hill, his former patient. Rob was completely healed of his cancer and had been in excellent health at his last appointment.

Rob answered on the second ring. "Hello, who is calling?"

"This is Angel."

"Doctor Angel, it is great hearing from you. I owe you, my life. What can I do for you?" Angel hated to continue but knew he must.

"I have been arrested for a triple homicide, and the judge has set my bail at a million dollars. The bail bondsman requires ten percent down to provide the bail. I hate to ask, but I need to borrow a hundred thousand dollars. It is a loan, and I will pay you back with interest."

"Of course, I will loan you the money. Just have someone call me and provide the wiring instructions."

"Thank you. I am sorry to impose on you like this, and I will pay you back as soon as possible."

"Doctor Angel, I would not be alive without you. I am happy to help you since you have done so much for me. Plus, thanks to you, I expect to go to heaven, and I cannot wait to try the heavenly brew you mentioned. Also, I have gotten to know you over the past year. I am an excellent judge of character, and I know you are innocent."

Angel thanked him again, and they both hung up. George contacted the bail bondsman and arranged the bail.

It took most of the day before the bail was posted and the ankle monitor attached. They retrieved Angel's personal property from lockup, but the police refused to return his cellphone or computer. George insisted on giving Angel a ride to his apartment, which Angel gladly accepted.

Angel was committed to doing whatever was necessary to avoid prison since he planned to keep the promise to his deceased father.

Angel was in high school when his father was diagnosed with cancer. He had spent many hours researching cancer and the various treatment options. Angel watched as his father underwent surgeries, chemotherapy, and radiation treatments. The treatments were horrible, and Angel felt there must be a better way. He had spent every night praying for his father's recovery. His father got better for a while.

After high school, Angel attended Florida International University, and upon graduation, he had planned to enter the veterinarian college at the University of Florida. He had dreamed of becoming a veterinarian for his entire life since he loved animals. Then his mother let him know his father's cancer had returned and had spread. As a result, Angel's life changed to an entirely new path. He needed to become a medical doctor so he could save his father. He stayed enrolled at Florida International University since they had an excellent medical college.

Several weeks later, they were having dinner together. "As I explained, my cancer has come back," his father said. "My doctor wants to start me on chemotherapy and then follow with radiation. I am not going through that again. I asked my doctor to be completely honest with me, and he told me it was unlikely the treatments would make any difference. He estimates I have less than a year. I do not plan to spend it being sick from the treatments. I love the two of you and want you to remember our good times. I have vacation days saved up and I can take a medical leave of absence at half pay when I can no longer work. I want some additional memories with you two."

Angel remembered his response to his father. "In the fall, I will enter medical school at Florida International University. Mother and I need you to stay alive. There is a new immunotherapy cancer treatment we want you to try. It uses the body's immune system to fight cancer cells. The side effects are minimal compared to traditional treatments. The cure rate is extremely low, but I believe we can succeed by adding a holistic diet, proper exercise, meditation, and prayer. It will be a family effort. It will also give me an incentive to study extra hard in medical school. I assume you want me to do well in school."

Angel remembered his father laughing as he accused him and his mother of conspiracy, but they spent an extended joyful time together until his father passed away. His father passed away two months before he graduated from medical school. His mother assured Angel that his father was watching as the dean presented him with his medical degree.

After his father's passing, his mother gave him a sealed envelope with his name on the outside. The envelope contained a letter from his father. Angel unfolded the letter and read.

"Angel, you are reading this letter because I have passed away. You already know how much I love you and your mother. God blessed me with a loving wife and blessed me a second time when an angel was left on our doorsteps. I know you became a doctor to cure me of my cancer. Because of your efforts, I had three additional years with you and your mother. Promise me that you will continue to work toward finding a cure for cancer and helping others. Even though I am gone, you need to continue your research. Do not mourn for me. God blessed me with a wonderful family. I will look down on you from time to time. You will do great things. Look after your mother. She is wonderful, and I still cannot believe she married me. I will see you again in heaven, but I expect to wait a long time for our reunion. Goodbye for now."

His father was a good person but had a short life. After reading the letter, tears were flowing down his face. He promised his father he would dedicate his life to finding a cure for cancer.

Angel remembered his father's doctor expressing surprise that his father had survived for almost three years. Angel started explaining how his family had coupled a holistic approach with immunotherapy. He stopped when it became apparent the doctor was not interested in listening to a medical student.

Angel had kept the promise to his father, and they were close to FDA approval for a new blockbuster cancer drug. This arrest could destroy everything. Angel had difficulty concentrating on his patient files. It would get worse unless they dropped the case. He knew who murdered the first victim but divulging the identity of the murderer would not help his case.

CHAPTER 5 NO PLEA

Angel was still shocked by the Judge's decision to require a million-dollar bail. He was relieved Robert Hill had loaned him the money to pay the bail bondsman, but it would take a long time to pay it back. He was thankful George was willing and able to handle his case. Angel twisted his ankle from side to side. It would take time to get used to the ankle monitor. The monitor was small and would not be noticed since it was covered by his pants. He was glad George had insisted on giving him a ride to his apartment since it gave him time to think about his predicament.

Angel and George rode in silence for a while before George shook his head. "I always knew that gun was going to be a problem."

They arrived at Angel's apartment and got out of the car. "Let's look at the damage," George said.

They took the elevator to the fourth floor and walked down the hallway. The door to Angel's apartment was shattered and lay just inside the apartment. Angel stood in the doorway. His apartment was a disaster. He entered the apartment closely followed by George.

"I cannot believe they destroyed all my furniture. It was not expensive furniture, but it was not cheap either. Replacing this is going to cost thousands of dollars. I do not have insurance since I did not think I needed it for an apartment. Can I sue the police for the damage?"

"You would be wasting your time," George said while shaking his head. "The police have qualified immunity for actions under a search warrant. It is not right, but it is the law. I can show you a case where the police used a flashbang device and burned down a suspect's home, but they were not liable under the law. I am sorry."

The police had confiscated Angel's desktop computer and tablet, but fortunately, everything had been backed up to the Cloud with a second backup on the hospital server. The police refused to return his computers or cellphone even when he offered to give them a backup of both computers and the phone.

After examining the room in his apartment, Angel looked at George and asked to borrow his phone. He then called the hospital to inform them he was taking Monday off. They arrested Angel on Thursday night, and it was now Friday afternoon. Angel handed the phone back to George and thanked him.

"I have a contact who will fix the door," George said. "I will keep you posted on the case. Send me a text message when you get a new phone."

George had offered to let Angel stay at his home, but he declined. The bedding was on the floor and had been walked on by the police during the search. He put all the bedding in the washing machine and left the apartment. Angel drove to an electronics store where he purchased a new phone, tablet, and desktop computer. He returned to the apartment and started the cleanup. He transferred the bedding to the dryer and put a load of clothes in the washer. Angel uploaded the backups to the phone, desktop computer, and tablet he had just purchased. He took the bedding out of the dryer and ran two more loads of laundry. He stacked his clothes in the closet and finished cleaning the apartment. Angel slept on the floor since his bed was destroyed. It was only 9:00 PM, but he was exhausted and fell instantly asleep.

The following morning, Angel ordered new furniture online from a local store. He made sure each piece of furniture was in stock and could be delivered on Monday. Just as he finished, a man wearing a tool belt knocked on what was left of the door. Angel had leaned the shattered door against the door frame.

"Good morning, my name is Harry. George called me and told me what happened. I took a guess and brought a standard door. It looks like I guessed right. It will take me a couple of hours to complete the installation. I will replace the doorknob and add a matching deadbolt. I can provide you with new keys or key the locks to an existing key."

Angel thought for a minute. "Go with new keys."

True to his word, it took a little less than two hours to install the new door. Harry examined the old door and pulled off a scrap of wood.

"I will use this scrap to buy some matching paint. I will be back on Monday to do the painting," Harry said as he gathered up his tools. He gave Angel two sets of keys. Angel took one key and gave it back to Harry.

"Keep one key in case I am not here when you return."

"The paint may be a little wet for a day or two, so just touch the doorknob," Harry said. "If you are not here, I will leave the spare key on the kitchen table. I will take what is left of your old door and put it in the trash dumpster."

Angel spent the day cleaning up the destruction to his apartment. Toward the end of the day, he called his mother.

"Hi, I would like to stop by if you are available?"

"Of course, I am available. What a silly question. I will cook, and we will have an enjoyable dinner together."

"Not tonight," Angel replied. "It will be my treat. I will order takeout from our favorite restaurant and pick it up on the way. See you soon."

Angel arrived and parked in the driveway. He had just removed the dinner bags from the car when his mother came out to greet him. She helped him with one of the bags.

They set down the two bags, and together they set the table. Angel's mother always said grace before eating. They ate a leisurely meal and enjoyed spending time together. She thanked him for bringing dinner and said it was excellent.

"It is good but not nearly as good as the dinners you prepare," Angel said.

"Well then, you can come over next Saturday, and I will prepare you a home-cooked meal. Surprise me by bringing a date."

"I will come, but I am not presently dating anyone."

"Son, you need a good wife, and I would like to have some grandchildren while I am still young enough to enjoy them. You recently turned twenty-four, and you need to find a wife before all the good ones are taken."

"I will," Angel responded since agreeing was the best way to deter further discussions about his personal life. Angel dreaded telling his mother about his arrest. No one spoke for several minutes.

"I am your mother, and I can see something is bothering you."

"I do not want you to worry, but I was arrested today. A gun was involved in a triple homicide, and the gun has my fingerprints on it. I handled the gun back when I was the leader of the Angels." His mother knew he was referring to the local gang called the Angels. Also, she was aware the gang was named after her son.

"There must be lots of fingerprints on the gun. Why did they arrest you? You are a doctor. How could they think you would murder someone?"

"They are just doing their job. I wanted to tell you before you found out from someone else. Hopefully, they will realize I did not commit those murders and drop the charges."

"Do you have a good lawyer?"

"Yes, I have an excellent attorney. Do you remember George Martinez? You attended his graduation when he received his law degree. He is my attorney."

"Of course, I remember George. He used to join us for dinner on a regular basis. He always had an enormous appetite. I am glad he is your attorney."

"Do not worry. Justice will prevail, and I will be exonerated."

"I always worry about you. It is a mother's job to worry about her children. I cannot believe they arrested you on a ridiculous murder charge. No jury is going to think you are a murderer."

"I have explained my arrest. Tell me, how are you doing financially?"

"As you know, your father had good medical insurance, which covered most of his medical bills. His life insurance policy covered his funeral expenses and our credit card debt. I sold his car, which took care of the car loan on his vehicle. My car is paid off, and I plan to drive it until it falls apart. I still have sixteen years remaining on the mortgage. It has not been easy without your father's income, but I am doing fine. Also, I have a small amount in an IRA. I hope to leave it alone until I can withdraw it without penalty. You have not asked about my finances since the funeral."

"Please tell me if you need help with bills or anything else," Angel said with concern.

"No, I have a little left each month to add to my savings account." Angel was not sure he believed her. He was finally working as a full-time doctor and was earning a decent salary. His student loans were nearly paid off, but now he had the debt from the bail. Still, he would find a way if his mother needed help.

"Promise me, you will let me know if you need anything, and I mean anything! I promised father I would look out for you, and he will be disappointed in both of us if I break my promise."

"I promise, if I need anything, I will tell you. I am glad you came to see me. You do not have to wait for an arrest to visit your mother. I am here every night, and it is lonely without your father. I am trying to give you a guilt trip so you will visit me more often. Is it working?"

Angel chuckled. "It is working quite well," Angel assured her. "I will see you for dinner next Saturday, but I will be alone."

They finished eating and put the leftovers in the refrigerator. Angel gave his mother a goodbye hug and headed back to his apartment. He hoped his visit would keep her from worrying.

Stone called the Criminal Division of the Eleventh Circuit since they handled murder cases in Miami which was in Dade County. It would be up to the State Attorney's office to determine who would try the case since only one murder occurred in Dade County. The other two murders took place in Broward County, and Broward was in the Seventeenth Circuit.

As detective Stone had expected, the case stayed in the Eleventh Circuit with the local State Attorney's Office in Miami. The Florida State Attorney General could have assigned a statewide special prosecutor but decided to let the local State Attorney handle the case. First-Degree Murder cases had to be presented to a Grand Jury before being tried locally. The Senior Assistant State Attorney reviewed the case. He knew it would receive some publicity since it involved a serial killer. After reviewing the file, it appeared to be a straightforward case since they had the suspect's fingerprints on the murder weapon.

Several weeks later, George informed Angel that the State Attorney had obtained an indictment against him from the eighteen members of the Grand Jury. George told Angel the State Attorney considered him a serial killer but would not seek the death penalty if he would change his plea to guilty. Defendants and their attorneys are not allowed to attend a Grand Jury hearing. Since he could not attend, George had some concerns there might be evidence other than the gun or potential witnesses that could hurt their defense. Angel informed George he had no intention of changing his plea, so they continued to prepare their Defense.

"It will probably be a year or more before the start of the actual trial," George stated.

Angel was puzzled. "Why will it take so long?"

"Because I will file motions, discovery requests, requests for extension, requests for admissions, and other documents to delay the trial. I will do everything to maximize the delays."

"Why would you intentionally delay the trial?"

George sighed. "Well, in most cases, when the trial ends, my clients go to prison, so I try to maintain their freedom for as long as possible."

Angel was silent for a moment before he responded. "George, I want you to do everything possible to speed up this case, and I do mean everything."

George explained why it was a mistake to speed up the case, but in the end, Angel refused to change his position. George finally capitulated.

"Okay, I will sit down with the prosecution and let them know we will assist in going forward with a speedy trial, but I still think it is a mistake."

George called the office of the State Attorney and set up a meeting for the following week.

Angel had not told anyone at the hospital about his arrest since he hoped the indictment would fail and the nightmare would disappear. After his conversation with George, Angel sent emails to all his patients saying he had been indicted for murder and asked them if they still wanted him to continue being their doctor. He then reviewed the files for the patients he would see the following day. It was close to midnight when he went to bed.

The following morning, he awoke at his usual time and took a shower. He sat at the kitchen counter and reviewed his emails. He scanned his emails as quickly as possible. Angel had received over a hundred emails since the previous afternoon. He read about half of the emails before he headed for the hospital. All except four of the emails were from his patients, and every email he reviewed had responded positively to keep him as their doctor.

Angel used his new phone to call his primary contact at Tyzugmod and told him about the murder indictment. He explained how all of his patients wanted to continue with the cancer drug trial and still wanted him as their doctor. Angel said he would understand if Tyzugmod wanted to replace him. Tyzugmod's representative said he would discuss the situation with the executives but advised Angel to continue the drug program as planned.

Angel called Doctor Stanford and gave him an update. Angel arrived at the hospital and started his rounds. He was only halfway through the morning when Doctor Andrew approached him.

"I am surprised you showed up today," Doctor Andrew said with a sneer. "I assume you will resign from your position here at the hospital. I am prepared to take over your patients and continue with the cancer drug trial." Angel took a minute to digest Doctor Andrew's proposal.

"I have no intention of resigning. I have notified my patients of the situation involving my arrest. All of my patients want me to continue as their doctor. The drug company has been similarly advised and told me to continue the drug trial. I notified the Chairperson of the Board of Directors for this hospital, and he confirmed his support. Also, everyone is familiar with your opposition to the holistic approach, and you will never be allowed to take charge of this drug trial. If you do not have any other matters to discuss, I need to continue making my rounds and caring for my patients. Good day."

Angel sent a precautionary email to Doctor Seneca. He advised him to take over the holistic cancer drug trial should anything prevent him from continuing the cancer treatments. When he started the drug trial, Angel provided Doctor Seneca's profile to the Tyzugmod Corporation as a precaution. Doctor Seneca had good bedside manners, fully supported Angel's holistic approach, and was ecstatic about the results. The week passed quickly.

George and Angel showed up at the State Attorney's office at the appointed time and waited in the lobby for less than ten minutes before being directed to a conference room. Four attorneys were in the room. The Senior Assistant State Attorney was Samuel Davis, and he asked them to take a seat. Two young Assistant State Attorneys appeared to be right out of law school, while the remaining attorney appeared to be in his thirties.

"George, this is Marilyn Ross and Daniel Ellis," Samuel said. "You already know John." George nodded to the attorneys.

"Samuel, congratulations on your promotion to Senior Assistant State Attorney," George said. "I cannot believe you are still working here. With your experience, you would do well with any firm, or you could start your own practice." Samuel could not help but frown at the comment.

"This is not the time for discussing my career," Samuel said. "You called the meeting, and I assume you are here to discuss a plea deal. You surely realize you are holding a weak hand. I am going to be completely honest with you and show you some of our cards. As you know, we have the murder weapon with your client's fingerprints all over the gun. We have two witnesses who will testify they saw your client murder the three victims. Also, we know your client is a former gang member. We can show a motive for all three murders. We will take the death penalty off the table if your client changes his plea to guilty and confesses to the three murders."

Samuel expected George to ask for a reduction from First-Degree to Second-Degree Murder, and he would agree to the lesser charge so they could close this case. They had just lost a dozen attorneys since the state budget did not provide for any raises. Thus, his department was extremely shorthanded. All of his staff were grossly underpaid compared to private practice. This would be a straightforward case for an experienced attorney. However, with his reduced staff, he would have to assign the case to inexperienced attorneys. His attorneys were assigned double the number of cases they should be handling and averaging over fifty hours per week. Also, he would have to redistribute the cases left behind by the attorneys who had just resigned. Miami was still the murder capital of the world. However, he believed they could close this case with a plea of a life sentence without parole. He gave a false smile and waited for George to make a counteroffer.

George looked around the room and knew he was about to surprise everyone. "My client is not interested in your plea offer. We are here to present two proposals. First drop the case since my client is innocent."

"That is not happening," Samuel said as he shook his head.

"Option two is we wish to cooperate in speeding up this case and start the trial as soon as possible. You have my word. I will not do anything if it would only serve to slow down the proceedings. My client is entitled to a speedy trial under the law. Let us set a date, with the court, to start the trial in two months."

Samuel was surprised at what he heard since defendants always want to slow the proceedings. "George, I am going to level with you and give you our best offer. We will reduce the charge to Second-Degree Murder for all three victims. It is an excellent offer, and you know it. Would you like a few minutes to discuss the offer with your client?"

George looked at Angel. Angel was very calm as he looked at the prosecuting attorneys. "There is no need for a discussion. I am not the least bit interested in any plea agreement. I am innocent and will not confess to crimes I did not commit. As my attorney just said, we wish to expedite this case so I can return to treating my patients full time with no distractions. I would like the trial to start tomorrow, but George advised that my desire was unrealistic. So, let us start in two months or the soonest a court date is available."

"It is your funeral," Samuel said. "This will be a capital case, and we will seek the death penalty. I will check the docket and see what dates are available."

George motioned to Angel. They stood up, nodded, and left the conference room. Samuel failed to hide his disappointment as he looked at his staff.

"I am not sure why they did not take the plea deal," Samuel said. "We have a case to try. Daniel, you will be the lead attorney. Marilyn, you will assist. Normally, I would assign a murder case to a more senior attorney, but no one else is available. Get to work. You have a case to win." Daniel and Marilyn left the office.

Samuel was tired both physically and mentally. "John, you have been with me for eight years. You are my best attorney, and I do not know what I would do without you. Daniel has been with us for eleven months and Marilyn for only nine months. They have both handled plenty of minor cases and know their way around a courtroom, but they should not be handling a capital murder trial without a senior lead attorney. You have more cases than anyone else, but I need you to review any documents they file with the court. Also, I want you to contact the four local law schools and get their help to set up interviews. We need to hire twelve attorneys as soon as possible, even though they will not be much help for a while.

Unfortunately, after we train them, they go into private practice, and we face them in court. The Public Defender's Office is the only agency worse off than us. We do not have time for both of us to interview each candidate. If you see a good applicant, hire them. Right now, we just need bodies."

John did not reply and had a pained look on his face. "Samuel, I am sorry."

Samuel did not want to hear it. "Please don't say it."

"I am sorry, but I have to turn in my notice. I start my new job in two weeks. I hate to leave you like this, but I could not turn down the offer. The starting salary is more than double what I am making now, and I will have fewer cases resulting in less stress. I have a wife and two children. I have not had a raise in two years."

Samuel shook his head. This could not have come at a worse time. "I do not blame you," Samuel stammered. "If not for a promise I made, I would leave with you. Do as much as you can before you leave."

After John left, Samuel lowered his head. He was wondering how the legislature could again not approve a budget increase. Everyone wants a good judicial system, but no one wants to pay for it. Everyone in their agency had significantly improved their efficiencies through increased utilization of technology. Still, these gains were offset because the experienced attorneys were leaving at a higher rate. Plus, it took time to train new attorneys. Florida was the third-largest state by population, and the growing population meant more cases.

Samuel decided he would let the case proceed quickly as requested by the Defense. Daniel and Marilyn would learn enough from this case to become experienced attorneys for the more complex cases they would handle in the future.

The newbies they planned to hire would learn by handling the routine cases. With ten law schools in Florida, there was no shortage of inexperienced attorneys. Unfortunately, law schools teach theory, but not the application of the law, which only comes from experience. Under normal circumstances, a new attorney would learn by working with an experienced attorney, but the experienced state attorneys did not have the time to provide the training. Therefore, the new attorneys would learn by making mistakes, resulting in some guilty defendants going free. Also, losing winnable cases could have negative political consequences.

However, the Angel Carpenter case looked to be an easy win. Samuel felt the case would draw little attention since all the victims had criminal records. It was time to get back to work. It would be a late night.

On the Bailiwick of Jersey, located off the coast of Normandy, the five trustees of a multibillion-dollar trust were having their monthly meeting. Their stated motto was world peace. In contrast, their unstated goal was to diminish and ultimately eliminate all forms of religion. The wealthy founders of the trust considered religion to be the harbinger of most wars and the single most significant contributor to human death. They used their wealth and power to support political candidates throughout the world. The trustees helped the careers of individuals who could shape public opinion. They took the long-term approach to destroy the religious foundations and were succeeding. They unquestionably believed their success was preventing another world war.

The Bailiwick of Jersey was the perfect location with major financial advantages for corporations, trusts, and foundations. The island provided financial privacy, and taxes were low compared to the rest of the world.

The Trust had successfully supported such subtle things as the elimination of prayer in schools and at public gatherings in the United States. They had supported Hitler because of his opposition to Judaism. They considered withdrawing their support when he started the war, but it was too late. Fortunately for them, the Israelis had failed to trace their involvement. They sometimes had assassins eliminate individuals who were having too much of a positive impact on religion. In certain situations, the assassins received extra pay to make such eliminations appear as unfortunate accidents or death from natural causes.

A detailed history listed their accomplishments. They considered their greatest achievement as preventing a nuclear war during the Cuban Missile Crisis. Their archives said they had agreed to eliminate the President of the United States if Russia would back down and remove their nuclear weapons from Cuba. They considered their archives to be absolute regardless of the histories presented by others.

Traditionally, the Trustees maintained a low profile by intent since they did not want to jeopardize their position on the island. However, the current Trustees were not as conservative or as patient as their predecessors. The Trustees began the meeting by discussing their investments, including their significant holdings in the Americas and Europe. Next, they discussed the advancement of key individuals who would be instrumental in further eroding the role of religion. Toward the end of the meeting, a trustee brought up the trial about an angel in the United States and mentioned it was starting to get limited worldwide attention. They agreed to have one of their operatives monitor the court trial. They had several operatives who held executive positions within the media. Their operatives would be directed to bring the matter to the attention of key individuals within the media to shape public opinion against this doctor. A doctor masquerading as an angel. They felt the Defendant was likely to be found guilty, and extensive press coverage could adversely impact religious beliefs. An angel convicted as a serial killer would contribute nicely to their ongoing propaganda. They agreed to use their influence to move cameras into the courtroom to increase the exposure of the criminal proceedings. They adjourned the meeting and enjoyed a gourmet meal at an exclusive, members-only restaurant.

The various media were looking for something to add to their news since nothing sensational was currently available to maintain their viewership ratings. They received directions from the top to check out the recent grand jury indictment of an angel who was, in reality, a serial killer. They got the typical statement from the Defendant's attorney stating his client was innocent. The Prosecution gave the expected, no comment, response. They then started calling the directors and doctors at the hospital with the same no comment, or they would hang up.

Then, one of the networks contacted Doctor Andrew, who agreed to give an interview. The interview with Doctor Andrew lasted four hours. They created several ten-minute segments showing the hatred of Doctor Andrew toward Doctor Angel Carpenter.

Doctor Andrews continued to be contacted by the press and felt like a celebrity. He was leaving the hospital when a news crew accosted him and asked if he had any additional comments regarding Doctor Angel Carpenter.

"It does not surprise me that Doctor Carpenter is a serial killer. Doctor Carpenter is delusional and requires everyone to call him Doctor Angel or simply Angel. He is closer to being a demon than an angel and is taking personal credit for the lives saved by a new cancer drug. Doctor Carpenter requires patients to pray each day, or they do not get access to the cancer-curing drug. He should have his license to practice medicine revoked."

Doctor Stanford was appalled when he saw Doctor Andrew on the news channels. Not only did Doctor Andrew disparage a fellow doctor, but he made the hospital look bad. Also, Doctor Andrew was not the spokesperson for the hospital and had not received authorization to speak on their behalf.

CHAPTER 6 TRIAL PROSECUTION

Angel kept asking George to speed up the start of the trial, but George informed him that starting a capital trial in only two months was exceptionally fast. The Chief Judge assigned Judge Terrell to handle Angel's case. She had served as a judge for over ten years. George told Angel the Judge had a reputation of being hard but fair.

George and Angel worked together on the opening statement. George knew it was essential to have a strong start for the trial. He rewrote the opening a dozen times, but even with Angel's help, he did not like the results. George explained to Angel how some jurors could form a mental bias based on the opening statement. Then George had an unconventional idea. He decided to let Angel present the opening statement. Using this approach would allow Angel to testify to the jury without the prosecuting attorney being able to conduct a cross-examination. Angel had given many presentations and knew how to sell an idea. After all, he had convinced a corporation and a charitable trust to fund his cancer drug trial. George had Angel rehearse the opening statement several times. They made a few modifications, and Angel made the presentation several more times. George provided feedback on maintaining eye contact with the jurors and mentioned when he should pause during the presentation. George felt they were ready.

In the final pretrial meeting with Judge Terrell, George mentioned that Angel would give the opening statement for the Defense. This surprised the prosecution, and Daniel Ellis objected without thinking, but the Judge overruled since there were no grounds for the objection.

"Is there any chance for a plea agreement," the Judge asked.

"We offered to drop the death penalty and reduce all three charges to Second-Degree Murder," Daniel said. "Yesterday, we offered to let the three sentences run concurrently with a recommendation for the minimum sentence of twenty-five years without parole."

"Your Honor, we have asked the Prosecution to drop all charges since my client is innocent," George replied. "My client will not commit perjury by entering a guilty plea."

Judge Terrell shook her head. "I see nothing has changed, but I wanted to give you one last chance to settle this case. The trial will start Monday morning at nine o'clock."

George had asked the judge to let the potential jurors fill out a modified questionnaire to include a potential juror's religious affiliation, but the Judge refused. Therefore, he was stuck with reviewing the information provided by the potential jurors on the Florida Standard Juror Voir Dire Questionnaire. The short questionnaire did not provide any information to show a person's religious leanings. While some of the prospective jurors would take time to fill out detailed answers to the questions, most would provide answers so brief as to be worthless.

During the voir dire, an attorney cannot ask about a person's religious beliefs or lack thereof unless the judge grants a waiver. George considered asking the Judge for a waiver but figured the Prosecution might decide to eliminate the jurors he was trying to select. Therefore, he did not raise the issue. There was no way of doing any advanced research since the potential jurors would only be presented at the beginning of the trial.

George interviewed and then hired two university students to assist him during the voir dire. They were to use the internet to research each potential juror to determine quickly if the juror would be sympathetic to his client. He explained to each of them precisely what he was looking for regarding potential jurors. His first preference was jurors with strong religious beliefs who were protestant or catholic. He wanted to retain jurors who would have a positive feeling toward Angel while eliminating jurors who might have a bias or prejudice against his client.

During their interview, he had given them several names to research as a test, and these two were extremely fast. One was a female law student who had been a paralegal before entering law school. The other was majoring in Information Technology. He gave them each a typing test. They both used all of their fingers in the proper position on the keyboard, which gave them an advantage in keyboarding speed. The law student typed over ninety words per minute, and the IT Student typed seventy words per minute. They were both adept at getting quick results so as not to slow down the voir dire. Social media and advanced search tools made it possible to obtain massive amounts of data on an individual. George had a wireless computer with a split-screen so his assistants could immediately send summaries of their findings to his laptop.

In addition to the twelve jurors, the Judge had decided to have four alternates. Under the Florida Statutes, each side would have ten regular peremptory challenges plus one for each alternate juror. Therefore, George had fourteen peremptory challenges to eliminate jurors.

On the first day of the pretrial, thirty potential jurors were brought into the courtroom. Judge Terrell asked if any of the jurors had circumstances preventing them from serving as a juror. Four jurors asked to be excused, but the Judge only allowed two to leave the courtroom. Twenty-eight potential jurors remained.

It became immediately apparent that the jury selection was going to be problematic. George wanted Christian jurors with a positive feeling toward doctors and without prejudice against gang members. The Prosecution wanted the opposite, and they wanted to eliminate anyone who believed in angels. The Prosecution attorneys were taking turns interviewing the potential jurors. George used his two assistants to great advantage as he eliminated jurors who might be predisposed against his client.

Out of the remaining twenty-eight potential jurors, George used nine of his challenges, leaving him with five. He felt good since the Prosecution had used eleven challenges with only three remaining. However, they had only elected eight jurors. It was late afternoon and the Judge announce they would reconvene the following morning at nine o'clock to continue jury selection.

The following morning, thirty more potential jurors entered the courtroom. Five of the new group were dismissed by the Judge. George lost his advantage when he used four challenges in a row. Only three additional jurors had been selected when the Prosecution and the Defense used up their remaining peremptory challenges.

The Prosecution and Defense were worried since they still needed to select one additional juror and four alternates. George stepped over to the Prosecution's table to speak to Daniel Ellis and Marilyn Ross.

"We need more challenges," George said. Daniel and Marilyn agreed.

"Your Honor, may we approach," George asked the judge.

"Yes," Judge Terrell replied. All three attorneys approached the bench.

"Your Honor, both the Prosecution and Defense agree we need additional peremptory challenges," George said. "We would like to request an additional six challenges each."

"Your Honor, we completely agree with the Defense," Daniel blurted. "Additional challenges are necessary to arrive at a fair and impartial jury."

"What a surprise, both the Prosecution and Defense are actually agreeing on something," Judge Terrell said. "I will give you two additional challenges each."

George spoke up. "Your Honor, we still need an additional juror to reach twelve, and we have to select four alternates. Two challenges are not enough to select five more jurors."

Marilyn added her support. "Your Honor, we agree." Judge Terrell frowned. She did not want to provide ammunition for an appeal this early in the trial.

"You will each get four additional challenges and no more," Judge Terrell said.

Unfortunately, George used up all four of his challenges without adding to the jury pool. The next candidate was female and had a police officer as a brother. George was given permission to approach the bench and asked Judge Terrell to dismiss the juror for cause, but she refused. The twelfth juror was an acknowledged atheist and was male. The four alternates were selected without issue. George was satisfied with the four alternates and would have taken any of them over the atheist. Overall, he had ten out of twelve jurors who had some exposure to religion. He could not determine the faith of the female whose brother was a police officer. Being religious prevented bias against his client but would not keep a juror from finding him guilty.

The trial would start at nine o'clock the following morning. George told Angel to meet him outside the courtroom at eight o'clock.

The following morning the sky was overcast and raining. Angel used an umbrella but was still partially soaked when he met George outside the door to the courtroom. They entered together and took a seat at the Defense table.

"All rise, the Court is now in session, the Honorable Judge Terrell presiding," the Bailiff shouted.

The Judge took her seat. "Please be seated. Good morning, ladies and gentlemen. Calling the case of the People of the State of Florida versus Angel Carpenter. Are both sides ready?"

"Ready for the People, Your Honor," Daniel Ellis replied:

"Ready for the Defense, Your Honor," George Martinez replied.

"Bailiff, please swear in the jury?" Judge Terrell said. The Bailiff approached the jury.

"Will the jurors please stand and raise your right hand?"

The Bailiff waited until all the jurors were standing. "Do each of you swear you will fairly try the case before this court, and you will return a true verdict according to the evidence and the instructions of the court, so help you, god? Please say, I do." All the jurors responded with the standard, "I do."

"You may be seated," the Bailiff said.

"Is the State prepared to give an opening statement?" Judge Terrell asked.

"Yes, Your Honor," Attorney Ellis replied.

Angel listened carefully to the opening statement given by Attorney Daniel Ellis. Attorney Ellis told the Juror the Defendant was a serial killer who had murdered Owen Ward, Randolph Snead, and Vern Dorn. He explained how the first murder of Owen Ward occurred six years ago, while the recent murders of Randolph Snead and Vern Dorn occurred three months earlier. The Opening Statement was well organized from the first sentence to the timeline and then to the last sentence, where he asked the jury to return a guilty verdict.

Angel had performed a final practice of the Opening Statement before coming to court. He had worn his hospital scrubs to court instead of a suit since George knew most people had favorable feelings toward physicians. Also, he was more comfortable wearing his work clothes. Angel took his time approaching the jury. He made eye contact with each juror.

"Much of what the plaintiff said is correct. My fingerprints are indeed on the murder weapon since I handled the gun. Also, it is true I knew one of the victims since we lived in the same neighborhood. First, I will tell you a little about myself. I come from a deeply religious, middle-class family. I have never been in trouble with the law except for several speeding tickets."

Several of the jurors chuckled while the rest smiled and nodded. Everyone on the jury was familiar with speeding tickets.

Angel continued. "I worked part time in high school and while obtaining my undergraduate degree. While in medical school, I worked part time at a research facility for a major drug company since I was undecided if I wanted to go into medical research or become a practicing physician. Like many students, I have student loans I have been paying off. I am currently a practicing physician caring for cancer patients. I have dedicated my life to helping people by providing them with the best available medical care. I work every day to extend the life of my patients. I would never take another person's life. My attorney has asked me to remind you, under the law, I am presumed to be innocent until proven guilty, but I am innocent. Thank you."

He looked again at each juror before returning to his chair. Several jurors were nodding their heads. No one could doubt Angel's sincerity.

Daniel shook his head, leaned over, and said to Marilyn. "What a joke, do you believe that?"

Marilyn whispered in Daniel's ear. "He just won over most of the jurors, and yes, he was very believable."

"The Prosecution may call its first witness," Judge Terrell stated.

"The People call Diana Webb," Daniel said.

"Will the witness approach the bench and remain standing until sworn in by the Bailiff," Judge Terrell said.

"Please raise your right hand. Do you swear to tell the truth, the whole truth, and nothing but the truth?"

"I do," she replied after raising her right hand.

Diana Webb went to the witness stand to the left of the Judge and sat down. Diana was the Prosecution's forensic expert. She was in her mid-forties, with average height, and was dressed professionally in a light brown dress. She wore glasses, sat up straight, and looked very poised.

Diana answered questions establishing herself as a forensic expert. She testified how all three victims were killed by bullets fired from the same gun marked as Exhibit 1. She explained the two-step process of identification in terms the jurors could understand. First, the class characteristics allowed the bullet to be matched to a unique type of gun barrel. Second, the individual characteristics were used to check the bullet against the distinctive marks within the barrel of the suspect firearm.

"Ms. Webb, please tell the jurors about your analysis of the fingerprints."

"The fingerprints on the gun were mathematically an exact match to the Defendant under the twelve-point rule guideline."

"Please explain what it means to have a twelve-point match."

"With twelve points matching between the fingerprints, the odds of a mistake are one in a million billion. For this case, there were fourteen matches between the fingerprints on the gun and the Defendant's fingerprints. The high number of points is why we say it is an exact match."

"I have no further questions, Your Honor." Daniel returned to his seat and was pleased with Diana's professional testimony.

"Does the Defense wish to cross?" Judge Terrell asked.

"Yes, Your Honor," George replied as he approached the witness.

"Ms. Webb, exactly where are the fingerprints located on the gun?"

"On the barrel."

"Were there any fingerprints or partial fingerprints anywhere else on the gun?" George asked.

The witness paused before answering. "No," she replied.

George stated the obvious. "So, the rest of the gun has been wiped clean of any fingerprints?"

Daniel responded: "Objection, calls for speculation."

"Sustained," the judge said.

"Ms. Webb, how old is the gun?" George asked.

"There is no way of telling since the serial numbers have been removed."

"How long ago was the first victim killed?"

Diana did not hesitate. "Six years ago."

"If the gun killed the first victim over six years ago and the same gun recently killed two other victims, then is it safe to assume the gun has been handled at least twice as a minimum?"

"Yes," Diana answered.

"Since there are no fingerprints or partial prints anywhere else on the gun, would you concur the person handling the gun either wore gloves or someone wiped off every part of the gun except for the barrel?"

Daniel immediately spoke up. "Objection, Your Honor, calls for an opinion."

"Your Honor, the prosecution has already qualified the witness as being an expert in this field, and Rule 702 clearly allows an expert witness to give an opinion," George said. "We are asking for her expert opinion on how a gun would only have fingerprints on the barrel."

"Objection overruled. You may answer the question."

"Yes, those are the two most likely explanations," Diana stated.

"Of the two possibilities, in your expert opinion, would you say the most likely scenario is that someone wiped the gun clean except for the barrel?"

"Yes, that is the most likely explanation, but there are other possibilities."

"Ms. Webb, exactly where on the barrel are the fingerprints located, and what is the orientation of the prints," George asked.

Diana Webb explained where the fingerprints were located and how the prints were oriented. George handed her the gun.

"Please show the court how Angel held the gun, for the fingerprints to be on the gun in that pattern."

It took the witness several minutes before she held the gun by the barrel with the gun pointing toward her chest.

"Thank you," George said. There were whispers throughout the courtroom concerning the orientation of the gun.

"If a person was trying to wipe off their fingerprints, wouldn't they wipe off the whole gun?" George asked.

The prosecution immediately objected since it would require speculation by the witness. The judge sustained the objection, but George knew the jury would consider the question and how the witness would have answered.

"Please demonstrate for the jury how the defendant would have been able to wipe off the fingerprints on the rest of the gun without wiping the fingerprints off the barrel."

"Objection, calls for speculation," Daniel shouted. "There is no way the witness could know how the Defendant would have wiped off the gun."

"Your Honor, I am not asking how a person actually wiped off the prints but was trying to ascertain how it might have been done," George replied.

"Objection sustained."

"I have no further questions," George said.

"Does the Prosecution wish to redirect?"

"Yes, Your Honor," Daniel replied.

"Ms. Webb, in your expert opinion, is it possible there are no fingerprints on the rest of the gun because the Defendant did a poor job wiping the gun clean, and in your expert opinion, what would be a plausible reason for such carelessness?"

"Objection Your Honor. I actually have two objections. The Plaintiff asked a compound question, and the first question was leading."

"Both objections are sustained."

Daniel knew the objections were proper and restated his question. "In your expert opinion, what is a plausible explanation for fingerprints being on the barrel of the gun and nowhere else.

"If the Defendant was in the process of wiping the gun clean and heard someone coming, he could have panicked and pitched the gun before he finished."

Daniel looked at the Jurors. "Thank you, Ms. Webb, for your expert explanation."

Daniel turned toward Judge Terrell. "Your Honor, I have no further questions."

Judge Terrell looked at the witness. "You may step down."

A clerk entered the courtroom and gave Judge Terrell a message. After reading the note, the judge dismissed the jury for the day and informed everyone the trial would reconvene at ten o'clock the following morning.

Judge Terrell then asked for the attorneys from both sides to meet in her chambers. After everyone took a seat, she informed them that camera crews would be in the courtroom starting the next day, and it would be a live broadcast. Daniel objected and stated several reasons why a camera crew should not be allowed.

"The decision is not open to debate," the judge responded. "The decision was made without my input. I am providing the information as a courtesy."

As they were leaving the courthouse, Daniel told Marilyn they needed to go back to the office and discuss the matter with Samuel, but Marilyn said she needed to take care of some personal matters.

This was a significant change, and Daniel knew he needed to inform Samuel about the live broadcast. Samuel was on the phone when Daniel arrived at his office. Samuel pointed at a chair, and Daniel sat down. When Samuel finished the call, he immediately handed Daniel a collection of computer printouts. The various articles and blogs all stated an Angel was on trial in Florida. Some responses to the blogs were humorous, but most contained derogatory comments regarding the State Attorney's office.

"How is the trial going?" Samuel asked.

"It is going okay."

"When you walked in, I was on the phone with the State Attorney discussing the Angel Carpenter case. He is extremely disappointed with the negative publicity and how this case could hurt his reelection campaign. So, I am asking you again. How is the trial going?"

"There have been a few minor issues, but it is a winnable case," Daniel said while frowning.

Samuel pulled up the case on his screen and located George Martinez's cellphone number. Samuel dialed the number, and the call was answered on the fourth ring.

"George, this is Samuel, I have Daniel with me, and you are on the speaker."

"I know this is not a social call, so why are you calling?" George asked.

"We expect to win the case but would like to avoid further publicity."

George laughed. "So, you heard the remainder of the trial is going to be televised."

Samuel was shocked. "George, I need to place you on hold for just a moment."

Samuel looked at Daniel. "Is he right? Is this case being televised?"

Daniel grimaced. "That is why I came to your office. The judge just told us. Starting tomorrow, the trial will be televised."

Samuel looked like he wanted to kill someone. "Damn!"

Samuel tried to regain his composure as he took George off hold. "Yes, I am aware the trial will be televised starting tomorrow."

"Daniel had not told you, so you just found out." George laughed again. Samuel controlled his anger.

"George, we are still going to win the case," said Samuel. "However, there is always the remote possibility the jury could ignore the facts and decide to acquit, or we could wind up with a hung jury and have to retry the case. Therefore, we will offer you a gift. We will drop two of the murder charges if Doctor Carpenter pleads guilty to one count of Second-Degree Manslaughter. We will ask the Judge to use the sentencing guidelines of fifteen years, and your client could be out after serving the mandatory minimum of only nine years."

"I am with Angel, and the answer is no deal," George replied. "You need to dismiss all charges against my client."

Samuel was shaking his head. "George, I cannot dismiss all the charges. In the next election, the opposing candidate would say the State Attorney is weak on crime by allowing serial killers to go free."

"Samuel, I appreciate the call, and normally, I would jump at such a generous offer on your part. There is one critical problem with your offer. My client is innocent, and I cannot ask him to commit perjury. Daniel, we will see you and Marilyn in the morning." George pushed the button to hang up.

Samuel looked at Daniel. "You need to win this case!"

Daniel nodded and headed to his own office, which was nothing but a booth with dividers in place. He opened the folder for the second witness for the prosecution and reviewed his notes to prepare for the next day. He wondered why Marilyn had not returned to the office with him. They planned to call four witnesses the next day if time permitted.

The next day as Daniel entered the courtroom, he saw several camera crews spaced around the courtroom and noticed the courtroom was full of spectators. He took a seat at the Prosecution's table and turned to speak to Marilyn.

"My god, Marilyn, are you wearing a new dress, and your hair? What is going on?" Daniel asked.

Marilyn looked at Daniel like he was a complete idiot. "We are being televised and need to look like professional attorneys. You do not look like a professional. You are wearing the same suit you wear every day, and it looks like you slept in it. At least you could have gotten a nicer-looking tie, and you should comb your hair." She then moved her chair to put a little distance between herself and Daniel.

Daniel leaned over toward Marilyn. "Is that why you took off yesterday afternoon?" He asked in a disgruntled voice. "So, you could go shopping and to a hair salon while I was at the office working."

Marilyn gave him a disgusted look. His question did not merit an answer. He did not need to know she had a manicure and a pedicure. She had purchased new shoes and a new purse to match her dress. She had purchased several more matching outfits for the coming days. It was apparent Daniel did not have a clue how the dynamics of their case had just changed. She was going to look good on camera and hoped to get a job offer with a good firm. Regardless, she had colleagues, friends, and relatives who might see her on camera. She wanted to look good and enhance her professional image. Her credit card had taken a major hit, and it would take a while to pay it off, but after looking at herself in the mirror, it was money well spent.

The judge entered the courtroom, and everyone stood. Marilyn looked at the judge and smiled. She was not the only one to prepare for the cameras. The judge looked great. Everyone took their seat when directed by the judge.

Judge Terrell looked around the courtroom. "The Prosecution may call their next witness."

"Thank you, Your Honor," Marilyn Ross said. "I call to the stand, Edward Tobin."

"Will the witness please take the stand," Judge Terrell said.

Edward Tobin was wearing dress slacks and a dress shirt, but in this case, the clothes did not make the man. He slouched in the chair and had a permanent scowl on his face. His huge biceps were straining against his shirtsleeves. Also, his shaved bald head, along with his other attributes, gave him a dangerous look. The Bailiff swore in the witness, and he took the stand.

"Mr. Tobin, in a deposition, you stated you were present on the night Randolph Snead and Vern Dorn were murdered," Marilyn said. "Please tell the Court what you saw."

"I was visiting some friends in South Beach on the night of April 21 when this guy came into the house. The guy walked up to Vern

Dorn and Randolph Snead. Then he pulled out a gun and shot both of them in cold blood like a contract killer. He then turned around and rushed out of the house. I immediately left the house since I did not want to be around when the cops showed up. Later, I found out Vern and Randolph died from their wounds."

"Is the person who shot Vern Dorn and Randolph Snead in this Courtroom?" Marilyn asked.

"Yes, it is the guy with the blond hair." Edward Tobin pointed at Angel.

"Let the record show the witness identified the Defendant, Angel Carpenter, as the person who shot and killed Vern Dorn and Randolph Snead."

"How can you be so sure it was the Defendant?" Marilyn asked.

"It is impossible to forget the blond hair. Plus, he was wearing hospital scrubs."

"Your Honor, I have no further questions."

"Does the Defense wish to cross?" Judge Terrell asked.

"Yes, Your Honor," George said as he approached the witness.

"Mr. Tobin, is it true you were recently convicted of armed robbery?"

"Yes," Edward said with a smirk.

"Mr. Tobin, how much time were you going to serve for this felony?"

"Twenty years," replied Edward.

"As a result of your testimony, how many years are you going to serve?"

Edward answered candidly. "Three years."

George appropriately asked a leading question. "So, by testifying, you shorten your prison sentence from twenty years to three. Therefore, testifying allows you to reduce your prison time by seventeen years. Is that correct?"

"Yes."

George was facing the jurors as he shook his head. "Your Honor, I have no further questions for this witness."

"Does the Prosecution wish to redirect?" Judge Terrell asked.

"No, Your Honor," Marilyn replied.

Judge Terrell turned to the witness. "You may step down."

"The Prosecution may call their next witness."

"The Prosecution calls Cecil Segal," Daniel said as he stood up.

Cecil Segal was wearing faded jeans with a red pullover shirt. He had tattoos covering his arms, neck, and part of his face. His tobacco-stained teeth were showing through his puffy lips, and his squatty nose was at a slight angle from being broken several times.

After the witness was sworn in, Daniel asked an open-ended question. "Mr. Segal, please tell the Court what you remember regarding the murder of Owen Ward."

"I forget the exact date, but it was around six years ago when I witnessed the murder of Owen. I was a member of the Warlocks and Angel was representing a rival gang. The two gangs were meeting to work out a peace agreement. Angel had a disagreement with Owen, our second in command, and they got into a fistfight. Owen lost and was sitting on the ground when he pulled a gun. Angel took the gun away from Owen. Owen was still sitting on the ground when Angel shot him dead."

"Was Owen getting up or trying to attack Angel when he was shot?" Daniel asked.

George interrupted. "Objection, Your Honor, leading the witness."

"Objection sustained," Judge Terrell ruled.

"Mr. Segal, what was Owen doing immediately before he was shot and killed?" Daniel asked the witness.

"He was not doing anything. Owen was on the ground. He was not attempting to get up. He was just sitting there."

"Mr. Segal is the person who shot Owen Ward in the courtroom, and can you point him out for the Jurors?"

Cecil Segal pointed at Angel. Daniel smiled and nodded. "Let the record show the witness identified Angel Carpenter as the person who shot Owen Ward."

"Your Honor, I have no more questions for this witness."

"Does the Defense wish to cross-examine the witness?" Judge Terrell asked.

"Yes, Your Honor," George replied.

George approached the witness. "Is it true you are currently serving time in the state prison for DUI manslaughter and leaving the scene of an accident?"

"Yes," Cecil responded.

"Mr. Segal, were you sentenced to five years for leaving the scene of an accident plus an additional fifteen years for DUI manslaughter?"

"Yes."

"How much time have you served so far?" George asked.

"Six years."

"As a result of your testimony, how many more years will you serve?"

"Two years."

George scrunched his face. "Mr. Segal, by testifying, you get to shorten your prison sentence by twelve years. Is that correct?"

"Yes."

George looked at the Jurors while rolling his eyes and shook his head. "Your Honor, I have no further questions for this witness."

"Does the Prosecution wish to redirect?" Judge Terrell asked.

"No, Your Honor," Daniel answered.

Judge Terrell looked at the witness. "You may step down."

The Prosecution had initially planned to call a witness who had shared a jail cell with Angel Carpenter on the night of his arrest.

The witness was going to say Angel bragged about killing the victims. However, Attorney George Martinez had provided depositions from the other two individuals in the same lockup who said Angel told them he was innocent. The two rebuttal witnesses seemed more credible and were not being offered any incentive for their testimony. Marilyn and Daniel figured if all three witnesses testified, it would be more helpful to the Defense. They quickly learned George Martinez was an excellent attorney. His experience gave him a noticeable advantage in questioning the witnesses.

"The Prosecution may call their next witness," the Judge said.

"The Prosecution calls Doctor Steven Andrew," Marilyn said. Judge Terrell saw the Prosecution had skipped the witness who was next on the list.

Doctor Andrew was sworn in and took a seat. "It is my understanding you work for the same hospital as Doctor Carpenter," Marilyn said. "What can you tell us about the Defendant?"

"He is a poor excuse for a doctor," Doctor Andrew replied. "He does not follow normal medical procedures and puts his patients at risk. Doctor Carpenter lucked out by being selected to head up a cancer drug trial. The drug trial should have been assigned to a more experienced doctor. The medical drug is curing the patients at the hospital, but he is taking all the credit. He gets away with violating hospital rules by telling everyone he is an angel. He has the entire hospital staff calling him Doctor Angel, and some of them are convinced he is an actual angel. In order for patients to get access to the cancer drug, they are required to pray each day. If you do not pray, then you do not get access to the cancer drug. He is disrespectful of the senior doctors. He is a charlatan and should not be allowed to practice medicine."

After hearing the testimony of Doctor Andrew, the jurors were looking at Angel with a suspicion they had not previously displayed. The atheist was nodding his head.

"No further questions, Your Honor," Marilyn said with a slight smile. She was quite satisfied with the testimony of her witness.

"Does the Defense wish to cross-examine the witness?" Judge Terrell asked.

"Yes, Your Honor," George said as he stood up and approached the witness.

"How many patients has Doctor Angel Carpenter treated at the hospital?" George asked.

"I am not sure," Doctor Andrew replied.

"Doctor Andrew, if I told you Angel has treated over four hundred terminally ill cancer patients in the past twelve months, does that sound right?"

"Yes, it seems about right."

"Have you treated about the same number of patients during the same time?"

"Yes, I have," Doctor Andrew replied with pride.

"Doctor Andrew, I believe you know that prior to Doctor Carpenter's cancer drug trial, only about forty percent of the patients using the cancer drug survived."

Doctor Andrew sneered. "Yes, I am aware of the prior test results."

"Doctor Andrew, I understand that over two-thirds of your patients have died during the past year. Is that correct?" It was apparent Doctor Andrew was uncomfortable with the question.

"I am not sure. I would have to check my records."

"How many of Doctor Carpenter's patients have died during the past year?"

Again, Doctor Andrew said: "I am not sure."

"Doctor Andrew, you are under oath, and lying under oath is perjury. You are on the Board of Directors of the hospital and know exactly how many of Angel's patients have died. Now, I ask you again. How many of Angel's patients have died?"

Doctor Andrew, with a red face, angrily replied. "None."

Everyone on the Jury and in the courtroom was stunned by the admission, and everyone in the audience was whispering. At first, the Jurors had begun to question whether Angel had deceived them, and now they turned their distrust toward Doctor Andrew. It started softly at first, as the people in the courtroom began booing the witness. Several individuals in the back of the courtroom started shouting to get Satan off the witness stand. Then, it got out of control as everyone was screaming at the witness, the Prosecution, and the Judge. It took several minutes to reestablish order in the courtroom.

Judge Terrell pounded her gravel. "If there are any more disturbances, I will clear the courtroom of all non-essential personnel."

"Does the Defense have any more questions for this witness?" Judge Terrell asked.

"No, Your Honor."

Judge Terrell looked at the Prosecution while trying to maintain a neutral look. "Does the Prosecution wish to redirect?"

Marilyn appeared pale as the blood drained from her face, and she felt faint. "No, Your Honor," she said in a weak emotionless voice.

Judge Terrell looked at the witness with disdain. "You may step down."

Daniel looked at Marilyn, and she nodded. "Your Honor, the Prosecution rests," he said.

"Your Honor, based on the evidence provided by the Prosecution, I move for a directed verdict of not guilty," George said.

"Defense Motion is denied," Judge Terrell responded.

Judge Terrell looked at the clock. "We will recess for today and reconvene tomorrow at 10:00 AM."

As the courtroom was emptying, Daniel turned toward Marilyn in anger. "You were horrible. You may have just lost the case."

Marilyn was distraught. She had gone over the testimony with Doctor Andrew several times. Doctor Andrew's testimony should have discredited Angel, but like a bomb, it had blown up in her face. Marilyn remembered her excitement when she graduated from law school and passed the bar on her first try. Now, she felt like a failure. Marilyn was getting so many negative comments on her social media accounts that she no longer bothered reading them. She had hoped this case could lead to better things. Now, she wanted to quit and go into hiding. She sat with tears in her eyes, and then she heard footsteps. The elderly Bailiff had walked over and was standing next to her. They were the only ones left in the courtroom. He had an understanding expression on his face that reminded her of her father.

"It is hard prosecuting an angel," he said. "Just think, all your future cases will be easier, and anytime you have a rough time in the future, it will not be as bad as today."

Marilyn chuckled half-heartedly as she dried her eyes. "I think you are right," she said as she sat up straighter in the chair. "I need to go to the office and prepare for tomorrow."

She put everything into her case file. She looked at the kindhearted Bailiff. "Thank you."

She drove to the office and parked her car. Just inside the lobby, Daniel was waiting for her. "I am sorry for what I said. It was very unprofessional and wrong. Samuel wants to see both of us in his office. Again, I am sorry."

"It is okay," Marilyn replied. "I am frustrated too. I guess we should go to Samuel's office and get our butts kicked."

When they arrived at Samuel's office, he was on the phone. He motioned them into his office, and they sat down.

"They just walked into my office. I will put you on the speaker," Samuel said.

The State Attorney, Luke Abbott, said: "Your attorneys handling the case looked like amateurs."

Samuel grimaced. "Sir, they have been with the state attorney's office for less than a year. Based on experience, they are amateurs! They are doing their best on what has turned out to be a difficult case."

"Then you should have assigned a more experienced attorney to this case," Luke said.

Samuel was getting mad. "Sir, I do not have any experienced attorneys available for this case. We are extremely shorthanded because of the recent resignations. I have twelve openings to fill. If you want my resignation, I will happily send it to you."

"Samuel, I do not want your resignation," Luke said in a more controlled voice. "I know the only reason you are still here is because of the promise you made to me when you were helping with my campaign. I am sorry for coming down on you. I just got off the phone with the State Attorney General, and she let me know how extremely displeased she was with the progress of the case. Both of us are elected officials, and the polls show the voters are not happy with the prosecution of this Defendant. Your two witnesses to the murders did not look good on the air, and the attempt to discredit Doctor Carpenter backfired completely. The case looks weak, and the Defense has not even started with their witnesses. Is there any chance of any type of plea for this case?"

"They are not willing to accept any plea," Samuel replied. "Believe me. I have tried. Sir, would you like to take over the case and try it yourself?"

"My campaign manager told me to stay as far away from this case as I can get. Try to discredit their witnesses and hope for a hung jury. Retrying the case will give you a chance to fix the holes in your prosecution. Daniel and Marilyn, I am sorry you have to try a case like this so early in your career, but you have to do better."

"We will," Daniel and Marilyn replied together.

"Samuel, I have been asking the governor to use his influence to provide additional funding for the judiciary, but it does not look promising."

"Thanks for trying," Samuel said. "We will do the best we can with the limited budget."

Luke sighed. "I know you will, goodbye."

Samuel looked at his two attorneys. "Pull out all the stops in challenging the Defense witnesses. It is not the time to play safe. Daniel, never attack your co-counsel. The cameras were still rolling after the Judge left the courtroom, and your comments to Marilyn went viral. If you were in private practice, you would be getting fired right now. Marilyn, learn to control your facial expressions. On camera, you looked like you had already lost the case. Get to work."

As they walked down the hallway, Daniel turned to Marilyn. "I am truly sorry. It will not happen again."

"Apology accepted. I am also sorry. I have made derogatory comments to you, and I promise to be a better co-counsel."

"We need to get to work and prepare for tomorrow," Samuel responded.

Marilyn added strength to her voice and said with a bit of optimism. "It is time for payback. We need to do the same thing to his witnesses that he did to ours. Also, I still think we can win this, but if we get a hung jury, I can promise you, we will not make the same mistakes we made in this trial."

Everyone in their department were giving them sad looks and shaking their head. They were receiving negative comments from colleagues, friends, and relatives. They knew it was unlikely a good firm would want to hire them because of their poor performance on this case. The only positive was job security, but that was associated with poor pay and long hours. Initially, they were excited to have a high-profile case, but now they just wanted the case to be over.

Regardless, they planned to be prepared for the next day and hopefully get some revenge.

CHAPTER 7 TRIAL DEFENSE

The following morning, Judge Terrell took her seat, and stared at the Defense table. "The Defense may call their first witness."

"The Defense calls Susan Wilkerson to the stand." Susan took a seat in the witness chair and was sworn in.

"Mrs. Wilkerson, please tell me how you came to know Doctor Angel Carpenter," George asked.

"I met Doctor Angel when he approved my daughter for a new cancer drug about a year ago.

"Objection, Your Honor," Daniel said with a raised voice. "Please direct the witness and all future Defense witnesses to refer to the Defendant by his professional title as Doctor Carpenter."

"Your Honor," George said. "I am unaware of any rule of law preventing a witness from referring to someone they know by their first name. Angel is the Defendant's legal first name. Everyone who knows the Defendant calls him Angel or Doctor Angel."

Judge Terrell nodded. "Objection overruled."

"Mrs. Wilkerson, will you please continue?" George said.

"My daughter, Paulina, had chronic myelogenous leukemia and had not responded to any of the treatments we had tried before meeting Doctor Angel. We were told Paulina had less than a year to live. Angel accepted Paulina into his cancer drug test trial. After three months, my daughter was completely healed. She is attending college and wants to become a doctor. If you get Doctor Angel as your doctor, you get well. If you get Doctor Andrew, you die."

"Objection, Your Honor," Daniel shouted. "The witness is not an expert and is stating an opinion."

"Objection sustained," Judge Terrell said. "The Jurors are to disregard the comments by the witness that all of Doctor Carpenter's patients get well or that another doctor's patients all die." It took considerable effort for George to keep from grinning since the Jurors got to hear the comments twice.

"Tell us about other patients of Doctor Angel you have met."

"There were fifty patients in the initial group with my daughter," Susan replied. "My daughter would meet other patients during the group sessions, and sometimes I would attend as an observer. My daughter and I became acquainted with all forty-nine of the other patients. They are all still alive. None of them have died. Also, my daughter and I met other cancer patients at the hospital who were not on the cancer test trial who have died. The cancer patients find out who are good doctors and who are bad. Doctor Angel gets to know all of his patients. He knows how to get you to want to live. Then, he gets you to believe you are not going to die. From the moment my daughter met Doctor Angel, she knew she would get well. As far as my daughter and I are concerned, Doctor Angel Carpenter is an angel."

"Thank you, Mrs. Wilkerson," said George. "Your Honor, I have no more questions for this witness." George was pleased with Mrs. Wilkerson's testimony and knew the jurors would be moved by her unquestionable love for her daughter and her admiration for Angel.

"Does the Prosecution wish to cross?" Judge Terrell asked.

Daniel looked at Marilyn, and she shook her head. "No, Your Honor."

"You may step down," the Judge said. "The Defense may call their next witness."

"The Defense calls Martha Carpenter to the stand."

The witnesses were sequestered and unaware of what other witnesses said on the witness stand. Mrs. Carpenter entered the courtroom when she was called. She took the witness stand and was sworn in.

"Mrs. Carpenter, please tell the Jurors your relationship to the Defendant," George said.

"Angel is my adopted son," Martha said with a big smile.

"How did you come to adopt Angel?"

"My husband and I were unable to have children. We tried several medical procedures to have a child but were unsuccessful. We finally gave up and were trying to adopt. One Sunday morning, we were leaving our home to go to church. I opened the front door, and on the steps was a baby in a small bassinet. I looked around and did not see anyone. I took the bassinet inside and found a note. The note said: 'Please give my baby a good home.' The baby was so beautiful and so angelic. I just said to my husband, someone left us an angel. It took a while, but we successfully adopted the baby. We thought about what to name our new baby, but no other name fit."

"What can you tell us about Angel's character," George asked.

"Angel has always lived up to his name. He is smart, ambitious, and competitive, but in the right way. Angel has a kindness within him. He always wanted to help people, and I think he was destined to be a healer. As he was growing up, he planned to become a veterinarian. I brought several pictures with me. I believe these pictures will show you what my son was like."

Martha reached into her purse, pulled out an envelope, and handed the pictures to George.

"I took these pictures during various trips to the local park," Martha said. "Angel would sit at a table, and the birds would fly up, land on the table, and take French fries out of my son's hand."

Martha pointed to one of the pictures. "There is a picture of Angel feeding peanuts to the squirrels. We have a cat, and the cat follows Angel around. Angel would occasionally go to sleep on our couch. Anytime that happened, the cat would crawl up on the sofa and go to sleep on Angel's chest. There are several pictures in the stack with Angel and our cat. Animals can sense the goodness in a person. Here are pictures of his gang eating Thanksgiving dinner at our home. My son is, and always has been, a good person. The same is true for the members of the gang. They are all angels."

"May I keep these pictures?" George asked.

Martha's face lit up. "Yes, those are an extra set just for you."

"Your Honor, I move to add these pictures collectively into evidence as Defense Exhibit 11."

"Objection, Your Honor," Daniel said. "The Prosecution has not seen those pictures, nor do we have a copy of the pictures."

Martha reached into her purse and pulled out another envelope. "Your Honor, I brought an extra set of the pictures." Martha held up the envelope.

"Bailiff, please take the envelope from Mrs. Carpenter and give it to the Prosecution," Judge Terrell said.

The Bailiff took the envelope to the Prosecution. Daniel and Marilyn looked over the pictures and there were no grounds for excluding the photos.

"Does the Prosecution wish to have a separate hearing on the admission of the pictures into evidence," Judge Terrell asked.

Daniel and Marilyn did not want a separate hearing on the admission into evidence of the childhood pictures of the Defendant. A hearing they would lose, and which would bring more positive attention to the Defendant.

"We withdraw our objection, Your Honor," Daniel said.

"The court will accept into evidence the pictures presented by the Defense," Judge Terrell said. "Bailiff, please mark the envelope and the back of each picture as Exhibit 11. Also, please number each picture and put the total number of pictures on the back of each photo." It only took the Bailiff a few minutes to number the pictures.

"The Defense may continue questioning the witness," Judge Terrell said.

"Mrs. Carpenter, tell me about your son's affiliation with the gang called the Angels."

"They were mostly good kids, and we considered all of them to be our adopted children. We used to have them come to our home for dinner. Sometimes, they would join us at church on religious holidays. We would have them over for Thanksgiving dinner and Christmas, but they knew to join us for dinner anytime. At Christmas time, we always made sure each of them received a present. Angel, my husband, and I helped many of them find jobs. Some of them attended college, and others took up a trade. We even had a gang member who became an attorney."

That was an inside joke between them since George was the former gang member who became an attorney.

Martha grinned at George and continued. "I am extremely proud of the accomplishments of all the angels in the gang. If any of the angels are out there listening, you are all invited to our home for Thanksgiving dinner." She saw several of the gang members in the audience. They were all grinning.

"Mrs. Carpenter, you stated your son wanted to become a veterinarian. Why did he change his mind and decide to become a medical doctor?"

"His father got cancer when Angel was in high school, but it went into remission. When Angel was close to graduating from college, my husband's cancer came back. That was when Angel decided to go to medical school and specialize in cancer research to find a cure for his father. Unfortunately, his father died right before he graduated from medical school."

"Your Honor, I have no further questions for this witness."

"Would the Prosecution like to cross-examine the witness?" Judge Terrell asked.

"No, Your Honor," Daniel replied.

"You may step down," Judge Terrell said to Martha with kindness. "The Defense may call their next witness."

"The Defense calls Doctor Mark Seneca to the stand." Doctor Seneca took the witness stand and was sworn in.

"Doctor Seneca, please tell the Jurors and the court how you came to know Doctor Angel Carpenter."

Doctor Seneca explained how Angel combined holistic medicine and faith with the cancer drug test trial. He gave Angel his highest praise for his innovative approach to medical treatment and the success achieved because of this approach. Again, the Prosecution declined to cross-examine the witness.

"The defense may call their next witness."

"The Defense calls Robert Hill to the stand." George approached Robert after he had been sworn in. "Mr. Hill, please tell the Jurors and the court how you came to know Doctor Angel Carpenter."

"I was one of the fifty patients to become part of the first group to be accepted into Doctor Angel's cancer drug trial. Initially, he would not let me become part of the trial because of my behavior."

"Mr. Hill, how did you get Angel to accept you into the drug trial?"

"I had to promise to stop cussing, be nice to the hospital staff, write something I was thankful about each day, eat only the organic food specially prepared for me, take Tai Chi lessons each day, attend a meditation class each day, participate in daily exercise classes, and see a chiropractor once a week. To improve my faith, he suggested I see a minister once a week and pray each day. I decided if prayers were going to help me live, then I would pray twice a day."

"What did you think about doing these unusual things?" George asked.

"At first, I did not like it, but after several weeks I noticed how well I felt. I just started feeling healthy. I started developing friendships with the other patients in the program since we saw each other in the classes. I even started looking forward to the exercise classes. Also, I liked the way my whole body was feeling. Before meeting Doctor Angel, I was going to die from my cancer. Now I am cancer-free, and I feel great. Doctor Angel saved my life. He is an angel."

"What do you know about Doctor Andrew?" George asked.

"Objection, Your Honor, Doctor Andrew is not on trial," Daniel said.

"The Prosecution used Doctor Andrew to question my client's character," George replied. "I wish to show Doctor Andrew was biased against my client. The Prosecution opened the door."

"The objection is overruled. The witness may answer the question."

Rob continued. "Everyone, including myself, knew Doctor Andrew hated Doctor Angel. If you had Doctor Angel as your doctor, you lived. If a patient had Doctor Andrew, they died. We referred to Doctor Andrew as Doctor Death."

Daniel shouted. "Objection, Your Honor, hearsay."

"Objection sustained. The Jury will disregard the comments made by the witness concerning what others may have thought about Doctor Andrew, the comments regarding Doctor Andrew's patients, and the comment referring to Doctor Andrew as Doctor Death."

"Would you say Doctor Andrew was jealous of Doctor Angel's success?" George asked.

"Objection, Your Honor, calls for an opinion, and the question is leading," Daniel shouted again.

"Objection sustained," Judge Terrell said.

"I withdraw the question. Your Honor, I have no further questions for this witness."

"Does the Prosecution wish to cross-examine the witness?" Judge Terrell asked.

"Yes, Your Honor," Marilyn answered.

"Mr. Hill, you believe Doctor Carpenter is a real angel and can sprout wings?"

"Yes, I believe he is an angel. Not because of wings, but because he knows things about heaven that no one else knows."

Marilyn smirked. "Indeed, and what things does Doctor Carpenter know that no one else knows?"

"He knows the location of a bar in heaven that serves beer."

The whole courtroom burst out in laughter. Even the Judge laughed. Marilyn closed her eyes for just a second as she silently berated herself.

Marilyn opened her eyes. "No more questions, Your Honor."

Judge Terrell was trying unsuccessfully to control her laughter. "Does the Defense wish to redirect?"

"No, Your Honor."

George had not planned to bring up the beer the witness consumed at the hospital but was prepared if the Prosecution brought it up. He even had a small ice cooler with a sample of the non-alcoholic beer. Security thought it was funny when he mentioned it was evidence. A trial lawyer only uses about twenty percent of the information he collects, but the eighty percent on standby can prevent a fatal error in court.

Judge Terrell turned to the witness, still laughing. "You may step down."

Judge Terrell got her laughter under control. "The defense may call their next witness."

"The Defense calls Nephi Sorenson to the stand." Nephi Sorenson took the witness stand and was sworn in.

George approached the witness. "Ms. Sorenson, please tell us how you came to know Doctor Angel Carpenter."

Nephi explained how her husband became a patient of Doctor Angel and the results of his treatment. She also ended by saying Doctor Angel was an angel. This time the Prosecution decided not to cross-examine the witness.

After the witness stepped down and before the Defense could call the next witness, Daniel addressed the court. "Your Honor, I see no reason for the Defense to continue to call character witnesses since it does not relate to the three murders."

"Your Honor, the Prosecution opened the door when he presented Doctor Andrew as a witness who made many allegations concerning my client's character and abilities as a doctor," George said. "I have approximately four hundred patients of Doctor Angel who have a positive opinion of my client's character and his abilities as a physician. There is a long list of employees at the hospital who have a positive opinion of my client's character and abilities as a physician. I have a list of individuals from the corporation that developed the cancer drug who will testify to my client's character and abilities as a physician. If the Prosecution admits in open court that my client's character and abilities as a physician are exemplary, we can cease calling character witnesses. Otherwise, the Defense will continue to call character witnesses to offset the damage done to my client's reputation by Doctor Andrew."

Judge Terrell looked to the Prosecution. "Does the Prosecution have anything to say regarding Doctor Carpenter's character and abilities as a physician?"

"The Prosecution believes Doctor Carpenter is a serial killer who murdered three individuals," Daniel said. "However, we will attest that Doctor Carpenter's character and practice as a physician are not in question."

"Very well, I want the Prosecution to state for the record that my client's outstanding character as a human being and his abilities as an excellent physician is beyond reproach," George said. "If so stated, we will cease calling character witnesses but reserve the right to call additional character witnesses if my client's character and reputation are questioned later in the trial."

Judge Terrell addressed the Prosecution. "Does the Prosecution have any objection to the Defendant's character and abilities as stated by the Defense?"

Daniel knew he had painted himself into a corner. "We have no objection, Your Honor."

"The Defense may call their next non-character witness," Judge Terrell said.

"Your Honor, the Defense expected to spend several weeks calling character witnesses. Therefore, our next witness is not available at this time. I would ask for an adjournment to give us time to reschedule our additional witnesses."

"It is Thursday," Judge Terrell said. "If we adjourn for today and reconvene on Monday morning at nine o'clock, will that give the Defense sufficient time?"

"Yes, Your Honor," George said.

Judge Terrell stayed with standard protocol. "Does the Prosecution have any objections?"

The Prosecution knew better than to object because their request resulted in the need for the Defense to rearrange their witness schedule.

"No, Your Honor, we have no objections," Daniel said.

"There being no objections, the court will adjourn and reconvene on Monday morning at nine o'clock."

Daniel and Marilyn were in the office on Friday reviewing the files of the Defense witnesses. While reviewing the files for Miguel Swartz, Daniel saw he was a former member of the Angel Gang. After working for almost an hour, Daniel received a call from an administrative assistant saying a caller on Line 3 had information on the Angel case. Daniel pressed the pickup button on the antiquated phone system. The department needed new phones, but there were no funds. He answered the phone and stated his name.

"Monday, you may wish to ask the defense witness about his nickname," a male voice said.

"Can you give me your name?" Daniel asked.

"No, you do not need my name. I do not want to get involved."

"Give me a moment, I am on another call, and it will take a minute to finish the call." Daniel placed the caller on hold. He then stood up and motioned to the attorney in the next cubicle to have the call traced. He then waited for another minute before reconnecting with the caller.

"Sorry to keep you holding. What about his nickname?"

"Just ask him about his nickname. All gang members have nicknames."

"Can you just tell me his nickname?"

The caller hesitated. "His nickname is the Undertaker."

"And why is he called that?"

"You figure it out. Also, Angel and all his gang members have the same tattoos on their arms."

Daniel heard the dial tone and knew the caller had hung up. He put down the phone in disappointment since the caller likely had additional information.

Martin Moore took the burner phone, removed the batteries, and threw it into the lake. He intentionally made the call near the lake, so he could permanently dispose of the phone. He calmly turned away and disappeared among the other pedestrians walking along the sidewalk. Doctor Carpenter had saved his life. He knew his mother would approve but decided not to tell her since she liked to talk and could never keep a secret. After being released from the hospital, Angel had introduced Martin to several Angel gang members. They helped him get a job, and he enjoyed spending time with them. He learned about Miguel Swartz and realized he had an opportunity to help Angel.

Daniel stood up. "Did they get a trace?"

The attorney in the next cubical nodded. "Yes, and the police are on the way. They will call us back when they get there."

Daniel was not surprised since it only took seconds for the police to trace a call using the current technology. The police called back a couple of minutes later and let them know there was no one at the location where the call originated, and no cameras in the area. Also, the phone was a burner phone, and it appeared the caller destroyed the phone since they could no longer get a lock on its location. Daniel thanked them for their help and quick response.

The court reconvened on Monday morning. The inside of the courtroom was packed, and the crowd outside had grown.

"The Defense may call its next witness," Judge Terrell said.

"Defense calls Miguel Swartz to the stand." The witness was sworn in.

"Mr. Swartz, do you know Angel Carpenter?" George asked.

"Yes," Miguel answered.

"Mr. Swartz, how long have you known Angel?"

"For over six years."

George handed Miguel an eight-by-ten photograph listed as Prosecution Exhibit E. "Here is a picture of Owen Ward. Do you recognize him?"

"Yes, he was a member of the South Bay Warlocks."

"Mr. Swartz, do you know how Mr. Ward died?"

"On a Saturday morning, Angel, me, and five other gang members went to meet with the Warlocks on their turf. Four of the gang and I arrived early and crawled on top of the surrounding buildings. Angel and one of our members met with the Warlocks face to face. At a signal from Angel, we beat on metal buckets to let the Warlocks know Angel was not alone. Angel separated from the group and talked with one of the Warlocks privately. After a few minutes, they rejoined the other Warlocks. The guy in the picture started arguing with the leader. He was a big guy, bigger than everyone else. All of a sudden, Angel and this Owen guy were fighting. However, it was not much of a fight. Angel was standing, and the other guy was on his back on the ground. Then Owen pulled a gun and shot Angel in the chest. Angel took the gun away from the guy, and I heard him shout, you cannot kill an angel with a bullet. Then Angel threw the gun to a Warlock. That guy walked over and shot Owen."

"If the other guy was so big, how did Angel beat him in a fight?" George asked.

"Angel has a Black Belt in karate. He is strong and fast. After he became our leader, we all took martial arts, but none of us were ever as good as Angel."

"Do you know the identity of the person who shot Owen?"

"No, he was too far away,"

George looked at the Judge. "Your Honor, I have no more questions of this witness."

"Does the Prosecution wish to cross-examine the witness?" Judge Terrell asked.

"Yes, Your Honor," Daniel replied.

Daniel approached the witness stand and turned on a projector. The projected image showed an aerial view where the meeting between Angel and the Warlocks took place.

"I have placed letters in various places on the projection. Please tell the court the letter that best represents where you were during this meeting."

"Letter E," Miguel Swartz answered.

"Let the record show the witness designated a location on top of a building across the street from where the alleged meeting occurred between the Defendant and the gang known as the Warlocks."

"Mr. Swartz, I stood in the exact location where you claim the conversation between Angel and the Warlocks took place. Listen as I play you a recording of the conversation between two police officers standing where the alleged meeting took place."

The conversation between the officers was crystal clear.

"Now, I want you to listen to a recording of the same conversation taken from your alleged location."

Daniel played the second recording, and it was impossible to make out the words. He turned up the volume, but the conversation was garbled.

"Mr. Swartz, your alleged location would have prevented you from hearing what took place at the meeting, and it would be difficult to see who was firing the gun."

George spoke up. "Objection, Your Honor, does the Prosecution have a question, or is he giving his Closing Argument."

"Objection sustained. Does the Prosecution have any more questions?"

"Yes, Your Honor."

"Mr. Swartz, you are in a gang called the Angels. Is that correct?"

"Yes, you are correct."

"Is there anything your gang does to show their membership in the Angels?"

"Yes, we get tattoos on our arms with a picture of an angel."

"Mr. Swartz, please show me your tattoo of the angel."

Miguel had on a pullover shirt, so he pulled up his sleeve and showed the picture of the angel. Daniel thought for a moment and decided to take a risk.

"Mr. Swartz, do you have a nickname?"

"Yes, my nickname was digger, but now I am called the undertaker."

"Why were you called digger and undertaker?"

Miguel paused. "I was called digger because I would dig the graves. Now I am called the undertaker because I make sure people are properly buried."

Daniel, the Jurors, and everyone else in the courtroom were quiet and shocked.

"I think the police might want to ask you some questions."

Miguel made a dismissive hand gesture. "In my business, I have buried several police officers."

The courtroom became noisy as the spectators reacted to what they had just heard.

Daniel nodded. Finally, he had discredited a defense witness. "I have no further questions, Your Honor," Daniel said with satisfaction.

"Does the Defense wish to redirect?" Judge Terrell asked.

"Yes, Your Honor," George responded.

George approached the witness stand. "Mr. Swartz, the Prosecution said you could not have heard what was being said or seen during the shooting. What is your response?"

"I explained I did not hear the conversation. However, the gunshots were loud, and it was pretty easy to see what Angel was doing since he stands out in a crowd due to his blond hair. Also, I heard what Angel said because, after the shot, he was shouting."

"Mr. Swartz, when you were called digger, you said it was because you dug graves. Why were you digging graves?"

"The people in charge of the cemeteries paid me two hundred dollars to dig a grave. They used a backhoe to remove most of the dirt, but I would make the hole the exact size to allow the casket to move freely to the bottom of the hole. Now, everyone calls me the undertaker because I am a Licensed Undertaker."

There was scattered laughter throughout the court. The Judge let it go on for a minute before calling the court to order. The Judge managed to keep a straight face.

George looked at the Jurors to ascertain their reactions. Everyone was smiling except for the atheist. "I have no further questions, Your Honor."

"You may step down," Judge Terrel said as she looked at the clock. "We will adjourn and reconvene tomorrow morning at ten o'clock."

Daniel was beside himself. He made the mistake of a first-year law student. You never ask a question unless you know the answer. He was mad but remembered to control his facial expression. He wondered if the Defense was involved in the phone call that set him up. It was well planned. If they could find evidence of culpability on the part of the Defense, they could demand a new trial and file additional charges against the Defendant. Attorney Martinez would face disbarment. He knew it was wishful thinking on his part. He needed to stop daydreaming and get to work.

Marilyn leaned over and said: "It is not your fault. We were told to take chances. I would have asked the same questions. I will meet you back at the office."

Daniel nodded and gathered his belongings. He did not think Samuel would be as understanding as Marilyn.

Back at the office, Daniel and Marilyn examined the Defense witness list. It took them nearly an hour to review all the witnesses on the list. They agreed there were only two remaining witnesses who were not character witnesses. After reviewing their notes, they felt the defense witnesses would not be credible. One witness had multiple arrests and several convictions resulting in prison sentences. They worked together to arrive at the best questions for their cross-examinations of the remaining witnesses. Also, they prepared questions for the Defendant even though they did not expect Angel Carpenter to testify.

CHAPTER 8 ANGEL'S TESTIMONY

George said he would drop by later to discuss how they should proceed. Angel had just finished dinner when the doorbell sounded. As usual, they sat at the dining room table, and George discussed his take on the court hearing from earlier in the day.

"If the jury had to decide today, what do you think the verdict would be?" Angel asked.

George took a deep breath and shrugged his shoulders.

"It is hard to say. I do not believe the jurors will consider First-Degree or Second-Degree Murder, but they may consider manslaughter murder. However, I believe we currently have a hung jury. Worse case, my guess would be eight for acquittal, two for guilty, and the other two I cannot get a read on. Additional research on the atheist shows he has a forceful personality and will form his own opinion without regard to his fellow jurors. The humor helped us discredit several witnesses. However, it will no longer be humorous when jurors go to the jury room for deliberations. Deciding if a person is to be executed or spend years in prison is serious business."

George divided the file for each juror into one of three piles. He then pointed to the two witnesses he thought would be more likely to cast a guilty vote.

"These two are on the jury because I was out of challenges during the voir dire. The male juror is an atheist and was not the least bit swayed by anything religious. He continued to smile at the state's attorneys but frowned when I questioned the witnesses. The female juror has a brother who is a police officer, and she may believe you are guilty because you were arrested. She should not even be on the jury since the Judge should have dismissed her for cause. These two are more likely to go with a guilty verdict."

George pointed to the two jurors in the maybe pile. "I could not get a read on these two. They had neutral expressions most of the time. I believe they will go with the majority. If they do, we have a ten to two not guilty majority which is still a hung jury."

"What will happen if the trial ends with a hung jury?" Angel asked.

George shook his head. "The state has the option to retry the case or drop the case. If they retry the case, they will do much better the second time around."

Angel was thoughtful. "I know you do not want me to take the witness stand, but I need an acquittal. If we have a hung jury, a second trial would keep me from concentrating fully on my work for an extended length of time. I want this trial to be over so I can give my patients the care they need and deserve, with no distractions."

"Very well, let us go over the questions I plan to ask you and decide on the best responses. I will then ask questions I think the Prosecution will ask, and we will work on your responses to those questions. Tomorrow, I have two witnesses to call before I ask you to take the stand. I already have you down as a witness, but the attorneys for the state will have assumed I will not call you to testify. It may give us a bit of an advantage. However, we still have to assume they will come prepared to question you, and if you respond poorly to their questions, you could be found guilty."

"I still want to testify. There was a lot of negative media coverage of me before the start of the trial. Particularly the interview with Doctor Andrew. The televised coverage of the trial has helped to offset most of the initial negative coverage, but people need to see the real me, and I can only achieve this by testifying. Also, people will think I have something to hide if I do not testify."

George was silent for a few minutes. "I believe the two witnesses I call tomorrow may give us the reasonable doubt we need for an acquittal, and they may sway the four jurors who appear to be unfavorable to our side. Although I am concerned about you testifying, I will honor your decision and call you as the last witness for the Defense."

They worked several more hours before calling it a night since George had appointments to meet with the other two witnesses. The trial would resume the following morning at ten o'clock, so George would still have time to get sufficient rest for the next day. Angel was going to take a melatonin capsule to help him sleep since he was too worried and had trouble relaxing. As usual, he closed his eyes and said a silent prayer. After his prayer, he relaxed and decided he did not need the melatonin after all.

The next morning Angel arrived at the courthouse at around nine-thirty and noted the skies were clear and the sun was shining. He had a good feeling as he left his car in the parking lot and entered the courthouse. There was a large crowd outside the courthouse and camera crews from the media. Everyone expected today would be the last day of court before jury deliberations. There were extra law enforcement officers to keep order. Angel managed to slip past most of the crowd before anyone noticed him. Then he heard encouragement from various individuals in the crowd. He waved to them as he entered the building. He made his way to the assigned courtroom and took a seat next to George.

"Any last-minute questions?" George asked Angel.

"No, I just want this to be over."

The courtroom began to fill up. The camera crews inside the courtroom were ready to start another day with the live feeds. The viewership had increased each day, and the show had moved into first place in the ratings. Everyone stood as Judge Terrell entered the courtroom.

After everyone was seated, the Judge looked at George. "Attorney Martinez, you may call your next Defense witness."

"Your Honor, as our next witness, we would like to call Roger Hamilton to the stand." George waited until Roger was sworn in.

"Mr. Hamilton, what is your occupation?"

"I am a supervisor at Walmart."

"What is your relationship to the Defendant, Angel Carpenter?"

Roger answered with pride. "I was a member of his gang, the Angels."

"Do you have an explanation on how Angel's fingerprints got on the pistol allegedly used in three murders?"

Roger looked at the judge and then at the jury. "Shortly after Angel took over our gang, he set up a meeting with the leader of the Warlocks. This was a rival gang. The Warlocks had killed our prior leader. We scouted the meeting location in advance, and our members climbed on top of local buildings with empty metal cans and metal rods. We beat the cans at the proper time to let the other gang know we were there. We did this to keep them from harming our new leader. Angel and their leader had a private discussion. I do not know what they talked about, but it seemed they reached an agreement. However, when they returned to the group, the biggest guy in their gang took exception to the agreement. Then, Angel and this huge guy started fighting. The other guy was bigger than Angel, but Angel beat the other guy using his martial arts. The guy sitting on the ground pulled out a gun. He shot the gun two or three times before Angel twisted the gun out of his hand. Angel threw the gun to the leader of the Warlocks, and the gang leader shot the big guy several times. I was too far away to hear the conversation, but Angel did not shoot the guy."

The testimony corroborated the statement provided by the prior Defense witness.

"I have no further questions," George said.

The Judge looked toward the prosecution. "Does the Prosecution wish to cross?"

"Yes, Your Honor," Daniel said.

Daniel approached the witness stand. "Mr. Hamilton, is it true you and the Defendant are good friends?"

"Yes."

"You would do anything to help your friend."

"Yes, but."

Daniel did not give Hamilton a chance to complete his response. "I want a simple yes or no. Would you lie for your friend?"

"Yes," Roger answered truthfully.

"No further questions." Daniel got the answers he wanted and did not want any explanation from the witness.

George declined to redirect and called his next witness, Joseph Adler.

Joseph Adler took the witness stand and was sworn in.

"Mr. Adler, tell me about yourself and how you came to meet my client, Angel Carpenter."

"I am a member of the South Bay Warlocks. I met Angel Carpenter for the first time when he met with our leader to arrange a peace treaty between our two gangs. Our second in command, Owen Ward, took exception to the peace agreement and decided to teach Angel a lesson by fighting him. The leader of the Warlocks agreed to let them fight but told them no weapons could be used. Owen lost the fight, but he pulled a gun and shot at Angel twice. They were only a few feet apart. I still do not know how Owen missed him. Anyhow, Angel twisted the gun out of Owen's hand. Then he shouted at Owen: 'You cannot kill an angel with bullets.' Angel then tossed the gun to a member of the South Bay Warlocks, who walked over and shot Owen. On that day, I believed Angel was an actual angel since I felt sure both bullets had hit him in the chest. Later, I figured he must have been wearing a vest."

George nodded. "Your Honor, I have no further questions for this witness."

The Judge directed her question at the prosecution. "Do you wish to cross?"

"Yes, Your Honor," Marilyn said.

Attorney Marilyn Ross approached the witness stand. "Are you a friend of the Defendant?"

Joseph smirked, shook his head, and then lied. "No, I am not friends with the Defendant. In fact, I do not like him."

"Then why are you serving as a witness for the Defense?"

"I was subpoenaed," Joseph answered with a scowl.

"Is it true Doctor Carpenter recently provided medical care to Phillip Grainger, a member of your gang?"

"Yes, but I dislike Phillip. Phillip is a real pain." Joseph did not say he was the leader of the Warlocks and had murdered Owen Ward. He did not say how a member of his gang had used the gun to kill the other two victims. Joseph wished the gun had been properly wiped down before being pitched, but he could not undo the past. He owed Angel, and the Warlocks honored their debt. Plus, he or someone in his gang may need a doctor in the future. The agreement he made years ago with Angel had worked out well. Also, Attorney George Martinez had gotten him off on the drug dealing charge, which allowed him to come to court and give his testimony for the Defense. It was a given he would need an attorney at some future date.

"Isn't it true your testimony is payment for Doctor Carpenter's medical help for Phillip Grainger?" Marilyn asked.

"No, as I just said, I dislike Phillip." Joseph had just lied again, and the lie was quite convincing.

"No further questions."

"Attorney Martinez, do you wish to redirect?"

"Yes, Your Honor."

"Mr. Adler, why did Angel provide medical attention to a member of your gang?"

"Doctor Carpenter had an obligation to our gang as part of the peace agreement we made to stay out of the Angels' territory. However, I believe Doctor Carpenter would have provided medical help because of the Hippocratic Oath. If not, another doctor would have taken care of Phillip."

"No further questions." George felt the witness helped their case but did not know if it was enough to get an acquittal.

The Judge turned to the witness. "You may step down."

"The Defense may call their next witness."

"Your Honor, I would like to call Angel Carpenter as my final witness."

Comments were being made throughout the courtroom. Attorney Daniel Ellis was unable to hide a smirk since he was fully prepared to cross-examine the Defendant and could barely contain his excitement. Whereas Attorney Marilyn Ross had a guarded expression, and it surprised her the defense attorney was allowing his client to testify.

Angel took the stand. George took his time approaching the bench. He was glad his client appeared relaxed and hoped it would continue.

George asked his first question. "Please state your title and tell us about your qualifications."

Angel did his best to make eye contact with each of the jurors. "I received my medical degree from Florida International University. I am currently a cancer specialist at the non-profit Christian Health Hospital in Miami."

George asked the next open-ended question. "What is the nature of your work?"

Angel looked at the jurors with a serious expression as he replied. "I have treated over four hundred cancer patients using a new drug approved for human trials. The patients admitted to the trial had failed to respond to standard cancer treatments and were considered terminal."

"To make sure I understand, if the patients did not become part of this drug trial, what would be their likely outcome?"

"While no medical diagnosis is ever absolute, without becoming a part of the drug trial, they were not expected to live," Angel answered compassionately.

"Of these cancer patients who were expected to die, how many are still alive?"

Angel continued looking at the jury as he answered. "All the patients under my care, who became a part of the cancer drug trial, are still alive. Many have been healed and have left the hospital. While none of my patients have died, the actual cure rate is around ninety percent. We expect to lose some patients in the ten percent who have not been cured."

The jurors and everyone in the courtroom were duly impressed. Many had friends or family members who had died of cancer. They were thinking of people they knew with cancer and planned to tell them about this new cancer drug. George paused while giving the jury time to digest the last answer.

Angel had not mentioned the recent sad death of Mary Baker, who was no longer under his care at the time of her death. At first, he was surprised Mary had returned to Doctor Andrew, but then he realized what she was doing. He continued to visit her even though she was no longer his patient.

"What is your relationship to the three men you are accused of killing?" George asked.

"As I explained in the Opening Statement, I met one of the men who was killed, but I just met him once. I took the gun from him, but I did not kill him. I never met the other two victims. I have killed no one. I hope to spend my entire life helping people and doing everything possible to extend the life of my patients."

George was thoughtful as he considered all the additional questions they had rehearsed and decided they had succinctly made their point.

"Your Honor, I have no further questions."

"Does the Prosecution wish to cross-examine the witness?" Judge Terrell asked.

Daniel was surprised since he had expected the Defense to take all day questioning the Defendant, but he was ready. "Yes, Your Honor."

Daniel approached the witness stand with confidence. "Doctor Carpenter, you are a member of a gang called the Angels."

"No, that is not true," Angel answered.

Daniel looked at Angel with a sadistic smile. "Witnesses have attested to your membership in the gang called the Angels. Even your mother has mentioned your affiliation with the gang. Take off your shirt."

"Objection, Your Honor, relevance," George said.

"Your Honor, we wish to show Doctor Carpenter's prior statement was false," Daniel answered. "We wish to show he has a tattoo showing his gang affiliation."

"Objection overruled. The Defendant is directed to remove his shirt."

"Your Honor, I ask the Defendant be required to approach the jurors so they can get a good look at the gang tattoo."

The Judge turned to Angel. "Doctor Carpenter, please step down from the witness stand and approach the jurors. After taking off your shirt, turn so the jurors can see the tattoo on your arm."

"Yes, Your Honor."

Angel stood up, stepped down from the witness stand, and slowly took off his shirt. He placed his shirt over the banister next to the witness chair. Angel was young and physically fit from his daily workouts. His chiseled chest and muscles were pronounced with flat abs. Angel walked casually over to the jurors. The females on the jury were mesmerized as they moistened their lips and felt their heart rate increase.

Attorney Daniel Ellis was clueless about the impact Angel was having on the female members of the jury when he pointed to Angel's tattoo. Daniel spoke directly to the jurors.

"I want you to look at the tattoo on Doctor Carpenter's arm. The tattoo is the emblem for the gang known as the Angels."

"Doctor Carpenter, you can return to the witness stand."

Angel returned to the witness stand and was reaching for his shirt when he saw George shake his head no, so he did not bother to put on his shirt.

Attorney Ellis was satisfied with what he hoped would win over the jurors. "Doctor Carpenter, I am asking you again, are you a member of the gang called the Angels?"

"No. Would you like me to explain?" Angel asked.

Attorney Daniel Ellis threw his arms up in the air. "No, I do not want you to explain! Your Honor and members of the jury, the Defendant has just lied under oath. All of Doctor Carpenter's testimony should be discounted since he does not understand the concept of perjury."

George immediately spoke up. "Objection, Your Honor. Does the Prosecution have a question, or is he again giving his Closing Argument?"

"Objection sustained," the Judge said. "Attorney Ellis, you know better. The jury will ignore Attorney Ellis's comments. Attorney Ellis, do you have any additional questions?"

Attorney Daniel Ellis proceeded, and his next question surprised everyone. "Doctor Carpenter, do you consider yourself to be an angel?"

"It depends on."

Attorney Ellis immediately interrupted him. "Yes or No, do you consider yourself to be an angel?"

Angel nodded his head as he answered. "Yes."

The whole courtroom erupted into shouts and comments. The Judge used her gavel. "Order in the Court," she shouted. The noise slowly subsided.

Attorney Ellis turned away from the Judge and said loudly. "No more questions, Your Honor."

He intentionally passed near the jurors and softly said: "He is completely delusional."

Attorney Daniel Ellis returned to his seat next to Marilyn. He leaned over to Marilyn with a smug look on his face. "What do you think, pretty good cross?" He asked in a whisper.

She shook her head in disbelief. "You are a complete idiot. You just lost every female on the jury, and he is going to destroy you on the redirect."

The Judge looked at the Defense table. "Does the Defense wish to redirect?"

"Yes, Your Honor."

"Angel, what is your relationship to the gang called the Angels?"

"I was completely truthful in my answer to the Prosecution," Angel replied. "I was going to explain. I have never been a member of the Angels. I was their leader and continued to be their leader until I resigned."

The courtroom burst out laughing. The Judge could not help smiling herself. This time the courtroom quieted down without the Judge having to intervene.

"Why did you become their leader?" George asked.

"A rival gang had killed the former leader of the gang in a drive-by shooting. I convinced the gang to reorganize similar to an Angels gang founded years ago to combat crime. It protected certain areas of the city while giving the young people in the gang a positive direction for their lives. Our Angels followed a somewhat similar path. However, besides our primary goal of protecting our small community, our secondary goal was to find a paying job for every member. The size of our gang nearly doubled when it became co-ed. My father was a licensed plumber, and with help from others, some of our gang members got jobs as helpers in the trade. We also got paying jobs for our members in fast-food restaurants, babysitting, digging graves, and other available jobs. Also, our members got free group lessons in martial arts from a local dojo. The members worked in groups to protect the playgrounds, bus stops, and other areas around the community. We arranged a truce with the other local gangs by both sides agreeing to stay out of each other's territory."

"Please explain your answer to the Prosecutor when he asked you if you were an angel," George said.

Angel again looked at the jury. "The term angel has multiple meanings besides the use of the term in various religious texts. A person who is good or does a good deed is sometimes called an angel. I believe many people are angels. An angel can be a person who goes to work every day to provide for their family. An angel can be a person who donates blood, a person who shows kindness to a pet, a person who is kind to another human being, a person who supports a charity, or just a person who struggles not to be a burden to others. I believe we have people in this courtroom who are angels: the members of the jury, the judge, not so much the Prosecution."

This time everyone except the prosecuting attorneys burst out in loud laughter. The Judge placed a hand over her mouth to stifle her laughter.

"Objection, Your Honor," Daniel said with a moan.

"Your Honor, he opened the door when he refused to let my client explain how the word angel can have multiple meanings," George said.

The Judge rolled her eyes. "Objection sustained. The jury is to disregard any use of the term angel to describe various individuals within the courtroom except for a description of the Defendant with an understanding the term angel can have multiple meanings."

"So, you cannot sprout wings and fly?" George asked.

"No, but I believe prayers help, and I believe in God."

"Your Honor, I have no further questions."

Judge Terrell turned to Angel and looked at his gorgeous body again. "Doctor Carpenter, you are excused. The Defense can call their next witness."

Angel picked up his shirt and put it back on as he returned to his seat. George remained standing.

Marilyn leaned over and whispered to Daniel. "This case is over, and we just lost."

"It is not over," Daniel replied. "We still have his fingerprints on the murder weapon."

George was still standing and looked at the Judge. "Your Honor, the Defense rests."

After a brief pause, George addressed the Court. "Your Honor, I would ask again for a directed verdict of not guilty."

"Request denied."

George gave the jury a friendly smile as he returned to his seat. Failure to ask for a directed verdict would have waived any right to request a judgment notwithstanding the verdict at a later date. This would allow the Judge to set aside a guilty verdict from the jurors if she believed the Prosecution failed to present sufficient evidence for a conviction.

"Is the Defense ready with the Closing Argument?" Judge Terrell asked.

George looked over his notes one last time. "Yes, Your Honor."

"You may proceed," the Judge said.

George approached the Jurors. He took his time and made eye contact with each juror. He had practiced his Closing Argument numerous times and saw no reason to make any changes.

"Your Honor, ladies and gentlemen of the jury. Doctor Angel Carpenter has spent his entire life helping people. He is simply not capable of killing anyone in cold blood. The two eyewitnesses for the Prosecution were convicted felons. We, the Defense, have provided our eyewitnesses attesting to how another person killed Owen Ward. Angel has explained how his fingerprints got on the gun. Further, the Prosecution's expert witness supports the Defendant's explanation regarding the fingerprints by showing how the gun was pointed at the Defendant and not at the victim. Therefore, the fingerprints support the Defendant's testimony. We do not know who killed Randolph Snead and Vern Dorn. We know whoever killed these two men wiped their fingerprints off the gun before throwing it away. Another felon testified to seeing the Defendant kill these two men. His testimony is suspect and is not reasonable. Remember, under the law, my client is presumed to be innocent. The Prosecution must prove every part of its case beyond a reasonable doubt. The fingerprints have been explained, and the two eyewitnesses for the Prosecution are not credible. Other than the explainable fingerprints, the Prosecution has presented no evidence to show my client committed these murders. You have heard the testimony of witnesses for the Defense and the testimony of the Defendant. My client is innocent, but I do not have to prove Angel is innocent. All the Defense has to provide is reasonable doubt. Therefore, you must find Doctor Angel Carpenter not guilty. Thank you."

"Is the Prosecution ready with their Closing Argument?" Judge Terrell asked.

"Yes, Your Honor," Marilyn replied:

Marilyn was immaculately dressed. She looked like a professional attorney and projected confidence as she approached the Jurors. She also took her time to look at each juror.

"Your Honor, ladies and gentlemen of the Jury. The Defendant's fingerprints are on the gun. The Defense has tried to come up with an alternative explanation for the fingerprints, but the explanation is not credible. The Prosecution has presented not one but two witnesses who attested to seeing the Defendant commit the murders. Even the Defense pointed out how the Defendant is easily recognizable and could not be mistaken as to his identity. The Prosecution has provided a motive for each of the murders. In both cases, it was a gang-related revenge killing, and the Defendant admits he is a gang leader. The Defendant is accused of killing three victims. Based upon the evidence and the eyewitness accounts, you must find the Defendant guilty. However, you as Jurors may decide the Defendant is guilty of one or all three of the killings. The eyewitness accounts indicate the Defendant is guilty of First-Degree Murder. However, you as the Jurors can consider the lesser charge of Second-Degree Murder or even Manslaughter Murder. Again, based upon the evidence and the eyewitness account, the Defendant is guilty."

Marilyn projected confidence as she gave the jurors a final look before returning to the Prosecution table.

The Judge looked at the Jurors. "You have heard arguments from both the Prosecution and the Defense. Ladies and gentlemen of the Jury, I am going to read you the law you must follow in deciding this case."

"For First-Degree Murder, the State must prove three things, beyond a reasonable doubt. First, that the victim is dead. Second, that the Defendant committed the criminal act. Third, that the killing of the victim was premeditated."

"For Second-Degree Murder, the State must prove beyond a reasonable doubt three things. First, that the victim is dead. Second, that the Defendant committed the criminal act. Third, that a person of ordinary judgment would know their act is reasonably certain to kill or do serious bodily injury to another."

"If each of you believes the Prosecution proved all three of these things for either First-Degree Murder or Second-Degree Murder, beyond a reasonable doubt, then you should find the Defendant guilty. But if you believe the Prosecution did not prove any one of these things beyond a reasonable doubt, then you must find the Defendant not guilty. Reasonable doubt does not mean beyond all doubt. You must reach a unanimous decision."

Judge Terrell continued: "You may consider Manslaughter Murder if you do not believe the Defendant is guilty of First-Degree or Second-Degree Murder. To prove Manslaughter, the State must prove two elements beyond a reasonable doubt. First that the victim is dead. Second that the Defendant committed an act that caused the death of the victim. In order to convict the Defendant of Manslaughter, the State does not have to prove the Defendant intended to cause death, only an intent to commit an act which resulted in the death."

After the Jury instructions, the jurors were led out of the courtroom and to the jury room for their deliberations.

"What do you think?" Angel asked George.

George was thoughtful. "I am still worried about the atheist and the female juror with a police officer as her brother. I am not worried about a guilty verdict, but I still have a concern we may have a hung jury. However, I believe we will get an acquittal. I checked with a friend of mine in the State Attorney's office, and even in the event of a hung jury, they do not plan to retry the case. They are receiving hundreds of thousands of emails, letters, and phone calls about the case, and all the communications are negative against their prosecution of the case. We can discuss this further over lunch."

They decided to eat at a restaurant within walking distance of the courthouse. It was a little early for lunch, and the restaurant was not crowded. The server placed water glasses in front of them. They each ordered a sandwich and fries. George added a soft drink to his order.

After placing their order, George noticed how Angel seemed despondent. "You seem more troubled than normal," he said.

Angel frowned. "The witnesses all lied or told the truth in such a way as to mislead the jurors."

"Some witnesses lie because of the benefit they expect to receive," George said. "Others believe they are telling the truth but just remember things differently. There was a study several years ago proving the unreliability of eyewitnesses."

"George, you were there. You were the person who said you cannot kill an angel with a bullet. I shot Owen Ward. It was an accident. The fight was supposed to make Owen look bad in front of the other gang members since he was trying to take over the gang once he had more support. Losing a fight to me would allow Joseph Adler to continue as leader of the Warlocks, and Joseph was willing to agree to peace between our gangs. I never expected Owen to pull a gun. When he shot at me, I just reacted and grabbed the gun. The gun discharged when I twisted it out of his hand, and the bullet punctured his liver. Owen was just as shocked as I was, and the blood was pouring out of him. I threw the gun to Joseph. I was just about to call an ambulance even though I knew he would die from blood loss before help could arrive. Then Joseph walked over and shot Owen through the head. On the witness stand, I said I did not kill Owen, but I did shoot him. I was guilty of manslaughter for my shooting and possibly as an accessory to First-Degree murder by throwing the gun to Joseph."

"Angel, the gun discharged during a struggle with a person who had already fired at you with the intent to kill. Under the law, it is self-defense. Also, when you threw the gun to Joseph, there is no way you could have known he would use it to kill Owen. Let me ask you a question. If you thought Joseph was going to use the gun to kill Owen, would you have thrown him the gun?"

"No," Angel answered without thinking.

"Then there was no accessory to murder. You need to stick to medicine and let me handle the legal issues. If the jurors knew all the facts, we would have the same verdict. However, the hospital would probably terminate your employment, and you would no longer be able to help your patients. Angel, the Prosecution has done everything they could to win the case. If a jury decides upon a verdict of guilty, the attorneys for the Prosecution are going to celebrate. They do not care if you are guilty or innocent. All they care about is winning. In all modesty, you are fortunate. You have an outstanding attorney."

Angel chuckled as he said in jest: "You were always so modest."

"I care about winning," George said. "But, unlike the Prosecution, I care about you. We have been friends for a long time. Plus, we are both former members of the Angels, and our tattoos made us brothers. For as long as we are alive, I am your attorney, and you are my doctor. Now, cheer up and think about the lives you are going to save in the future."

Angel was thoughtful and nodded his head. "You are correct."

Angel raised his glass, and George did the same. They clinked their glasses together in a toast. "To the Angels," they said together.

A server brought their food with an added soft drink for George. Angel decided to enjoy the meal even though it did not meet his daily nutritional standards.

Angel would not stop worrying until the jurors reached a verdict. He was unaware that millions around the globe were praying on his behalf for an acquittal. Also, powerful players were waiting for the results and hoping for a verdict of guilty. Angel did not know his life was about to take a dramatic shift.

CHAPTER 9 JURY DELIBERATION

After entering the jury room, the twelve jurors took their seats around a large conference table to begin deliberations. They were looking forward to reaching a verdict and going home.

The jury foreperson, Alex Edson, took charge. "It is eleven fifteen. Why don't we order lunch before we begin deliberations? If we reach a verdict too soon, we will not receive the free meal."

Several jurors shook their heads but did not object since they were not opposed to another free meal. They ordered lunch.

Alex asked for everyone's attention. "The prosecution case was built around the Defendant's fingerprints being on the gun. Two possibilities exist. Doctor Angel Carpenter used the gun to kill one or more of the victims, or his prints were on the gun as presented by the Defense."

Their discussion centered on the fingerprints. Various jurors felt the explanation provided by the Defense would have provided reasonable doubt if there had been no witnesses. However, two jurors were playing devil's advocate. They felt if you believed the witnesses provided by the Prosecution, you would have to accept the explanation for the fingerprints, and the reasonable doubt would not apply.

The jurors agreed to consider the double murder first. After further discussion, they decided Edward Tobin, the witness for the double murder, was not believable. He was reducing his prison time by seventeen years which gave him a strong incentive to lie. Doctor Carpenter being an assassin for hire or acting on behalf of a gang as a retaliation was not believable. The Prosecution did not provide evidence of the Defendant receiving any money or identify who would have paid for such killing or give a reason for a gang retaliation for the double murder. They decided the double murder was not supported by any evidence other than the fingerprints on the gun. Plus, the fingerprints on the gun barrel occurred with the first murder, as explained by both the Prosecution and the Defense witnesses. This created a reasonable doubt as to the double murder.

The jurors were left with the single murder of Owen Ward. A revenge killing for that murder was believable. Doctor Angel Carpenter had admitted he was the leader of the Angels, and the Warlocks had killed the prior leader of their gang. Now they had to decide if the single witness for the Prosecution was more believable than the two witnesses for the Defense. They decided the witness for the Prosecution, Cecil Segal, had an incentive to lie since his prison sentence was being reduced by twelve years. They had a similar problem with the first witness for the Defense, Roger Hamilton, who admitted he would lie for his friend and his gang leader. That left the second witness for the Defense, Joseph Adler. They decided he was the most believable of all the witnesses since he was not receiving anything for his testimony and stated he was not a friend of the Defendant. Also, his explanation for the fingerprints was identical to the explanation given by Defense witness Roger Hamilton. This also made Roger Hamilton's testimony more believable.

"To sum it up, does everyone believe the witnesses for the Defense were more believable than the witnesses for the Prosecution?" Foreperson Alex Edson asked.

Most of the jurors were nodding to show they believed the Defendant's explanation. One juror stated how the positioning of the Defendant's fingerprints was explainable if the gun was pointed at the Defendant and pulled from the other person's hand. Again, most of the jurors nodded, showing their agreement with the speaker.

"Does everyone believe the explanation given by the Defendant on how his prints wound up on the gun is enough to create reasonable doubt?" Alex asked.

Again, most of the jurors nodded in agreement, and several spoke up, saying they believed the witnesses for the Defense and doubted the witnesses for the prosecution.

A female juror, Margaret, said what they were all thinking. "The eyewitnesses for the prosecution were self-serving, resulting in a lack of belief in their truthfulness. After all, who would not lie to reduce your prison sentence?"

Alex looked around the room. "Are there any more comments or discussions before we vote?"

No one spoke. "Time to vote," Alex said. "Please place the word guilty or not-guilty on the piece of paper in front of you, turn it over, and pass it down."

The foreperson pulled all twelve pieces of paper together, including his vote, and started flipping over the votes one at a time while reading each vote out loud.

"We have eleven for Not Guilty and one Guilty vote. Okay, will the person who voted Guilty please explain your reasoning?"

"All the religious talk offended me," Ralph Miller, the outspoken atheist, said. "Especially the comments about the Defendant being an angel. I do not believe in God or angels or heaven or hell. I do not believe in life after death."

"I understand your position Ralph," Alex said. "But do you think the prosecution proved Angel Carpenter is guilty beyond a reasonable doubt?"

"Of course not," Ralph said. "The Prosecution was pathetic, and the Defense did an excellent job. Also, the Doctor's testimony was very believable. I could not vote for acquittal on the first ballot with all this angel nonsense being tossed around. On the next ballot, I will vote not guilty."

A knock on the door signaled that lunch had arrived. While eating lunch, the ladies sat together at one end of the table and talked about family, local events, and the hot shirtless Angel. After finishing lunch, the foreperson called for another vote, and they arrived at a unanimous verdict of not guilty. Serving on the jury had occasionally been exciting and utterly boring at other times. They enjoyed the humorous parts of the trial, but they were all happy it was finally over.

At around two o'clock, George received a call on his cellphone. The jury had reached a verdict. They were just a few blocks from the courthouse, and it only took them fifteen minutes to walk back to the courtroom. The jurors were already seated. Everyone stood as the Judge returned to the courtroom and took her seat on the bench.

The Bailiff went over to the Foreperson. He took a folded piece of paper from the Foreperson and handed it to the Judge. The Judge looked at the paper.

Judge Terrell directed her question to the Foreperson. "Has the jury reached a verdict?"

"Yes, Your Honor."

"What is the verdict?"

"Not guilty on all charges."

The court erupted into an uproar. George and Angel hugged each other. When the courtroom settled down, Judge Terrell thanked the jury and dismissed them.

"Your Honor, I have an Order I need you to sign allowing my client to remove his ankle monitor," George said.

Judge Terrell motioned to the Bailiff, who took the Court Order from George and handed it to the Judge. Judge Terrell signed the Order and gave it to the Court Clerk. The Clerk fed the Order through her scanner and returned the Original to the Bailiff, who gave the executed Order to George.

"You can take off the ankle monitor," George said. "I will notify the monitoring company and email them a copy of the Order. I will also send you a copy. They will want the monitor back, so do not throw it away. I believe it is time to face the media."

There were hundreds of people waiting outside the courthouse. The crowd cheered when they saw Angel. Angel waved to the spectators. A dozen news reporters accosted George and Angel. George explained why the verdict was never in doubt and how Angel was one of the greatest doctors currently practicing medicine. Angel said he was thankful the trial was over so he could continue helping his patients.

"Is it true you have never lost a patient?" A reporter asked.

"So far, my patients and I have been blessed with the success of the cancer drug," Angel answered.

The same reporter asked a second question. "Doctor Carpenter, ten million people die of cancer each year. Please tell our listeners, how many of these can be saved?"

"As I said during the hearing, the drug is not effective against all forms of cancer. However, when the drug is coupled with the holistic approach, the results show it is possible to cut the worldwide death rate in half."

"When will this drug be available?" Another reporter asked.

"You need to ask Tyzugmod, the corporation that developed the drug and the FDA."

Angel suddenly realized he should not be answering these types of questions. "Please, I cannot answer any more questions concerning the cancer drug."

"Are you an angel?" A reporter in the back of the crowd shouted.

"You heard my answer in court. There are many angels who try to make the world a better place. You should talk to all those angels and give them the coverage you give to the small percentage of the population who commit undesirable acts."

"Was the verdict ever in doubt?" Another reporter asked George.

"There was never any doubt concerning my client's innocence," George answered.

George was continuing to answer questions when the Judge's judicial assistant approached Angel and told him Judge Terrell would like to speak with him. George was concerned, but the clerk said it was a personal matter unrelated to the trial. Angel was relieved to get out of the spotlight and let George handle the questions from the media.

Angel followed the judicial assistant to the Judge's chambers. Judge Terrell had removed her robes and was wearing a one-piece black dress. Angel took a seat as directed. The Judge's assistant closed the door as she was leaving.

"You are probably wondering why I wished to see you privately," Judge Terrell said.

"You have cancer and want to see if I will take you on as a patient."

His response startled the Judge. "So, you are an angel, and you read minds."

Angel chuckled and shook his head. "No, it was just deductive reasoning. I am a doctor specializing in cancer, and you said you would like to see me regarding a personal matter. Do you have a copy of your medical diagnosis?"

Judge Terrell handed Angel a copy of her most recent medical report. Angel reviewed the summary data. The prognosis was dire, and the last sentence stated that further treatment would not be effective.

"I would be happy to be your doctor. Call the hospital and tell them I have already agreed to take you on as a patient, and I would like to see you as soon as possible. You are in luck. Another group will start in four weeks, and we have a couple of openings. You need to take a leave of absence for at least three months. I will tell my assistant to expect your call." It was fortuitous for the Judge that three of the patients on the waiting list had died. Due to the trial, Angel had not selected their replacements.

Angel stood up and went toward the door. Judge Terrell was thinking that no doctor should look that good. Angel turned back and looked at the Judge. He was about to say she was going to be all right but decided he should wait until he had completed an examination before commenting. Instead, he smiled at her, then turned and walked away. The Judge thought, oh my god, he just read my mind. She realized she was letting her imagination get out of hand. She was a little embarrassed but felt better. Her doctor, upon request, had answered honestly. He told her she was going to die, but now she would be healed by an angel.

Judge Terrell had not been to church in a while and figured it was time to start back. She was thinking the trial was fortuitous, and maybe fate or faith had selected her as the Judge for the case. She enjoyed being a judge while staying busy outside of work attending judicial events, charitable gatherings, and governmental affairs.

Judge Terrell had a wonderful, understanding husband who had a personal injury law practice, but she was in a state of denial and had put off telling him that her cancer had returned. She knew it was time to sit down with her husband and tell him about her cancer and her commitment to being cured by an angel. Together they would decide how to tell their adult children.

She prepared a letter to the Chief Judge explaining she would be taking a leave of absence and attached it to an email. She then telephoned the Chief Judge on his cellphone, and he picked up immediately.

"Hi Kevin," Judge Terrell said. "I just emailed you a letter. I am taking a four-month leave of absence. The reason for my leave of absence was not provided in the letter. I have cancer, and Doctor Angel Carpenter is taking me on as his patient. Doctor Carpenter was unaware of my condition until after the case was closed, so there was no conflict of interest. I hope to keep my condition and treatment as confidential as possible, but I wanted you to know in the event someone raises the issue with you. My former judicial assistant retired last year, and my new assistant knows I am taking some time off, but not the reason for the absence."

"Joan, I am so sorry," Kevin replied. "Thank you for letting me know. I will keep your condition confidential for as long as possible. I watched as much of the trial as possible, and it was quite entertaining. If I had cancer, I would want Angel as my doctor. Amazingly, he has never lost a patient. We have known each other for many years. Please let me know if you need anything. Also, keep me posted on your progress. I am looking forward to your return in four months."

The Honorable Judge Terrell hung up the phone, picked up her purse, and told her judicial assistant she was heading home.

Angel went home to his apartment. He entered the kitchen and used a knife to cut the strap to the ankle monitor. After laying the monitor on the kitchen counter, he massaged his ankle. A text message said he would receive a prepaid box to return the monitor. It felt like someone had lifted a weight from his shoulders and not just his ankle. The stress of the trial and the uncertainty of the verdict had left him drained. Suddenly, the future looked bright again. He was looking forward to working without distractions.

Angel called the Tyzugmod Corporation and informed them of the decision. His contact said: "Everyone here has been following the trial, and we are already aware of your acquittal. We are having a little party here on your behalf to celebrate your win. The directors and executives are incredibly pleased with the positive publicity. As our marketing executive pointed out, we were getting free national advertising every day of the trial. The impact on our stock price is phenomenal. The stock price increased every day of the trial. Drug companies usually spend millions of dollars advertising a new drug, and it takes an extended period to gain public support. Your court trial allowed our company to bypass the initial advertising and marketing costs for our cancer drug. We have a worldwide market with no advertising costs."

"I am just thankful it is over," Angel said.

"I am glad you called. With the unanimous support of the directors, our Chairperson just approved an additional one hundred thousand stock options for you, based upon the stock price at the beginning of the trial."

"Thank you, I think," Angel said.

"You think? Everyone who owns stock in our company is in love with you, including me."

After the call, Angel used his tablet to check the stock price for Tyzugmod. The stock had more than doubled since the beginning of the court trial and had quadrupled since Angel started his holistic drug trial. In the past year, the market capitalization value of the Tyzugmod Corporation had increased from ten billion dollars to over forty billion. It was now the twenty-ninth largest publicly traded pharmaceutical company in the United States. The articles connected to the company were all touting the cancer drug as the next blockbuster drug to hit the market. He thought the stock information was interesting, but he was only concerned about the lives the drug could save if properly administered.

Angel called Doctor Stanford to tell him about his acquittal, but Doctor Stanford said he had already heard and was thrilled with the results. He also told Angel how the hospital had already received over five hundred thousand requests from cancer patients wanting to become part of the drug trial. Requests were coming in from all over the world. The hospital's voice and data lines were completely overloaded. Cancer patients worldwide wanted to be treated with a drug with a one hundred percent survival rate. Doctor Stanford had received calls from too many state and federal officials. Also, several governors had called. Quite a few had asked for preferential consideration to allow themselves or their loved ones to become part of the drug trial. No one wanted to be reasonable. The United States Embassies around the world were also being contacted and politically pressured.

The publicity resulted in the hospital receiving a considerable increase in charitable donations. The donations would allow the hospital to provide increased care to those who did not have sufficient healthcare or the ability to pay for medical services.

The Trustees in the Bailiwick of Jersey were irate when they had their monthly meeting. Their interference in the courtroom trial of Angel Carpenter had made matters worse. The polls showed improved positive feelings toward religions in general and specifically toward Christianity. The polls showed there were three significant contributors to the overall improvement. First, the Pope had become more active in his appearances, which impacted Europe. Second, the young minister in Argentina was gaining an audience throughout South America. Third, the televised trial of Angel Carpenter had the most significant impact within the United States, but viewership worldwide was increasing as the court trial continued to be translated and rebroadcast. They discussed various options, including the possibility of eliminating the minister in Argentina and Angel Carpenter. However, they ended the meeting without reaching a resolution. They next discussed various politicians they would support and current politicians they wished to replace by supporting opposition candidates. They then looked at business executives needing their help in advancing to the top ranks of their respective corporations. Historically, less than half of their efforts were successful, but often it only took a minor change to have a significant impact.

The following morning, Angel received a call from Doctor Stanford informing him there were two guests waiting to meet with him in the main conference room. This was the same conference room where the Board of Directors held their meetings. Angel arrived and was directed to go into the conference room by an administrative assistant. Two men were seated near the center of the large table who were unknown to Angel.

Angel approached the two men who stood up when he entered the room. The older man appeared to be in his mid-forties, while the younger man looked to be in his early thirties. Both men were physically fit. Angel thought they were military, possibly special forces.

"I am Angel Carpenter. How may I help you?"

The older gentleman spoke with an accent. "I am Lorenzo, and this is Domenico. Please take a seat. We are here to offer our help." Angel took a seat facing them.

"We are from the Vatican," Lorenzo said. "Specifically, we are members of the anti-terrorism unit established in 2012 as an addition to the Gendarmerie Corps of the Vatican. The Pope created the Gendarmerie Corps in 1816. Christianity has existed for over two thousand years. From the beginning, there have been groups opposed to such existence. Various religious faiths opposed each other resulting in much bloodshed on all sides. However, there was one group whose members opposed all forms of religion. They are known as the Diocletian Knights and were formed when Diocletian tried to wipe out Christianity. This group was irrelevant until the beginning of the nineteenth century, when they accumulated excessive wealth. They now operate using a front as Trustees of their financial holdings. Today, their worth is in the billions of euros, with financial holdings throughout Europe and the Americas. They have thousands of secret followers worldwide, but their main financial headquarters is in the Bailiwick of Jersey. While they accomplish most of their goals passively, assassins are used when they believe it will expeditiously advance their cause. We recently learned of their interest in you. Your exploits have brought a slight increase in the faith of Christians everywhere. We think your life is in danger since they have discussed your elimination."

Domenico took a small tablet and showed Angel photos of the five men who headed the organization.

"This group is a growing cancer, and it has spread throughout the world," Domenico said. "We came here to introduce ourselves and to warn you."

"Thank you for the warning, but if you know who they are, why have you not taken action to stop them."

"Recent Popes have passed edits only allowing for the use of deadly force to protect the Pope or the Vatican," Lorenzo explained. "While the church cannot take direct action against this group, we have an excellent spy network to monitor their activities."

"Others must know their existence," Angel said. "Why have they not exposed this group?"

"They have historically operated covertly, and they are careful so nothing can be traced back to them. A person who openly opposes them, either disappears or dies. Others support what they are doing and keep quiet. Those who do not support them are too afraid to act. You should not share this information with anyone since it would further endanger your life."

Angel asked them to transfer the file on the Diocletian Knights to his tablet. After the transfer was complete, Lorenzo handed him a card with an international phone number.

"Call the number on the card if you need our help. Your code name will be your first name."

Angel thanked them again. They left the conference room and went their separate ways. Angel was committed to curing cancer, and the Diocletian Knights were a malignant cancer.

Angel continued with his daily routine. It had been three days since his acquittal in court. The hospital's Board of Directors scheduled an emergency meeting the following morning at eight o'clock to discuss recent events.

CHAPTER 10 TOO SUCCESSFUL

Angel arrived at his apartment, worked out in the gym for an hour, and ate a light dinner. After eating, he reviewed the file of the Diocletian Knights. He was only through the first part of the file when he received a text message from Doctor Stanford. The hospital directors were meeting the following morning at eight o'clock and asked him to attend the meeting. Angel sent a text reply, confirming he would be there.

The news channels and the internet had little news to report. Therefore, they concentrated on an Angel who was curing terminal cancer patients. It was being picked up by every news outlet worldwide. The central theme was how an angel was healing every one of his patients and how none of his terminal cancer patients had died since he started treating them. His patients were being interviewed, and they all were saying how they had given up hope, how their prior doctors had told them they were terminal, and how an angel named Angel had healed them. The significant parts of the jury trial were being rebroadcast and were streaming on all the social media outlets.

Angel woke up at his usual time the following morning when his clock alarm sounded at five o'clock. It would be another two hours until sunrise. He proceeded to get ready for work. He took a shower and was partially dressed when his phone rang. Angel saw it was George calling as he answered his cellphone.

"Good morning, George. I did not expect to hear from you for a while. Please tell me we are not going back to court."

"No, your case is closed," George answered. "But I suggest you turn on your television and check the early morning news channels. Your apartment and the hospital are surrounded by thousands of people. They want to either see the angel or be healed by the angel. I recommend you get to the hospital without being seen."

While Angel was talking to George, he turned on his television. He flipped through the channels until he saw an aerial view outside his apartment. The area surrounding his apartment was overflowing with people.

"George, I have no idea how I am going to get to the hospital with all those people outside." George realized Angel needed his help.

"Put on some regular clothes and try to disguise yourself," George said. "I will pick you up. I will call again when I get there."

Angel put on a pair of jeans, a pullover shirt, and a ball cap. He located an old lightweight jacket with a hood and waited for a call from George.

It was still semi-dark, and so far, the crowd was still outside the building in the parking lot. There was no way to get to his car without being noticed. About forty-five minutes later, his phone rang.

"I am a block away," George said. "I cannot get closer with all the cars and people blocking the way."

George told Angel where he was waiting. He looked through the peephole that had been installed with the new door. The fisheye lens gave a good view of the hallway space outside his door. He did not see anyone in the hallway. Angel opened the door and exited the apartment with a small travel bag containing his tablet, some clothing, a toiletry kit, and other personal items. He locked the door and used the staircase instead of the elevator. He used the exit door at the bottom of the stairs. Angel pulled the hood of his jacket over his head and put his hands inside his pockets. It was twilight outside since it was an hour before sunrise. He was lucky no one paid attention to him as he left the building. Everyone was expecting a person in hospital scrubs since he had worn scrubs every day during the court trial.

Angel spotted George's car. He got in the vehicle, and George accelerated away from the area.

"What is happening?" Angel asked.

"My phone has been continuously ringing since we won the case," George said. "My number is listed on my website, whereas few people can find your number. There are four groups of callers. The first group are religious people who want to see the angel. The second group are people with cancer or who have friends or relatives with cancer. They want access to the cancer drug. The third group are angry people who question why we are withholding a cancer drug from people who are dying. The fourth group are individuals who have been arrested and want to hire me. I like the fourth group. I am letting all my calls go to voice mail. I am only returning calls from individuals who want to hire me."

"We are severely limited in the number of cancer patients we can help since the FDA has not approved the drug for general distribution," Angel said.

George sighed. "That is the problem. Taking a drug not fully tested is a risk a dying person is willing to take. If the person dies from the drug, they are no worse off."

"George, you are not the only person with that belief, but we still have to wait for FDA approval," Angel said and changed the subject. "I am surprised you are up so early."

"I needed to prepare for several court appearances today. I got behind working on your case, and I was doing additional research. While working on your case, I set up a subroutine with you as the search parameter. I opened the site and was going to delete it when I saw the news clips. I immediately turned on the television, and after watching for a few minutes, I called you."

They approached the hospital and had to slow down to a crawl since thousands of people were in the area. Fortunately, a dozen police officers were keeping everyone out of the hospital building who did not belong. Everyone was behaving peacefully, but the police were concerned the group could turn violent. Angel closed his eyes and said a silent prayer for a continuation of a peaceful gathering.

A police officer stopped George as he was entering the parking area. George let down the window. "Officer, we need access to the emergency room entrance. I have Doctor Angel Carpenter with me, and for everyone's safety, we need to get him inside the hospital as quickly as possible without anyone knowing."

Angel showed the officer his hospital badge, but he waved it away since he recognized Angel. The officer got on his communicator and explained the situation to his superior. George was directed through the parking lot. Two other officers directed the traffic to allow them to arrive at the emergency room entrance. Angel thanked George as he got out of the car with his bag and entered the hospital. His patients were in a different wing of the hospital building. It did not take him long before he arrived at the cancer center. He set about meeting with his patients since it would be nearly an hour before the Board meeting. Everywhere Angel went, the hospital staff and patients congratulated him on the results of the court trial. Most thought the whole thing was ridiculous and a waste of taxpayer's money. Angel noticed how everyone was now calling him Doctor Angel. In the past, there were people who still called him Doctor Carpenter, but not anymore. He was now the official hospital angel.

Angel made sure he arrived at the director's meeting on time. He was the first one there. He made a cup of coffee and took a seat. It was not long before the other directors arrived.

Once everyone was present, Doctor Stanford called the meeting to order. "Doctor Carpenter, congratulations on your acquittal, but as a result, the hospital has received too much positive publicity. We are now the center of attention for a cancer drug everyone wants. Unfortunately, we are still waiting for FDA approval. Also, some people think you are an actual angel and believe you can cure them of other diseases. I called this meeting so we can decide how to address these issues."

Doctor Andrew shouted. "We would not be having these issues if Carpenter had behaved like a doctor instead of calling himself an angel and requiring his patients to pray for God to heal them. He is the problem at this hospital, and the sooner we get rid of him, the better. This hospital should publicly denounce him as a charlatan, and we need to distance ourselves from him as soon as possible."

"Doctor Andrew, I am Chairperson of the Board of Directors of this hospital, and I have heard enough from you. This is a non-profit, religiously founded, and religiously supported Christian hospital. I have listened to your negative comments about Doctor Carpenter and derogatory statements about this hospital. You have an extremely high opinion of yourself and a negative opinion about everyone else. Your patient evaluations are the lowest of any doctor who has ever worked here. You can either turn in your resignation or be terminated for cause. The choice is yours. You need to grab your belongings and leave this hospital immediately. You should carefully consider any communications you make in the future that could be construed as libel or slander. Come with me."

Doctor Andrew was in a state of shock. Chairperson Stanford walked over, opened the door, and addressed a member of the hospital staff working at a desk near the conference room.

"Will you please escort Doctor Andrew out of this hospital? Be sure to retrieve his hospital credentials. Also, please delete his password."

"You will regret this," Doctor Andrew shouted. "I will sue you and this hospital."

"Steven, if you resign, no one will find out you are a poor doctor. If not, we will prepare a detailed reason for your termination, which could affect your future ability to practice medicine. From one doctor to another, I recommend you use this as a learning experience and become a better doctor, but the choice is yours. I will give you twenty-four hours to think about it. I will expect your resignation by this time tomorrow if you do not want to be fired. Your last paycheck will be transmitted to your account by the end of the day. Goodbye."

The Chairperson reentered the conference room, closed the door, and sat down. As he looked around the room, the other Board members were nodding to show their support.

One director said what they all were thinking. "It was about time."

"Back to business, we need to figure out a good action plan," Doctor Stanford said.

"Doctor Stanford, would you like me to resign?" Angel asked.

"Thanks for offering," Doctor Stanford said. "No, I do not want you to resign. I believe your resignation could hurt the hospital."

"If you change your mind, all you have to do is ask," Angel said.

"Any recommendations?" Doctor Stanford asked.

"We need to release a statement letting the public know the hospital is evaluating a cancer drug, but stress how the FDA has not approved the drug," a director suggested. "Advise them to check with the FDA for questions relating to the final approval of the drug for general use and refer all other questions concerning the drug to the Tyzugmod Corporation."

The other directors were nodding their heads in support of the recommendation.

"That sounds reasonable," Doctor Stanford said. "How do we address the questions concerning Doctor Carpenter?"

Another director spoke up. "Tell them the truth," she said. "Tell them Doctor Carpenter is a flesh and blood doctor who behaves like an angel when treating his patients. Remind them how this is a church-founded non-profit hospital."

Doctor Stanford nodded his head. "Would one of you put those two suggestions in the form of a motion?"

The motion was made, seconded, and unanimously approved. The hospital had an excellent spokesperson who handled media announcements.

"Any other comment or recommendations?" Doctor Stanford asked.

Angel raised his hand. The Chairperson smiled. "Angel, you do not need to raise your hand."

"The cancer drug trial is doing well. I was wondering if you might support increasing the size of the test to include more patients. Assuming Tyzugmod agrees, we would have to get approval from the FDA, but I do not think that will be a problem. We would need additional funding to cover the holistic costs. Also, there would be a need for additional patient rooms. I understand the new addition will be completed in a couple of months. It would be easier caring for the drug trial patients if all the patients were in the new addition. It would also provide the additional space we would need if Tyzugmod agrees to increase the trial size. It is just a thought."

The Chairperson nodded as he looked around at the other directors and addressed his response to the entire room. "That is an excellent thought. The donations to the hospital have doubled since Doctor Carpenter's experience with our judicial system. We need to announce how the hospital addition will allow us to double the

number of terminal cancer patients we can treat. As a result, our
new donors will most likely continue their charitable support of the
hospital. Thus, I do not believe funding will be a problem. However,
funding is secondary to the additional lives we will save. What do the
rest of you think?"

Everyone joined in the discussions and approved a plan of
action. They directed Angel to contact Tyzugmod as the first step
to see if they would support expanding the trial to two hundred
patients. Angel did not think it would be a problem getting the FDA
to approve the expansion of the test. A larger sample size would give
a better indication of the success of the cancer drug and provide a
more robust representation of possible adverse reactions. Assuming
they received Tyzugmod's support, they would use the new facility
to expand the drug trial.

Angel contacted Tyzugmod and explained the opportunity to
expand the drug testing to more patients. He was surprised his
contact did not seem excited by his request. At first, the
representative for the company tried to explain how expanding the
test was unnecessary to get FDA approval. However, Angel was very
persistent and finally received a positive response to his request. The
representative agreed to Angel's request pending approval by the
FDA. The Chairperson of Tyzugmod had told the representative
that his primary job was to maintain Angel's full support. He did
not want to do anything to reduce Angel's enthusiasm since their
stock price continued to go up. Three days later, Tyzugmod called to
let Angel know the FDA had approved the request to increase the
patient count to two hundred.

Angel was excited and immediately informed Doctor Stanford.
The press was notified, and the statement they approved at the prior
Board meeting was given in the afternoon. The person providing
the press release to the media did an excellent job presenting the
hospital's position and dodging other questions by directing them

to contact Tyzugmod or the FDA. The announcement included Angel's work, and it had the desired effect. Angel gave a friend at the hospital the key to his apartment. They brought him some additional clothes and personal items since he was continuing to sleep at the hospital.

The following day, Angel located Doctor Mark Seneca. "Mark, the drug company has just received authorization from the FDA to double the size of the cancer drug trial to two hundred. I was hoping I could talk you into working the trial with me. I think we would make a great team."

Mark was ecstatic. "I would love to work with you. I am thrilled with the results you are getting. Over half of my existing patients would be perfect for expanding the cancer drug trial." Angel was thankful Doctor Seneca had agreed to join him.

"That is fantastic. Doctor Stanford approved letting me choose the additional doctor. Also, we can transfer any of your existing patients to the program who can benefit from the drug."

Doctor Seneca had been hoping for a way to save more of his patients who were not responding to traditional treatments. "I look forward to reviewing my patient files with you."

"Also, part of the new addition to the hospital will be used for the cancer drug test," Angel said. "The second through the fifth floors will be for the main part of the trial. The sixth floor will be for those patients who are not cured during the twelve-week cycle. The seventh through the twelfth will be for general admittance."

"Then it looks like we have a lot of work ahead of us. Angel, I am excited to be working with you. I will see you at the end of the shift."

Doctor Seneca already knew that eighty-five of his terminal patients were prime candidates for the cancer drug and he presented the list to Doctor Carpenter. They spent the balance of the day reviewing the thousands of applications the hospital had received. Together, they selected one hundred fifteen additional patients. They now had the first group of drug trial patients to be housed in the new facility. They would work with the hospital administration to get experienced nurses and staff to join them in caring for the increased number of patients. They could now add two hundred patients every twelve weeks.

Angel continued to sleep at the hospital. By the weekend, only a small hardcore group was still hanging around the hospital. The people hanging around his apartment eventually gave up their efforts to see Angel and started leaving the area. Angel figured the people staking out his apartment had left by the eighth day, but he wanted to be sure.

Angel called Rick Grant. "Rick, this is Angel. Are there still people hanging around outside my apartment?"

"No, they finally gave up. I wanted to tell you. Paulina and I have been dating. We are like best friends. We even attended the high school prom together. Actually, we attended two proms, one at her school and one at mine. She is attending college at Florida International University, and I am attending Florida Atlantic University. We are both living at home and commuting to college. She can now solve the Rubric Cube. Of course, now we talk about other things. Are you aware she plans to become a doctor?"

Angel did know but did not want to reduce Grant's excitement. "That is great. What do you want to become?"

"I am not sure yet," Grant replied. "The first year is spent completing the required courses. I am very good with mathematics and thought about majoring in engineering with a minor in computer science."

"I think you will do great in either area. Are you still working at the burger restaurant?"

"Yes. I am working Friday nights and Saturdays flipping burgers while enjoying the free food. Also, I am now charging money to help people with their electronic devices. I access their computers remotely. In most cases, I fix their computers within a few minutes. I charge a minimum fee and my business is growing. My customers are willing to wait since my fee is so reasonable. Most of them are my former free customers. Thanks again for helping me with the scholarship." They talked a little longer before hanging up.

Angel arrived home and enjoyed being back at his apartment. At his apartment, he usually slept through the night. He never slept well at the hospital. He was happy his life was returning to normal so he could concentrate solely on the care of his patients.

Angel had gotten approval for two change orders to the new hospital addition. The first change order removed walls in several central locations on each floor. The larger rooms would be for the classes the patients would attend as part of the holistic approach to the comprehensive healing program.

The second change order added 2800 square feet to the kitchen and dining areas by eliminating 20 patient rooms. This change provided a separate kitchen to prepare organic, holistic food and allowed patients to eat in the dining area instead of their rooms.

The county quickly approved the change orders since none of the load-bearing walls were affected.

Even though there was a shortage of nurses, the administration had no problem recruiting the desired staff to expand the cancer drug trial. The publicity from the court trial had gone viral. Everyone in the medical community was aware of the cancer drug and wanted to be part of what was likely to become a historic moment in medicine.

Unfortunately, the publicity continued to cause problems within the hospital's administration with worldwide bombardment from individuals wanting access to the drug. They continued to divert such callers to Tyzugmod and the FDA, but many made impossible demands upon the hospital. The hospital administrators were praying for the FDA to speed up the drug's approval.

The hospital staff responding to the communications found it impossible to explain why the FDA had not approved the drug. Many of the callers were dying from cancer with less than a year to live. They understood the drug was still in the testing stage and said they did not care about undiscovered side effects. It was not helping that former cured patients were posting their results online, with most posts going viral.

The hospital staff was being offered bribes. Members of Congress continued to ask for preferential consideration for themselves, a loved one, or a major contributor to their reelection campaign. There were even personal threats.

Tyzugmod submitted the data accumulated over the previous twelve months from Angel's Phase Three Clinical Trial along with updated information from the Phase Two and Phase One Trials. They requested the application be given a priority review status. The FDA was being bombarded with calls and was also being pressured by members of congress. They even received a call from the President. The FDA approved the priority application. However, the early review was no guarantee of approval. The Phase Three Clinical Trial would continue in case the FDA decided more testing was needed before granting final approval.

Angel and Mark were screening cancer patients and going as fast as possible since they could now treat eight hundred patients over the next twelve months. They did not have to advertise for new patients since the hospital continued to receive thousands of letters each day. The entire staff helped with the letters and selected those individuals who seemed to be the right fit for the cancer drug. The letters with the greatest details received the most attention. Angel and Mark made the final selections. They had only gone through a small percentage of the mail before they had over a thousand names of individuals who fit the profile. The type of cancer was the first criteria since the drug was not effective against all forms of cancer. The second criteria required that traditional treatments had failed. The final criteria required a patient's prognosis be terminal. Also, they were required to be ambulatory since they could not participate in the physical part of the treatment if they could not walk unassisted. They made a conscious decision to give younger patients priority over older patients. It was a difficult selection process for everyone since those not chosen would die.

All selected patients were given the cancer drug, with no patients receiving a placebo. It took a lot of work for the staff. The first two hundred patients had been checked into the rooms in the new facility and were doing well. They continued to select future patients who would wait for openings as patients were healed and discharged. After reviewing the medical records, they schedule the best candidates for physical examinations. They had preselected another six hundred patients and separated them into groups of two hundred. With the next twelve months scheduled, they only needed to add a patient if someone on the waiting list died.

A dozen patients were given preferential acceptance at the request of Doctor Stanford based upon large donations or because they had powerful connections outside the hospital. Angel accepted these patients without objections because of the small number of patients involved and because he did not wish to oppose Doctor Stanford. Angel and Doctor Seneca refused to take calls since it would have taken all of their available time, and they would have no time for their patients. Unfortunately, Doctor Stanford had to take the calls the staff could not handle. Angel knew Doctor Stanford tactfully turned down numerous requests every day, and he trusted Doctor Stanford to make the best decisions for the patients and the hospital.

It had been a busy day, and Angel had just finished seeing his last patient. He proceeded to his office to review the daily test results. A woman and a child were sitting on the floor outside his office. The lady was wearing a nurse's outfit. Angel could tell the child was suffering from acute dyspnea, her hair was gone from chemotherapy, and she appeared thin and fragile. Angel knew she was in the final stage of cancer with only a short time remaining.

The nurse and child got to their feet as Angel approached. "I am Grace Chapel, and this is my daughter, Elisabeth."

Angel interrupted her. "Visitors are not allowed in this area of the hospital."

"I am aware of that," she said. "I am an RN. I acted as if I belonged, and no one stopped me. It was wrong, but I am out of options. My daughter is seven years old and has cancer. You are our only hope."

This was a nightmare all over again. Angel had been unable to forget the similar encounter with Carol Brittle and her daughter Cathi. He still remembered the frail, adorable little girl in the wheelchair asking for his help and how she tried to comfort her mother. Cathi had died shortly after their meeting. Rejecting applicants after reviewing their files was entirely different from looking a person in the eyes and telling them he would let them die.

"I am sorry. We are conducting a Phase Three Clinical Trial for adults. No date has been set for testing children, and testing is needed to establish a safe dosage. Also, we only have drugs for two hundred patients at a time, and all the patients for the next twelve months have already been selected."

"My daughter cannot wait. Any dosage is better than no dosage. She needs the drug now." She did not say that Elisabeth would be dead within a few months since she refused to use such words in front of her daughter.

"I am sorry. I sincerely wish I could help," Angel said.

Susan changed her tactic. "If this were your daughter or your father, you would find a way to help." She had done a lot of research before coming to see Angel. She had watched the court trial and knew Angel's father had died of cancer.

"We can care for your daughter in the oncology section of our hospital. She will be a regular cancer patient. I will include her in the holistic part of the program, but without the drug. Again, I am sorry. I wish I could do more."

She heard the sincerity in his voice. "Okay," she replied. "How do we get checked in?"

"Give me one minute, and I will have a staff member assist you through the admission process."

Susan looked at her daughter. "The doctor is going to help get us checked into the hospital. You are going to get well."

With difficulty, Elisabeth said to Angel: "Thank you." Elisabeth held her arms out, and when Angel leaned forward, she gave him a weak hug.

Angel made the call, and a nurse showed up a few minutes later. After a discussion with Angel, he asked the lady and her daughter to follow him. Angel had told the nurse to check Elisabeth into a private room on his authority.

Angel called his contact at Tyzugmod. "I need a three-month supply of the drugs for a female with terminal cancer."

"You need to replace an existing patient for the woman." Angel decided not to complicate the request by providing the patient's age.

"I am not replacing any of the patients. This will be in addition to the two hundred patients, and she will not be part of the test group."

"Doctor Carpenter, the FDA approved increasing the test size to two hundred. The FDA would crucify us if they found out we exceeded the number of test subjects they had approved."

"I know, but I need you to do this for me," Angel demanded.

"Very well, but you must make sure no one finds out about this unauthorized shipment. I will pack it myself in a generic box. I need an encrypted email from you requesting replacements for damaged drugs to protect the company. Are you sure you want to take this risk?"

"Yes, I am sure," Angel replied.

"The shipment will go out tomorrow with a requirement for your signature."

Angel when to the room assigned to Elisabeth Chapel. Grace was sitting in a chair by the bed. Angel closed the door quietly so he would not wake up Elisabeth.

Angel kept his voice low. "If I start Elisabeth on the cancer drug immediately, are you willing to keep it an absolute secret for the rest of your life?"

"Yes, absolutely yes," Grace said in a low excited voice.

"I will personally administer the drug each day. The drug is only ninety percent effective, and you need to understand the drug is less successful with Stage IV cancer. We do not know the adverse reactions for someone so young. There is no guarantee she will get well. I will pray this works and suggest you do the same."

"I will. There are not sufficient words to thank you for your help. I know my daughter will live, and I will pray a lot. I will keep your secret to the grave."

Elisabeth only weighed forty pounds, so Angel decided to give her half the normal dose. He would closely monitor her blood and adjust the dosage if needed. Angel knew he should not have risked everything for one patient. He could lose his license if caught. This action could land him back in court. Also, he had made an exception for one patient while rejecting thousands. He wondered, once you start breaking the rules, when does it end? He had honored the Hippocratic Oath, but the justice system would not see it that way. Giving a minor an unapproved drug was a felony. He had just broken all the rules and knew he should feel remorseful. Instead, he felt good.

Angel monitored Elisabeth's blood daily. At first the cancer cells were responding better than expected, but then the results declined. Angel reduced the drug to one-fourth the amount given to adults and after several days the results were again positive. Even at a one-fourth dosage, the results were better than the adults. He carefully continued to monitor Elisabeth's results. Angel wanted to share the results with Tyzugmod but knew he could not risk exposure. He theorized that four children could be cured of cancer using a single adult dosage. If correct, it would be possible to double the number of lives they could save by just using one-fourth of the available dosages on children. A Phase One Clinical Trial for children was desperately needed. A single test subject could not be used as a basis for his theory. Also, anyone could point out that he would not know that she was cured until the end of the twelve-week period.

Angel remembered working part time for a veterinary clinic while in high school. He had watched the veterinarian as he adjusted the amount of vaccine for each animal based on weight. It made sense. You would not give a Toy Poodle the same injection amount that is given to a Saint Bernard or a Great Dane.

Angel felt he was close to a breakthrough. However, any changes to the medication would have to be done with care if he decided to test his results on adults. He was wondering if it would be possible to save the ten percent of the patients who were not responding to the cancer drug by changing the dosage. He was stuck since if he approached Tyzugmod with his theory, they would start asking questions he did not want to answer. He decided to wait until Elizabeth was completely cured before attempting to convince Tyzugmod to modify the dosage for the adults who were not being cured. When time permitted, he would search the veterinarian records for vaccine dosage adjustments. The research for adjusting the dosage amounts to cure animals should provide the same results in humans. He would definitely pursue this further once Elizabeth recovered.

Two interns were hired to assist Angel and Doctor Seneca. Angel received a high volume of applications for the positions. The interns had graduated near the top of their class. They both excelled in their responses during their interview, but the deciding point was when he took them on a tour of the hospital. The applicants were unaware the tour was part of the interview. Most applicants wanted to discuss the cancer drug and asked questions about the facility. The two he offered employment had spent the entire time talking to and asking questions about the patients.

No one seemed bothered with Elisabeth Chapel's inclusion in the sessions, or they chose to enjoy having a child in the group. Angel scheduled a time each day to administer the cancer drug to Elisabeth. Her response to the drug was immediate, and she grew stronger each day. Her blood work showed a gradual but persistent reduction in cancer cells. She was improving at a faster rate than his other patients. Initially, she was showing up for the exercise classes but barely participating. However, after six weeks, she was leading the class.

Angel and Doctor Seneca were having a cup of coffee and getting ready to start their rounds. They were discussing their patients when a nurse asked Angel to come to the drug storage room. Doctor Seneca accompanied him.

When they arrived, Abigail Cross was standing outside the entrance to the medical storage room. "The duty nurse asked me if Tyzugmod had modified the cancer drug and showed me the most recent shipment," Abigail said.

The container had been opened, and she handed one of the vials to Angel. Angel noticed the description on the vial was the same. However, there was a slight variation in the labeling, and the shape of the vial was slightly different. Also, the fluid inside the vial had a slight pink tint when it should have been clear.

Angel immediately called Tyzugmod and asked if they had changed the formulation without advising him. He sent a picture of the vial. It only took a minute for his contact to determine the vial had not come from their company. Angel told his contact that he was sending him a vial for testing.

Angel handed two of the vials to Abigail. "Please tell everyone not to use any vials in this container. Take one vial to our lab and have it analyzed. Tell the lab supervisor we need a priority analysis. Please let me know the results as soon as the analysis is complete. I want the other vial shipped next day delivery to Tyzugmod."

Angel turned to Doctor Seneca. "Mark, what do you think?"

"This does not make any sense. I would rather not jump to conclusions when our lab can use their mass spectrometry to determine what is in the vials. I suggest we lock up these vials to eliminate any risk of someone using a vial by mistake."

Angel agreed. Together they took the container and placed it in a secured locker. It had only been about twenty minutes when a lab technician said the analysis was complete. Doctor Seneca joined Angel as they rushed to the lab.

A technician met them at the door to the lab. "I used our clinical mass spectrometer to test a sample from the vial. The sample contained thimerosal which is used as a preservative in some vaccines. Also, there was neomycin, an antibiotic to prevent the growth of bacteria, gelatin, and a stabilizer. These items prevent the deterioration of the primary ingredient. However, the sample contained a lethal dose of Oleander instead of a vaccine and trace amounts of Sodium Chloride. I took the time to research the poison.

Oleander is a beautiful flowering scrub, but even in its natural state it is extremely poisonous, and it is ubiquitous throughout Florida. All parts of the plant are deadly and eating a single leaf can result in death. The poison can be extracted using Sodium Chloride during distillation. It would be easy for someone to prepare the poison. The concentration in the vial would result in death in two days. For the record, the ingredients in this vial were prepared in a sophisticated lab."

Angel and Doctor Seneca realized they could have lost all of their patients if the Duty Nurse and Nurse Cross had not acted to prevent the tragedy that could have occurred. Angel called Doctor Stanford and explained what had taken place. Doctor Stanford called their attorney, who advised him to contact the FBI.

Doctor Stanford contacted several consulting firms and asked them for a recommendation to improve the security of the hospital. The consulting firms agreed to an expedited preparation of a comprehensive proposal. They were told of the attempt to poison the cancer patients. Two firms agreed to submit proposals to enhance hospital security at an emergency meeting of the Board of Directors to be held in one week.

The FBI assigned two agents to the initial investigation. They arrived the following day and spent all morning questioning Angel and other staff members, including employees at the receiving dock. The FBI escalated the case to an act of terrorism since two hundred people could have died from the poison. As a result, they assigned additional agents to the case.

The FBI had a criminal topologist and profiler approach the case assuming an individual had committed the crime. There were thousands of threatening letters from individuals who had not been accepted into the drug trial or who had family members who died from cancer after requesting assistance. Other agents examined corporations or investors who might have a financial motive to sabotage the drug trial. A smaller group looked at organizations that might want to halt production of the drug for non-financial reasons. Agents in the field were following physical leads.

The FBI got a major break in the case when they located the company that manufactured the vials. From there, they checked out all the deliveries made to their customers. They used the packing slip to locate the original shipping point. The delivery of the vials was tracked to a small company that made euthanasia medication for dogs. The euthanasia medication was provided to animal shelters and veterinarians. The euthanasia drug used was pentobarbital which acts within seconds to render a dog unconscious, and the dog dies within one to two minutes.

The FBI got a search warrant and raided the facility with the help of a local SWAT team. After five hours, they made several arrests. The FBI determined an outside party had paid a supervisor fifty thousand dollars to prepare the vials. The vials were prepared using their normal procedures for the euthanasia drug, but they received a substitute for the pentobarbital. The supervisor paid several employees in cash to assist him and help him create the labels. They were given the shipping container for holding the vials. They filled the vials and packed them in the container. Then they placed the shipping label on the container and delivered it to a local shipping store. The supervisor still had the empty cancer drug vial they used to duplicate the labels. The FBI took the vial and sent it to their lab to test for fingerprints. The box delivered to the hospital had already been tested for fingerprints and DNA. There were three employees at the company who handled the box. The box used to ship the poison was an actual box used to deliver the cancer drugs to the hospital. The box and label were nearly perfect. Fortunately, the slight difference in the vial and the color of the liquid alerted the nurse, or many patients would have died. If the vials had contained the dog euthanasia drug, the first patient they used the drug on would have died instantly, and only one patient would have died. However, the Oleander poison could have resulted in two hundred deaths since it would have taken several days for the patients to die.

The last arrest was at the hospital. There were quite a few fingerprints on the shipping container, but a custodian confessed to giving a man an empty box for a thousand dollars. He was released when Special Agent Darnell determined he was not involved in the plot to poison the patients. He could have been charged and prosecuted for aiding an act of terrorism since he knew or should have known that selling an empty box for a thousand dollars involved an illegal act. Also, the custodian confessed to knowing the box was used for shipping the cancer drug. Special Agent Darnell used his authority to decide the FBI could better use its resources pursuing the actual terrorists and released him. The hospital terminated his employment.

A sketch artist from the FBI worked with the two individuals who received the payments and created a composite of the person who paid the money. Several weeks later, a person matching the sketch was found dead in an alley. They considered it a professional hit with three bullets to the chest and one between the eyes. They failed to determine a motive for the attempt to murder two hundred cancer patients. Such deaths would have significantly delayed final approval by the FDA. The FBI filed the final reports and put Unknown under Motive. The file was closed, but the case would remain active for six months.

The Trustees on Bailiwick of Jersey received word their attempt to interfere with the cancer drug trial and discredit Angel Carpenter had failed. A motion was made to issue a private contract of a million euros for the death of Angel Carpenter. The motion was seconded and unanimously approved. They contacted an agent they had used in the past.

Angel was relaxing at his apartment when he received a phone call from Lorenzo. Lorenzo confirmed what Angel had feared. "The Diocletian Knights funded the attempt to poison your cancer patients," he said. "Unfortunately, we became aware of the attempt too late to send you a warning. We do not get our information in real-time. There can be a delay of two to four weeks before we receive a recording of their meetings. Watch your back and be extra careful. You might consider going armed, wearing a vest, and getting a couple of bodyguards."

Lorenzo let Angel know the Vatican would continue to monitor the Diocletian Knights and hoped to warn him of future actions against him before it happened. Angel thanked him. The Diocletian Knights were the worst kind of cancer. It would take a special vaccine to eliminate this scourge. Angel refused to consider carrying a gun. However, wearing a vest while away from the hospital might make sense. He knew his apartment was not very secure. Sleeping at the hospital for a short duration was okay, but he was tired of living at the hospital. Angel decided to discuss the matter with George.

CHAPTER 11 MEDIA

Angel and Doctor Seneca continued caring for their patients. The cancer drug was doubly checked each time a vial was removed. It now required two keys plus a passcode to access the special storage room containing the cancer drug. The hospital returned to its regular but hectic routine. Angel and Doctor Seneca were pleased with their interns.

One morning a lady was waiting outside Angel's office when he arrived. He was afraid it was someone wanting to become part of the drug trial.

"Can I help you?" Angel asked.

The lady responded thoughtfully. "I am here to help you," she said. "I am Doctor Benita Fredrick. I am a Medical Research Scientist. Besides my MD, I have a PhD in chemistry. My specialty is cancer research. I want to work with you or for you."

"We do very little research here," Angel said. "We provide medical care to our patients."

Doctor Fredrick had a stoic expression. "I can also take care of patients. In addition, I can provide direct analysis of any unusual results without waiting for statistical results from a remote lab. Here is a hard copy of my resume and letters of recommendation."

Doctor Seneca's office was across the hall from Angel's. "Mark, will you join us?"

Doctor Seneca came into Angel's office, and Angel introduced the two doctors to each other. Angel handed the resume to Doctor Seneca, who took several minutes to review the personal data.

"What do you think?" Angel asked.

While reviewing the resume, Doctor Seneca said: "I have been meaning to talk to you about hiring another doctor. However, I am not sure Doctor Fredrick is the right person for the job. Research and taking care of patients are completely different."

"Let me work with you for four weeks on a temporary basis," Doctor Fredrick said. "I will take four weeks of vacation from my current job. You can decide in four weeks if you wish to hire me. You may wish to review publications of my research listed on the last page of my resume."

"Why do you wish to work here?" Angel asked.

"What you are doing here may be the biggest medical breakthrough in the history of cancer research. I want to be part of it. Theoretically, your holistic approach should increase the cure rates for other vaccines. Everyone in the medical research field knows proper diet and exercise result in a longer, healthier life. However, we prescribe the drugs, and the patients seldom change their lifestyles. Here, you are forcing the lifestyle changes on your patients, and the change is doubling the healing power of the cancer drug."

Doctor Seneca had placed the resume on the desk. Angel glanced through her resume again and was surprised when he saw her current employer was Tyzugmod. It was on the last page of the four-page resume.

"You are working for Tyzugmod," Angel stated. "Why would you want to leave?"

"I helped develop the cancer drug you are using. In our previous trials, only forty percent responded positively to our drug. I have read the amazing reports you have been sending to Tyzugmod. I want to be directly involved in what you are doing here to make the drug more effective."

"Does Tyzugmod know you are here?" Mark asked.

"No, but I am on vacation, and it is not unusual for someone to vacation in Florida."

Angel was impressed with her resume but concerned about her ability to switch from research to patient care. "If you have read my reports, then you know religion and prayer are part of the approach we are using here."

"I know," Doctor Fredrick said. "I look forward to analyzing all aspects of your approach. I am a scientist, but I will keep an open mind. We need to understand why prayer is having a positive impact on wellness so we can determine how to accomplish the same or a similar effect for the non-believer. I hope you do not want the non-believers to die if we can save them."

Angel chuckled. "Oh, I want to save them. If not in this life, then in the afterlife."

"If it makes any difference, I am a Methodist," Doctor Fredrick said with a grin.

"I do not get to make the final hiring decision," Angel stated. "I can only make a recommendation. However, I can approve the hiring of a temporary employee. When would you like to start?"

"Right now." Doctor Fredrick answered with enthusiasm.

Angel was thoughtful. "Having you here may be a blessing. There are additional blood and urine tests I wish to pursue. I want to determine why some individuals who fit the profile do not get well."

"I would look forward to conducting a little research while assisting in the care of our patients." Doctor Fredrick had four weeks to earn a permanent position. She liked Angel, but she had an immediate attraction to Doctor Seneca.

Angel looked over at Doctor Seneca. "Mark, would you mind if Doctor Fredrick accompanies you on your rounds, while I contact administration to provide her with temporary employment."

"I would be pleased to have Doctor Fredrick accompany me," Mark replied with a smile.

Doctor Seneca turned to Doctor Fredrick. "Come with me."

Angel called Doctor Stanford and explained the arrival of Doctor Fredrick. Doctor Stanford responded positively and said he would look forward to Angel's recommendation when the four-week temporary employment ended. Then he changed topics.

"A television network show is continuing coverage of the cancer drug by interviewing your prior patients who are cured. It is called the Harrieta Connor's Show. Her followers are growing. Have you seen the show?"

"No, I am unfamiliar with the show," Angel said. "I seldom turn on the television. Thanks for telling me. I will check it out."

Angel performed a search on his tablet. The Harrieta Connor's Show was receiving more viewership each day. Two of the patients who had received the bad x-rays had been on the show. They told how they could feel the healing heat from Angel's hands as he healed them of their cancer. Angel hoped the station would switch to another topic as the court trial became old news.

Several weeks later, Angel was contacted and asked to be on the Harrieta Connor's Show to discuss the recent court trial and the cancer drug test. He declined and then notified Doctor Stanford of the contact. Doctor Stanford called him back the next day and suggested he should go on the show. Doctor Stanford was impressed with Angel's performance on the witness stand during the court hearing and believed he would do well on the network show. Angel called back the booking agent and agreed to be on the show.

Angel arrived early as requested and met with Harrieta Connor, the show's host. Then, he allowed the makeup specialist to apply an ultra-high-definition foundation cosmetic. The makeup specialist said her job was easy since Angel had no wrinkles to smooth out or scars to cover up.

Shortly after the show started, they called him out on stage to join the show's host. Harrieta gave an oral summary of Angel's background from when his mother found him on their doorsteps to the final verdict of the trial. Next, they showed a montage of short clips of the court trial. The audience considered some parts with thoughtful contemplation and laughed at other clips.

Harrieta paused and looked straight at the camera with the amused grin her audience had come to love. "Each night, we have asked, are angels real? We have a guest tonight who some claim is an actual angel, but first, I have a serious question for Doctor Angel."

Her acting ability took over, and her entire demeanor turned serious. "Tell us why the cancer drug treatment is so successful at your hospital compared to the earlier drug trials. My followers believe it is because an angel is administering the drug."

"I hate to disappoint your fans," Angel said. "It has nothing to do with the person administering the drug. There are five parts to the cancer healing method at our hospital. The first part is the cancer drug. Second is a proper diet to provide the body with the vitamins, minerals, protein, and other nutrients in the proper amount to maximize a person's health. Only organic foods are used, and the food is prepared fresh each day at the hospital. Our overweight patients lose on average thirty pounds with an increase in muscle composition. Plus, our underweight patients put on an average of fifteen pounds with a similar increase in muscle mass. The third part is a proper daily exercise routine to strengthen the physical parts of the body. Fourth is having a positive mental outlook, and we include religion as integral to this part. Fifth is using traditional methods such as surgery to remove an organ if it is too cancerous to be treated or remove a cancer tumor before it spreads to other areas within the body."

"The items described seem to be things the medical community has been recommending forever," Harrieta said.

"You are correct," Angel responded. "People need to listen to their doctors. If people adhered to proper diet and exercise, it would eliminate many of the health issues in the United States, including a significant reduction in the cancer rate. The medical establishment is mostly ignored when it comes to prevention. People should see their doctor while they are well and ask their doctor how they can maintain their health. People ignore their doctors unless they are sick."

"During the court trial, you said the drug treatment was only effective against certain cancers."

"Again, you are correct. The drug treatment does not work for all types of cancer. For example, it will not work for bone cancer."

"Is it true that none of your cancer patients have died?"

Angel was hesitant as he contemplated his response. "We expect the cancer drug to be ninety percent effective when combined with our holistic approach. The hospital has an excellent treatment facility, and so far, none of the cancer patients under my care have died while participating in the cancer drug trial. However, our drug trial has only existed for a little over a year."

The audience clapped and cheered loudly in accordance with the show's proctor.

There was a commercial intermission break. "Angel, you are doing well, and thanks again for being on our show. When the commercials are over, I will bring out additional guests to join in our discussions."

After the intermission, she introduced a guest with a PhD in mathematics, another guest with a PhD in physics, and a final guest with a PhD in religious history. Her introductions clearly showed each of the guests was an expert in their chosen field. As each guest took a turn speaking, it became apparent they were there to attack Angel personally and professionally.

The mathematician gave statistics showing how even though the odds of winning might be astronomical, it still happens. "The odds of winning the Florida lottery are three hundred million to one but someone always wins. The fact that none of Angel's terminal patients have died is statistically similar to a person winning the lottery." When he finished, there was some applause from the audience.

The scientist stated it was not possible for Angel to heal a person by touching them. He explained how Bigfoot, the Loch Ness Monster, and angels all fit in the same category.

"There is a scientific explanation for the ladies who claim Angel cured them of their breast cancer," the scientist stated emphatically. "I will stake my reputation on it. There is always a rational explanation when a miracle is thoroughly investigated using the scientific method."

The scientist then provided examples where miracles were later repudiated when scientists performed a proper investigation. He further explained how shared events became distorted in the retelling of what took place. Again, the audience followed the proctor and applauded.

The religious specialist reviewed the history of how there were no miracles in current times. "Today, it is easy to debunk people's exaggerations by checking the facts or videos of the event in question. Doctor Angel Carpenter is an excellent doctor. However, I say with complete confidence that Doctor Carpenter is not an angel as depicted in the bible." Again, there was light applause. The other two guests nodded in agreement.

The camera focused on a close-up of Angel and Harrieta. She gave her practiced look that conveyed a questioning innocence. "Doctor Angel, please respond."

Angel was not caught off guard. He had learned over the years how to defend his faith passively. The first step is not to argue but try to find common ground.

Angel took his time, relaxed, and looked thoughtfully at Harrieta. "Each of your guests is extremely smart and is a specialist in their field. I do not disagree with anything they said. Also, I do not have the amazing background of your distinguished guests. I am a cancer doctor and have a question. I would like you, your guests, and those in the audience to answer honestly. If you were dying of cancer, would you consider being treated at our hospital?"

There was complete silence as the other guests on the show looked at each other and then back at Angel.

The producer signaled it was time for a commercial break. "We will be back after the commercial break and find out if there are real angels," Harrieta said.

"Angel, you did well in responding to the attacks by my guests, but you are not helping my show. We need some drama, and I was hoping for a heated argument."

The young mathematician clapped his hands and looked at Angel. "Outstanding response! The answer to your question is yes, I would want to be treated for terminal cancer at your hospital. If I had cancer, the odds are one hundred percent that I would want you as my doctor."

The Producer announced when the show was back live, and Harrieta had one more card to play in the hope of generating some excitement. She took out a pair of special infrared glasses and asked everyone to put on the glasses given to them when they arrived at the studio. The three guests also put on the glasses, and the camera crews switched to special infrared lenses. At her signal, they turned the lights off. Angel looked at the monitor. Everyone else on stage was slightly visible from the heat of their body, but Angel was glowing brightly, and he knew what everyone would think.

"You should not have done that," Angel said.

Angel stood up and walked off the stage. He raised and lowered his arms quickly in frustration. Unfortunately, as he moved, the heat signature faded slowly, showing the path he was taking, and the fading heat signature from the movement when he raised and lowered his arms looked like wings. Angel found the exit light over a door and left the building. They turned the lights back on, and the audience was in an uproar.

Without prompting, the people in the audience were shouting. "He is an Angel!"

Harrieta was ecstatic. "Ladies and gentlemen, you can tell all your friends how you saw a real angel tonight," she exclaimed. "We will see you tomorrow night. Good night for now."

The Producer announced they were off the air and shouted to Harrieta. "Great show!"

The remaining guests were baffled. "How did you do that?" The scientist asked. "What type of special effects did you use?"

"There were no special effects," Harrieta answered. "I have no idea what he is, but he is undeniably not normal. He may or may not be an actual angel, but I do not care. I cannot wait to see the ratings tonight. I guarantee we will be on every media site."

"For the foreseeable future, we are going to have angels as the major theme for our show," the Producer said. "Each night, we will have someone claiming to have seen an angel or a religious person talking about angels, and we need to see about getting Doctor Carpenter back on the show. We will save the angel discussions until the show's last segment so the viewers will watch the entire show. We will tease them throughout the show to keep them watching." Everyone associated with the show was excited but also wondering if Angel was an angel.

When Harrieta arrived home, her husband gave her a big hug. "Tonight, was your best show ever," he gushed.

Both of them worked full time, but her husband arrived home at a more normal time and took care of the children at night while Harrieta took care of them during the day. She usually left home around five in the afternoon and returned home around ten o'clock each night. They usually turned in each night at eleven o'clock, which gave them less than an hour together, but they both had the weekends free to spend family time together. They had a rule to turn off the television at night and spend the time together without interruptions unless one of their children needed attention.

Harrieta was eating a late-night yoga snack since she only had a low-calorie salad for dinner before going on the air. Her husband gave her an update on the children and then wanted to talk about the show. He was surprised when she exclaimed there were no special effects involved with Doctor Carpenter. He just naturally glowed on the screen.

"If there are actual angels, then Doctor Angel Carpenter is exactly what I would expect an angel to look like," Harrieta said.

Her husband agreed. "He definitely looks angelic."

"Our producer expects us to move into the number one prime time spot. He wants to continue with the angel theme since it is connecting with the audience."

Harrieta put her empty bowl and fork in the dishwasher as they both decided it was time to head to the bedroom, but she was not thinking about sleep or sex. She was thinking of all the possibilities for covering angels and specifically covering Doctor Angel Carpenter.

CHAPTER 12 HOSTAGES

Angel awoke the following morning and was still upset with the previous night's appearance on the network show. It was still dark when he arrived at the hospital, and it gave the appearance of being a typical day. He parked his car in the parking garage and went to his office. He emailed Doctor Stanford to let him know he was at the hospital.

Angel was reviewing patients' files when he saw Doctor Seneca and Doctor Fredrick coming down the hall. They were currently meeting each morning before starting their rounds. This was the third week of the temporary employment for Doctor Fredrick, and she was proving to be just as good with patients as she was as a research physician. Angel had already asked Doctor Stanford to process the documents to provide her with permanent employment at the hospital. Doctor Seneca had similarly submitted recommendations to hire her.

Angel motioned them into his office and asked if they saw the show. They both nodded. "You were doing so well, right up till the end," Mark said.

Doctor Fredrick was more circumspect. "Why did your body glow in the infrared?"

"Greater skin blood flow and an active hypothalamus cause my body temperature to be higher than normal," Angel explained.

"May I touch you?" Doctor Fredrick asked with a quizzical look.

Angel nodded his head and held out his hand. "Sure."

Doctor Fredrick took his hand in both of her hands. After a moment, she smiled. "Your hands are very warm and comfortable. My hands and feet are always cold."

Doctor Fredrick let go of Angel's hand, and the three of them discussed issues with several patients who were not responding to their treatment. Doctor Fredrick said she would like to run some additional tests to see if she could determine why they were not responding. Angel encouraged her to proceed with the tests. Doctor Seneca agreed to take care of new patient orientations with Doctor Fredrick assisting. This would give Angel more time to review ways of increasing the cure rate.

Angel was examining a patient who was recovering from a surgical procedure performed two days earlier when he received a text from Doctor Stanford asking him to come to his office. When Angel arrived, the door was open, and Doctor Stanford motioned for him to come in and take a seat.

"I told you to go on the show last night, but in hindsight, it was a mistake," Doctor Stanford said with a sigh and shook his head.

Doctor Stanford turned his monitor so Angel could see. Security had done their best, but the parking lots and surrounding area were filling up with people. The police were assisting with crowd control, and so far, it was peaceful. Some people were carrying signs. Most of the signs were religious, but some had pictures of aliens. They were shouting for Angel.

"I am so sorry," Angel said and gave a gesture of helplessness with his hands.

Doctor Stanford was upset with himself. "This is my fault and not yours. I want you to know I fully support you. Hopefully, this will blow over in a few days like the last time."

"Let me know if there is anything you want me to do, and I will do it," Angel said.

"Thank you. For now, just take care of our patients." Doctor Stanford knew Angel always put his patients and the hospital first.

"I will. While I am here, did you get our recommendations to change Doctor Fredrick from temporary to permanent?"

"Yes, and I have already approved the change. We are fortunate to add such a fine doctor to our staff. She should receive the employment notification later today and a welcome letter. Please tell Doctor Fredrick that her position is now permanent. Normally, we would call together our key people to meet a new doctor. However, she is not really new since she has been working here for several weeks. Also, with this mutated virus strain infecting so many of our senior citizens, we cannot spare the time to pull the staff together, even for the few minutes it would take to introduce such a distinguished doctor."

Angel stood up and headed back to his patients. Doctor Stanford was feeling the stress from the worldwide attention they had been receiving since the court trial. He spent most of his time explaining to individuals why they could not get access to the cancer drug. He occasionally made exceptions, but it was becoming increasingly difficult to deal with people who would die without their help. Doctor Stanford fondly remembered when he was a young doctor and enjoyed coming to work. Now, he dreaded each day.

The crowd outside was adding to his stress. Also, the emergency room was over-run with the new virus strain, and they already knew the flu season would be severe. The antigenic drift of the influenza virus was immune to the flu vaccine. People complained they caught the flu even though they had received the flu vaccine. Doctor Stanford knew the average person did not understand how the vaccine did not protect against every variety of flu or against an influenza virus that mutated after creating the vaccine. This was just another item added to all the other problems associated with running a hospital.

Angel could not wait to tell Doctor Fredrick about her change in status. He called her and gave her the good news. Even though the hospital would not do anything special, he would make a token effort. He ordered a congratulations cake for delivery the following day. He spent the rest of the morning seeing patients.

It was early afternoon, and Angel was having a late lunch on the first floor when he heard what sounded like gunshots. He ran toward the sound. He passed medical staff and patients running in the opposite direction. Angel slowed down as he reached the area where a nurse was lying on her back and was unconscious. There was blood covering the right side of her chest. Angel felt beneath her and did not find an exit wound.

There were several patients and a nurse hiding in the opposite corner behind a desk. Angel got the attention of the nurse and saw that it was Michelle. When she saw Angel, she rushed over to assist him.

"Where is the person doing the shooting?" He asked.

Michelle pointed towards a room with a closed door. Angel went back the way he had come until he located a stretcher. He returned with the stretcher and lowered it to the floor next to the wounded nurse. Michelle helped him load the shooting victim onto the stretcher. They rolled her down the hall a short distance.

"Michelle, there is a medical supply room at the end of the hall. I need a Tactical Trauma Kit."

Michelle ran down the hallway and entered the supply room. She saw a trauma kit on the second shelf. She was reaching for the kit when she saw a case containing four trauma kits. Her training as a military nurse caused her to grab the case since it was always better to have extra supplies. She returned to the victim and handed

Angel one of the kits. Angel had his cellphone on speaker and was communicating with the emergency room.

Angel with Michelle assisting, packed the entry wound with hemostatic dressing which would cause the blood to clot. They then applied wound seal bandages. The victim revived and looked at Angel.

Angel saw the disoriented look. "You are going to be all right. You have been shot, but it is not bad." Angel lied to the patient. The wound was bad, and she would need emergency surgery to remove the bullet and repair the damage to her lungs.

The emergency room attendant had their location along with the condition of the victim. It was only a couple of minutes before two paramedics showed up and immediately started an IV. Angel had the attendant transfer his call to the ER nurse.

"Take her straight to surgery. A bullet is lodged in her chest. Her condition is severe," Angel said before ending the call. He was acquainted with the ER nurse and knew the victim was in capable hands. As they wheeled her away, the lead paramedic was already on the phone with the emergency room.

"Michelle, was anyone else shot?"

"The gunman started shooting after he entered the room. He fired three shots. One of the bullets came through the door and hit the nurse. I am unsure if anyone in the room was injured since the door was closed before he started shooting. That is all I know."

"I am glad you thought to bring the extra trauma kits," Angel said as a complement to Nurse Michelle's thoughtfulness.

A police officer crouched low and made his way across the floor to Angel. "Additional officers are on the way, and I requested a SWAT team. What is the status of the shooter?"

"The shooter is in the room across the hall," Angel said and pointed at the room. "One person was shot and has been taken to the emergency room. Nurse Michelle says three shots were fired and all the shots were fired after the door was closed."

They heard loud shouting coming from the other side of the closed door. "I want to see the Angel, and I want to see him now, or I will start shooting."

Angel picked up the case of trauma kits and started toward the room when the officer grabbed his arm. "What are you doing? You cannot go in there."

"I do not believe he intends to shoot me, or he would not be asking for me by name. He may start shooting if I do not go in. Regardless, there may be other people in there who need medical care." The officer let go of Angel's arm.

"Michelle, see if you can locate additional stretchers," Angel said as he approached the door.

"Four stretchers will be here shortly." Angel turned toward Michelle. She smiled and gave him a casual salute as she continued to converse on her cellphone.

When Angel reached the door, he stopped. "I am Angel. Hold your fire. I am coming in."

Angel turned the doorknob and carefully opened the door. He took two steps into the room, and the door was slammed shut behind him. Angel looked around the room. The man holding the gun was middle-aged. There was a young boy with similar features who Angel took to be the gunman's son. Angel took one look and knew the young boy had cancer. Two people had been shot. A man was sitting on the floor, leaning against the wall. The left side of his shirt was covered in blood. Another man was face down on the floor in a pool of blood. Angel started towards the victim on the floor.

"Do not move," the shooter shouted.

Angel turned cautiously and faced the man with the gun. "I am a Doctor, and I am going to check on the two people you have shot. I will talk to you about your son after I have attended to these patients."

Angel turned back around and walked over to the person on the floor. He dropped to one knee and checked for a pulse. Angel saw the person had been shot through the chest before falling facedown since there was an exit wound in the victim's back. This indicated the person was likely going toward the shooter when shot.

Angel looked at the person holding the gun. "He is dead."

"I am sorry. I did not want to hurt anyone. I just want help for my son."

Angel got up and moved slowly toward the other shooting victim. He wanted the shooter to calm down, so he kept his voice under control.

Angel reached the second victim and dropped to one knee again. Blood was flowing from a bullet wound in his shoulder.

"Is the shoulder your only injury?" Angel asked.

"Yes, the dead guy tried to play hero, and I got hit by a stray bullet."

"I am going to patch you up."

Angel turned toward the shooter. "I need to administer first aid to this man," Angel said with a calm but demanding voice.

Angel took a trauma kit from the case. He cut away the shirt and examined the wound. He used the same approached he had used on the female victim except there was both an entry and an exit wound. It only took a couple of minutes to packed and sealed the wounds. Angel put the arm in a sling and taped the arm against the patient's body. The patient was pale from loss of blood and shock, but it was not life threatening.

"You are going to be fine," Angel said. "I will try to get you out of here. If I am successful, please tell the police not to try anything. I believe I can get the shooter to give up."

Angel looked around the room at the other individuals. "Is anyone else injured?"

"I am having a heart attack," a man said who appeared to be in his forties. "I am dying," he gasped. "I need help. My chest is hurting, and I am faint."

Angel used his digital ultrasound stethoscope to check the patient's vitals. The advanced stethoscope was part of him, and he always carried it. Performing the tests took twice as long since the guy would not stay still. Angel read the numbers and looked the man in the eyes.

"You are not having a heart attack!" Angel said in a forceful voice. "You are having an anxiety attack because you are in a stressful situation. Also, you are hyperventilating, which is causing your other symptoms. Your heart rate is a little high for the same reason. I want you to keep your mouth closed and breathe through your nose. Lie flat on the floor and think about being in a peaceful, relaxing place."

Angel helped the patient lay down. "Close your eyes and keep breathing through your nose. Relax, this will be over shortly, and you will go home." The man seemed better, and Angel slowly stood up.

"I am asking again. Is anyone else injured?" The other individuals shook their heads, and several murmured no.

"I want all of you to remain calm and stay still," Angel said. "If everyone remains calm, we can resolve this situation with no one else getting hurt."

Angel turned around and approached the man with the gun. He did not come too close since he did not want the gunman to feel threatened. "I believe you are a good person since you are trying to get help for your son, but this is not the way to go about it."

"I tried everything else to get you to help my son," the shooter said. "My wife and I have sent over a dozen letters and have made at least a hundred phone calls asking for you to cure our son. You have not answered our letters or returned our phone calls."

"I have not seen any of your letters. Not counting the millions of emails, we have received over a hundred thousand letters and nearly as many phone calls. Let me get a stretcher and get this wounded man out of here so he can receive proper medical care."

"No, take care of my son first. You are an Angel. He needs your help."

Angel was thoughtful. "If I am an angel, then you know I am not afraid of you or your gun. I am going to the door and ask for a stretcher for the second person you shot. After I have taken care of the patient, I will talk to you about your son."

Angel walked over to the door and shouted. "I am Doctor Angel Carpenter, do not shoot, I am going to open the door. First, I want everyone to get away from the door."

Angel slowly opened the door. "I need someone to bring me a stretcher. We have a person with a gunshot wound who needs medical attention."

It was only a few minutes before a member of the SWAT team rolled a stretcher up to the door.

"Please do not take any action yet," Angel said. "Backup, and in a minute, I will bring the stretcher back with one of the victims."

Angel recognized the officer. "I remember you. You were with the group of police officers who broke into my apartment."

"I was just doing my job," the SWAT officer said without remorse.

Angel grimaced as he remembered. "I believe I can talk him into giving up, but it may take some time. Please do not try anything. I will be back in a minute."

Angel pulled the stretcher into the room and closed the door. He rolled it over to the far wall and helped the victim onto the stretcher. He then rolled it back over to the door and turned toward the shooter.

"The person who brought the stretcher was part of a SWAT team. I met him previously. He was one of the police officers who arrested me. I do not want him coming close to the door again. I would like you to select someone to pull the stretcher out of here." Angel held his breath, hoping the shooter would agree. The shooter pointed to a female hostage.

"You, do what Doctor Angel says." The female hostage approached the stretcher.

"Tell them the gunman is behaving rationally," Angel said. "I believe we can resolve the situation with no one else getting hurt. Tell them to give me some time, and I believe the shooter will surrender. Do not tell them about the relationship between the boy and the shooter."

Angel directed her to take the end of the stretcher closest to the door. Angel shouted again for everyone to hold their fire. He opened the door, and the female hostage walked backward as she pulled the stretcher out of the room. She continued to pull the stretcher until she was a good distance from the door. Two paramedics stepped forward and relieved her of the stretcher. They loaded the victim into an ambulance for the short distance to the emergency room. She saw eight police officers in heavy combat gear with their rifles pointed toward the door where the hostages were being held.

A SWAT officer stepped forward and accosted her. "I am SWAT Supervisor Garrett, and I need to ask you some questions."

"Okay, what do you need to know?"

"First, describe the gunman."

"He is around forty years old, about six feet tall, a little overweight. He has brown hair with a little gray."

"Is he threatening to shoot anyone else?"

"No, he calmed down after Doctor Angel entered the room. Doctor Angel believes he can get the gunman to surrender if you will just give him some time."

"Doctor Carpenter may be a good doctor, but he is not an expert on hostage situations," the SWAT supervisor said. "Who else is in the room?"

"There was a middle-aged man who said he was having a heart attack, but Doctor Angel said he was just having an anxiety attack, and when I left, he was relaxing with his eyes closed. There is a female nurse assistant in her early twenties, a young male in his thirties, an elderly male patient with his wife, and a young boy who I would guess to be about ten years old."

"Here is a drawing of the room," the supervisor said. "Show me where each person is located."

She pointed to various locations and told the officer where each person was situated within the room. He thanked her and asked her to go with one of the regular officers so they could take her statement.

He met with two of his senior officers, and they discussed various strategies for entering the room. In each rescue scenario, they were to kill the shooter to protect the lives of the hostages. They would not risk further deaths by asking the shooter to surrender. They had their tech specialist working on getting a camera into the room through an air conditioning duct.

After closing the door, Angel grabbed a chair, dragged it over in front of the shooter, and sat down.

"Do you have your son's medical records?" Angel asked.

The shooter reached over and opened a gym bag. He pulled out a five-inch expandable file folder that was stuffed full. Angel was close enough to the shooter to use his martial arts training to disarm him but decided to wait.

He handed the folder to Angel. "I just brought the most recent medical reports. We have an entire file cabinet at home full of his medical records. Here is my son's electronic file." The gunman handed Angel a flash drive. "We made a point of saving copies of everything."

Angel removed the documents from the folder. It only took a moment for him to locate the relevant documents. He realized the gunman's son fit the profile of a patient who would benefit from their cancer drug.

"I believe we can cure your son," Angel said.

The shooter took a deep breath and started crying. It was several minutes before he stopped crying and dried his eyes with the back of his shirt sleeve.

"My wife and I have been praying for a miracle. We sent in several applications to become part of the cancer drug trial. No one responded to the applications, our letters, or our phone calls. We saw you on the Harrieta Connor's Show and knew you could cure our son. I was desperate and did not know what else to do. When I came here today, they would not let me see you without an appointment, and when I tried to make an appointment, they told me the first available appointment would be in eleven months, but my son will not be alive in eleven months."

"We have a problem," Angel said. "I cannot let people think all they have to do to get treatment for a loved one is to come in here and start murdering people. However, I still plan to help your son. I need to make a phone call."

The shooter nodded his head as more tears rolled down his face. Angel made his call to Doctor Seneca.

"Mark, I believe you are aware of my current situation."

"Yes, how can I help?"

"One of our young cancer patients is here," Angel said. "We need to have him returned to his room. I would like you to bring a stretcher since he is unable to walk. Let me know when you arrive. If anyone asks, make sure they understand he is an existing patient by the name of Thomas Bailey, and I am his physician until he gets well. He is not part of the cancer drug test but will participate in the holistic program. I alone will provide his medication. I believe his medical file has been inadvertently deleted. Tell me when you are ready, and I will provide you the information so you can reload his personal data."

Angel provided the information from the file he had been given, and Doctor Seneca entered the data on his end. He also understood the need for the subterfuge.

"If this ever becomes a problem, I am the Department Head, and you were following my orders," Angel said. "We need to keep quiet about what we are doing. I am concerned the police may arrest the son as an accessory to murder. Bring a sedative."

"I understand," Mark said. "I will be there shortly."

Angel explained to Mr. Bailey what he had in mind. Angel moved his chair over to Thomas Bailey. "In a few minutes, we are going to put you on a stretcher. You will be taken to one of our rooms so we can make you well. Your father will need to stay here. Where is your mother?"

"She is at home," Thomas answered. "Do you want me to call her?"

"Not yet, but would you mind giving me her phone number?"

Thomas looked at his father and saw him nod his head. Angel put the number into his cellphone and then sent a text message to Doctor Seneca.

Angel moved to the door and shouted. "One of our cancer patients is uninjured but needs medical care. I have a doctor who should arrive shortly."

"We cannot let more people enter the room and add to the number of hostages." Supervisor Garrett said.

Angel was genuinely upset and lost his temper. "We need to get this child some medical attention, or he could die, and it will be your fault. The shooter has agreed to release the child and two additional hostages. Or would you just prefer to kill everybody?" At the end, Angel was shouting.

Just as Angel got his temper under control, there was a knock on the door. Angel opened the door slightly before opening it further when he saw Doctor Seneca. Doctor Seneca pulled the stretcher into the room. Doctor Fredrick was pushing the other end of the stretcher. They had Thomas lie down on the stretcher, and Doctor Fredrick administered a sedative. Thomas' eyes fluttered and then closed. Angel handed the medical file and the flash drive to Doctor Seneca. Doctor Seneca placed the file under the pad on the stretcher and placed the flash drive in his pocket. Doctors Seneca and Fredrick wheeled the stretcher out of the room.

Angel looked at Bailey, and he nodded his head. Angel pointed to the elderly couple, and they left the room right behind the stretcher.

"Who is the kid?" An officer asked.

"He is one of our cancer patients." Doctor Seneca replied. "He has only been with us for a few days, he missed his meds, and I do not have time to discuss the matter now." The officer scratched his head as the doctors rolled the stretcher down the hallway to the nearest elevator.

Angel made eye contact with Mr. Bailey. "I have done my part. I need you to release all the hostages."

Mr. Bailey nodded his head and handed the gun to Angel, but Angel did not want his fingerprints on another gun. Angel reached over and picked up the gym bag. He checked and saw there were no other weapons in the bag. He held the bag opened and Mr. Bailey placed the gun in the bag. Angel set it on the floor.

Angel went to the door again and shouted. "Hold your fire. The hostages are coming out."

The hostages thanked him as they were leaving, and several hugged him. Angel and Bailey were the only two remaining.

"The police are going to come in, and they will not be gentle," Angel said. "Do not resist. I want you to lay face down on the floor and put your hands behind your back. Tell them immediately, you want an attorney, and do not say anything else. I have an attorney friend of mine who will represent you. His name is George Martinez. Again, do not say anything except to ask for an attorney. Do you understand?"

"Yes, I understand. Thank you."

Angel walked over to the door. "Do not shoot. The shooter is unarmed. I am opening the door."

Angel opened the door and barely got out of the way as four SWAT team members barged into the room. Two of them quickly handcuffed their suspect and took him out of the room. Angel pointed to the bag with the weapon. An officer examined the contents of the bag and left with it. Additional crime scene investigators came into the room and started taking pictures.

"Doctor Carpenter, we need you to come to the station and make a complete statement." SWAT Supervisor Garrett said.

"Unless you are placing me under arrest again, I am going home. I will come to the station tomorrow and provide a complete statement. Unless you plan to break down the door to my apartment again and drag me to the station."

"I was just doing my job," Officer Garrett said again.

Angel was angry. "Did your job require you to injure my back? Did your job require you to do thousands of dollars in damage to my apartment? Did your job prevent any of you from apologizing?"

Then the officer did something Angel did not expect. He apologized, then he turned and left. Saying Angel was surprised, would have been an understatement.

Angel called George Martinez. "I have a client for you. Mr. Bailey was just arrested here at the hospital for murder. His son has cancer, and he can explain the rest."

"I will handle it," George said. "You should start sleeping at the hospital again. There are thousands of people surrounding the hospital and your apartment."

"Not again," Angel sighed and shook his head. "Thanks for telling me."

After finishing the call with George, Angel called Mrs. Bailey. "Mrs. Bailey, I am Doctor Angel Carpenter. I was just calling to update you on your son's progress here at Christian Health Hospital. He is doing well. I will put you on the visitors' list, but it may take a considerable amount of time for you to get through the traffic. I will meet with you when you arrive. Do not talk to anyone about your son before our meeting."

"God bless you. You truly are an angel. Can you tell me anything about my husband?"

Angel decided it would be best to tell her the truth since it would quickly be on the news media outlets.

"Your husband is in police custody. He shot three individuals, and one of them died. Your husband's attorney is George Martinez. I will text you his phone number. I want you to promise you will not talk to the press or the police about your husband or son. Talk only to your husband's attorney."

"I promise," Mrs. Bailey said. "My husband is a good man, a good husband, and a good father. Thank you again."

They hung up. Angel had only used a little over one-fourth of the cancer drugs he had got for Elisabeth Chapel. The one-fourth dose had successfully cured Elisabeth, and he was confident it would do the same for Thomas. Using the leftover drugs from Elisabeth's treatment meant he would not have to involve anyone else.

It would be twelve weeks before they would find out if Thomas would be cured of his cancer. However, Angel believed his young patient would be in the ninety percent who survived.

Angel was physically tired since it had been a long day. Also, he was mentally exhausted from not knowing what to do about all the people who desperately wanted the cancer drug. Today he saw a good Christian man commit murder to save his son. What about the ten million people who were going to die from cancer over the next twelve months? What were they capable of doing? Was everyone at the hospital in danger from the crowd waiting outside the fence?

Angel called his mother. "I need you to take a vacation. Please go some place remote and leave as soon as possible. I am worried about your safety.

"Tell me why I need to go on a vacation and are you okay?"

"Yes, I am fine," Angel said. "Earlier today, a father wanted his son to be part of the cancer drug trial. He shot three people at the hospital, and one died. There is a large crowd outside the hospital and outside my apartment. It could turn violent. I will sleep at the hospital until things settle down."

"None of this is your fault, but what does that have to do with me taking a vacation?"

"Someone could decide to hold you hostage and threaten to kill you unless I give them the cancer drug. You need to go to a safe place until things settle down. Please do this for me."

"I have a lot of vacation and sick time saved up. You do your job and do not worry about me. I will call you once I am ready to leave and let you know where I will be staying."

Before hanging up, his mother told him how much she loved him and how proud she was of all he had accomplished. After she hung up, Angel said a silent prayer that she would be safe.

Several hours later, George Martinez called. "I have already talked to Mr. Bailey, and it will be a difficult case, but I do not believe the District Attorney will want to take this to trial. The gun went off several times while he was struggling with the victim who died. There was no intent to kill anyone, so I believe we can get the charges reduced to involuntary manslaughter. In Florida, the minimum sentence is nine years and four months. Under the Florida statutes, he will have to serve at least 85 percent of the sentence before being eligible for parole."

"Do you think you could win in a court trial?" Angel asked.

"Probably not, and a loss would result in a much longer prison sentence. The prosecution would likely charge him with First-Degree Murder. They will allege he knowingly drove to the hospital intending to kill if he did not get his son accepted into the drug program."

"Thank you for taking the case. I have to go to the police station tomorrow to make a statement. Is there anything I should say to help your case?"

"I will go with you, and no, you will answer only the questions when I tell you it is okay."

"Is that necessary? I am not on trial. I am just a witness."

"Angel, you should know better. They still want you behind bars. If you answer a question incorrectly, they can prosecute you for perjury. I will meet you at the station, and you will not say a word to anyone until I get there. Do not even say your name. Better yet, meet me in the parking lot."

The following morning Angel and George met in the police parking lot and discussed their strategy. George gave the same explanation he had given Angel when he was on trial. George told Angel to give short answers, no opinions, and only answer medical questions. Angel was not to answer a question unless he received a signal from George. They wanted to avoid inconsistencies which could lead to a charge of providing false information to the police.

They entered the police station and checked in at the front desk. They waited approximately twenty minutes before being escorted to a meeting room to meet with two detectives assigned to the case.

George told the detectives his client would only answer medical-related questions and plead the fifth on any other type of question.

"Do you have something to hide?" The younger detective asked.

George gave Angel the sign they had agreed upon. "Under the advice of counsel, I assert my Fifth Amendment privilege."

"So, it is going to be adversarial," the older detective stated. "We are just trying to find out what took place at the hospital. Doctor Carpenter could be called as a witness by the Prosecution. Therefore, there appears to be a conflict of interest for you to represent both Mr. Bailey and Doctor Carpenter."

"There is no conflict unless you decide to charge Doctor Carpenter with a crime. Doctor Carpenter is a witness for the Defense, which allows me to represent him. Ask your questions."

The questioning continued for several hours. George continued to provide the hand signal when Angel needed to plea the Fifth. Angel pleaded the Fifth Amendment on over eighty percent of the questions.

Angel was relieved there were no questions regarding Thomas Bailey. He had told George how they had moved Thomas to the cancer treatment facility. George told him not to answer any questions about Thomas.

Finally, at the end, the older detective asked: "Did you tell Mr. Bailey not to talk to the police?"

"I assert my Fifth Amendment privilege."

"Did you tell Mr. Bailey to call Attorney Martinez to represent him?"

"I assert my Fifth Amendment privilege."

The older detective was frustrated. "We are done. Get the hell out of here."

After Angel and George left, the younger detective asked: "I do not understand. It seemed you were going after Doctor Carpenter instead of treating him as a witness."

"You are correct. I was absolutely going after our fine doctor. A doctor who got away with murder and embarrassed the police department."

Once they were alone in the parking lot, Angel wanted an explanation. "Will you please explain why you had me plea the Fifth on so many questions?"

"He already had the answers to the specific questions he was asking," George said. "If you gave an incorrect answer to any of those questions, they could charge you with giving false statements to a law enforcement officer in a criminal investigation. That is a First-Degree Misdemeanor punishable by up to one year in jail and a thousand dollar fine for each statement. If you answered a question incorrectly, they could also charge you with obstruction of justice, a felony punishable with up to five years in prison. Answering yes to the last two questions would have resulted in two charges of practicing law without a license with a punishment of one year in jail and a ten thousand dollar fine for each violation. The detective would have immediately arrested you. If you so much as hiccupped, they would have charged you with resisting arrest without violence, adding another year plus a thousand dollar fine. They recorded the entire questioning and mounting a defense would have been problematic. You could have been looking at spending considerable time in prison with a sizable reduction in your bank account."

"Wow, I am glad you were with me, and I am glad I have a great attorney," Angel stated.

"You finally got it right!"

Angel chuckled. "Thank you for all your help. How much do I owe you?"

"Nothing, but I expect preferential medical treatment if I need a doctor."

"Anytime," Angel replied, but he had another concern.

"How about the Bailey family?" Angel asked. "Will they be able to pay you?"

"My fee is not the problem. The family has been receiving donations that will cover my fee and their living expenses for a short time. Plus, I am discounting my fee. However, they are going to have financial problems long-term. Mrs. Bailey quit her job to care for their son. She is looking for a job, but any future job is unlikely to replace Mr. Bailey's income. However, both Mr. Bailey and his wife are happy since their son is going to live. Mr. Bailey understands he must pay for taking a man's life."

They separated and headed to their separate vehicles. They each had a long day of work ahead of them. Angel hoped there would be no more violence.

Angel barely got through the crowd at the hospital by using the emergency room access. Fortunately, he now kept a bag at the hospital with extra clothes and personal items.

Angel asked Doctors Seneca and Fredrick to join him for a short meeting. Once everyone was seated, Angel closed the door.

"I have improperly admitted two patients into the cancer drug trial. If either of these two patients becomes a problem, they were admitted into the hospital under my authority. If anyone asks, I was the only person involved in their medication. I will take full responsibility for the consequences."

Both doctors nodded in agreement and promised to abide by all the rules. They had tremendous respect for Doctor Carpenter. They failed to understand why Angel had given two individuals access to the drug trial and exceeded the number of test subjects approved by the FDA while rejecting thousands.

Angel did not provide a political or financial reason to take the added risk of treating two minors. Also, unlike Angel, they would never have put themselves in personal danger by rushing into a room with a shooter. While questioning his recklessness, they admired his courage. Regardless, they were thrilled to be part of what could be the most significant breakthrough in medicine since the MRI.

Angel administered the cancer drug to Thomas Bailey each day. Thomas weighed seventy pounds and Angel initially gave him half the adult dosage. He saw the same adverse reaction from the drug that he observed in Elizabeth. He reduced the drug to one-fourth but this time the blood test showed a lack of response by the cancer cells. Angel adjusted the dosage to one-third the adult dosage. He was relieved when the blood tests showed the daily reduction in the cancer cells were within the expected range.

CHAPTER 13 ASSASSINATION ATTEMPT

Angel continued to practice his martial arts each night. The lease at his apartment would be up for renewal in three months. He located another apartment closer to the hospital but wanted to keep the location a secret. A secret location would prevent people from surrounding his apartment, and he would no longer have to sleep at the hospital.

Angel contacted George for assistance, and George helped Angel form a Limited Liability Company which leased the new apartment. George served as the Registered Agent and Manager for the company. Angel was not listed on the documents filed with the state. George opened a bank account in the name of the LLC, and Angel deposited cash into the account. The utilities and rent were set up for automatic payment. His bank accounts, credit cards, and magazine subscriptions were all paperless. Therefore, he had no physical mail going to the new address. He paid the rent for the balance of the lease at his former apartment and notified the landlord he would not be renewing the lease.

Angel sold his old car and purchased a used car in the company's name. Each day he arrived at the hospital wearing street clothes and changed into his hospital scrubs after arriving. He changed back into street clothes before leaving the hospital. Finally, he wore lightly tented sunglasses and a ball cap when away from the hospital. Angel donated the like-new furniture from his old apartment to the Salvation Army since moving the furniture to his new apartment could be traced. The company purchased quality furnishings for his new apartment.

Due to the attempted poisoning, the hospital followed the recommendations from a consulting firm and the firm supervised the replacement of their antiquated security equipment. The security budget was increased, and additional guards were hired to supplement the upgraded security system. Angel wondered if all his activities to become anonymous were needed until he received another phone call from Lorenzo.

Angel was in his apartment when the caller ID identified Lorenzo. "Angel, we just received a communication from our agent in Bailiwick. The Diocletian Knights have offered a million euros for your death. For that kind of money, they can hire a top assassin."

"I have taken precautions," Angel said. "I have moved into a different apartment leased in the name of a company that cannot be traced back to me, and I purchased a different car in the company's name. Also, I wear civilian clothes with sunglasses and a ball cap when I am not at the hospital."

"I am glad you have taken some precautions, but it may not be enough. I have been authorized to offer you sanctuary. The Church can protect you if you move to the Vatican."

"Thank you for the offer, but if my work here is successful, it will save millions of lives."

"Contact me if you change your mind. You need to get rid of your cellphone and switch to untraceable burner phones. Each time you switch phones, send me a text message with the new number so I can keep you posted on any additional threats to your life." After a few pleasantries, they hung up.

Angel called Rick Grant. "Doctor Angel, how are you?"

"I am fine. I need to make my phone untraceable. Is that even possible?"

"No, you cannot make your phone completely untraceable, but you can make it more difficult to trace. You need to turn off most of the apps on your phone. Also, you need to eliminate ads, mapping, and other hidden features that track your movements and shopping habits. I can tweak your phone's location settings, keep internet browsers from tracking your every move, switch to a private browser on your phone, opt-out of ads, modify your virtual assistants, and eliminate all GPS-related software. Essentially, you need to use your phone only for phone calls and text messaging, but that is just the first part."

"What else?" Angel asked.

"We also need to put in a triple passcode to access your phone, which requires your fingerprint, voice verification, and passcode. We can install a messaging encryption app and spy protection app. Even with all those modifications, the police can still track you unless you turn off your phone and remove the battery. This can be problematic if you have an iPhone since the battery cannot be removed. The best approach is to get rid of your regular phone, pay cash for cheap prepaid phones, and only use those phones in an emergency."

"I would like you to fix my phone, and I will only use it at the hospital," Angel said. "I will use burner phones when I am away from the hospital. When would you be available to fix my phone? Also, I will pay you whatever you think is fair."

"I would normally do it for free, but I am attending college and need every penny I can get," Grant said. "How about two times the minimum wage?"

"That is a bargain. Include your travel time."

"I do not have any classes tomorrow morning. I can drop by around eight o'clock in the morning if that works for you."

"I will see you in the morning at the hospital," Angel replied. "Thank you."

Angel looked at the time and went to Walmart since they stayed open late and would have a large selection of prepaid cellphones. He arrived at the store and was pleasantly surprised that the phones were cheap. He bought two phones and paid cash. The phones allowed unlimited talk and messaging for thirty days after activation.

Angel arrived at the hospital at his usual time and informed Security to put Rick Grant on the visitors' list. Rick arrived a little before eight. Angel gave him his cellphone and the burner phones.

Rick held out his phone. "Take my phone. I will call you when I am done. This will take a while." Rick called him in less than two hours, and Angel returned to the office.

"As we discussed, leave your regular phone at the hospital," Rick said. "You can review your messages and voice mail each morning. Use your burner phones when you are away from the hospital and only use them for emergencies. Let me see your tablet. The best way is to stay off the internet as much as possible. I will make the same type of changes to your tablet."

The tablet took a little longer. It was lunchtime when Angel returned, and Rick had just finished the modifications.

"I have switched your phones and computer to a virtual private network, which everyone refers to as VPN. It gives you online privacy and anonymity by creating a private network from a public internet connection. I did additional research last night and added all the most recent phone and computer security apps. The apps are designed for anonymity, but someone who is good and persistent may still locate you. Also, you should not answer any calls from a number you do not recognize and do not open any attachments to any tech messages. The same goes for your tablet regarding emails. I will come by once a week to check your phones and tablet spyware. Here is a flash drive. Plug it into your desktop computer when you get home, and it will secure your computer. Do not send any messages or receive any messages on your home computer and do not buy anything using it. Use a hospital computer if you need to buy anything online and have it delivered here."

Rick explained the changes he had made and how to use the apps. Angel paid Rick and thanked him again. After completing his afternoon rounds, he sent a message to Doctor Seneca and Doctor Fredrick to meet in his office. They arrived when the shift ended and took a seat.

"You know about the attempt to poison our patients, but I need to provide you with additional information," Angel said. "The FBI made several arrests but failed to catch the person who orchestrated the attempt. It is unlikely they will ever find the person. They believe the person was part of a group and not acting alone. The money used to pay various individuals shows the group is well-financed. The poison attempt has resulted in greater security at the hospital. However, we need to maintain our diligence."

"We will keep a careful watch for anything unusual," Mark said. "Does the FBI have any idea who attempted to poison our patients?"

"Just some theories. I wanted to talk to you because I have received several death threats. I am taking some extra personal precautions and plan to leave my cellphone in my office when I leave the hospital. I will use prepaid phones when I am not at work. Here is my burner phone number so you can reach me in an emergency, but do not give the number to anyone for any reason."

Both doctors agreed to keep the number confidential, but their facial expressions showed their concern. Angel did not tell them about the Diocletian Knights. He heeded Lorenzo's warning that even the knowledge of the organization could put their lives in danger. They then spent nearly an hour reviewing patient files before going home.

Doctor Seneca and Doctor Fredrick remained somber throughout the following days as they wondered who would try to stop or delay a drug trial that could save millions. They were very concerned about the threats against Angel. Maybe someone was upset because they were excluded from the drug trial and were just venting. However, they kept thinking about the recent triple shooting that resulted in the death of a patient.

Lilith Talon caught a 2:05 PM connecting flight on United in Frankfurt. It was a ten-hour flight, but it would arrive at 10:05 PM at the Miami International Airport because of the time difference. Lilith flew first class and caught up on her sleep. She was twenty-eight with an athletic build due to her daily workouts. She was five foot six inches tall with short dark reddish-brown hair and blue-green eyes. However, she had wigs to change her hair color and various colored contact lenses to change the color of her eyes. She had a reputation for never failing an assignment. She was attractive and sometimes used her sexual charms to lure prey to a private area to be eliminated with no witnesses. Once, she even had a romance with a victim. It had lasted several months before she could separate him from his bodyguards. Lilith enjoyed watching him as he realized she had outsmarted him. She put three bullets through his heart and one between his eyes.

Lilith was proficient with guns, knives, and poisons. She had never failed to complete a contract because she always took her time and was selective in the contracts she accepted. Also, she used a code name, and no one knew her identity. Her employers always assumed she was male, and she found it humorous since it allowed her to demand a male assassin's salary. However, this job was not a private contract. She had been contacted and told to complete the assignment in forty-eight hours. When she declined, they posted an open contract. The funeral request had been posted on the Mortality List. Lilith would be competing against other assassins. She still expected to collect the fee but would proceed at her own pace. Lilith thought this assignment might prove interesting. She had never killed an angel.

Lilith's flight landed without incident. She exited the plane and entered the main corridor of the airport. Lilith saw her limo driver had followed her instructions and held a sign with the word NACHT printed in all caps, which was the Dutch word for night. They collected her two bags at the claims area, and the limo drove her to the luxurious hotel Setai on Miami Beach. She would do her research before moving to a different location with an alternate identity. She had multiple passports and other identifiers in a hidden compartment in her luggage.

Lilith spent the first week researching her prey. She had watched the entire courtroom proceedings, which she found entertaining. Her respect for Doctor Carpenter increased when she read about him rescuing hostages and getting a shooter to surrender. She studied his appearance on the Harrieta Connor's Show and the articles on his efforts to cure cancer. She would regret killing him but knew he was already dead. Someone else would earn the fee if she developed a conscience.

Lilith checked every social media on the internet, and millions of individuals routinely discussed Doctor Angel Carpenter. Angel surprised her by not having a single social media account or a website. Lilith located his apartment and decided to pay him a visit. This might be the easiest fee she had ever earned. She found a black-market gun supplier and paid four times the retail price for a pistol with a silencer and a rifle with scope. She purchased several hunting knives from Walmart.

Lilith rented a car and watched the apartment building for three days but failed to see Angel. She finally hurried to the entrance of the building and greeted a lady who was leaving.

"Good morning," Lilith said. "I have traveled here, all the way, from California to meet Angel. Does he still live here?"

"He has an apartment on the fourth floor, but I have not seen him in a while. He often sleeps at the hospital." Lilith already knew Angel lived in apartment 412.

"Thank you. I will try to contact him at the hospital."

Lilith watched as the lady got in her car and drove away. She was only a few steps from the door when a mother with two children left the building. She caught the door before it closed and entered the building. Lilith took the elevator to the fourth floor. She located the apartment, and it only took a minute to pick the lock. Lilith entered the apartment and realized instantly that Angel no longer lived there. She concluded this would not be an easy kill.

Lilith used the portable computer she had brought with her, and after locating Angel's phone number, she called him. The call was blocked. She sent a text message to the number with an embedded tracker app. Several days passed, and the app had not been activated. She finally decided Angel had some excellent spy software blocking her calls. The phone would only accept calls from a list of specific numbers. She used a forwarding tracker and called Angel's mother.

"Hello, may I help you?"

"Yes," said Lilith. "I am trying to locate your son, Angel Carpenter. My daughter has cancer, and I would like to talk to him about getting her accepted into the cancer drug trial. I have not been able to reach him by phone."

"My son told me not to give his number to anyone. You can reach him at the hospital."

"The hospital will not forward my calls. My daughter is three years old and has terminal cancer. As a mother, surely you understand. Would you at least give him my phone number? Please, you are my last hope."

After the caller hung up, she called her son's regular cellphone and left a detailed message. She did not call his burner phone since it was not an emergency. She hoped her son could help the desperate caller's child. She had experienced the pain of losing her husband to cancer and felt the caller's pain for her daughter.

Lilith knew the tracking app was successful when she located the phone at the hospital. The tracking app would also attach to the phone of any person called by Angel's mother, but she would ignore the other numbers. She monitored the tracker for several days, but the phone never left the hospital. Lilith searched the county records and found no homeownership in his name. She searched the public records for the state. There were no businesses in Angel's name and no businesses with him listed as an officer.

Rick continued to visit the hospital weekly to check Angel's phones and tablet. This time Rick saw the regular cellphone had been hacked. It took a while, but he thoroughly cleaned the phone and told Angel the app invaded his phone from a call he received from his mother. They called his mother, and while they were on the line, Rick cleaned her cellphone and put spyware blocks on her phone to prevent a future occurrence. Angel's mother was distraught when she learned someone had hacked her phone, but Angel calmed her by telling her there was no harm.

Lilith noticed the tracker had stopped working. Her only option now was to track him physically. She had already tried unsuccessfully to schedule an appointment to meet with Angel. The hospital said Doctor Angel was not meeting with patients except through the normal application process. She was told an appointment might be available in a year if she passed the initial screening. She tried to get a job at the cancer center, but there were no openings. Then she tried to get a job anywhere in the hospital. Her fabricated resume did not hold up since they performed a thorough background check. Under the hospital's new security protocol, everything on a resume was verified which included calling the prior employers. Her resume was discarded.

Lilith started hanging out at the restaurants and bars close to the hospital until she found several locations popular with the hospital staff. It became another dead end. No one seemed to know where Angel lived, and they never saw him away from the hospital.

Lilith noticed a middle-aged man with a camera bag and a camera hanging from his shoulder. He was sitting at the bar drinking beer. She guessed he was paparazzi. Lilith sat next to him and waited for the bartender to notice her. Today she was wearing a blond wig with blue-tinted contact lenses.

As the bartender approached, the photographer asked, "May I buy you a drink?"

"Yes, you may, and thank you." She ordered a light beer since he seemed impoverished.

"You appear to be a professional photographer. Have you taken any interesting pictures lately?"

"No, I am having a dry period. I got some splendid pictures several months ago and sold them for a good price."

"Let me guess," Lilith said. "You took pictures of Doctor Angel Carpenter."

"Yes, I did. Would you like to see them?"

"I would love to." He pulled a viewer out of his bag and inserted a flash memory card into the slot. He showed her dozens of pictures of Doctor Carpenter, and she pretended to be impressed by the quality of the shots.

"These are brilliant pictures. Do you have any idea where Doctor Carpenter lives?"

"If I knew, I would be staking out the place and not enjoying your company. By the way, my name is Brett Farber."

"What a lovely name. I have a brother who works for an online tabloid in Germany. Brett, if you get some additional photos or find out where Angel lives, he will pay you well for the pictures or the location."

"How much," Brett asked. Lilith knew she had to give a number high enough to get his interest but not so high as to be unbelievable.

"For original good quality pictures, ten thousand of your dollars. Plus, I would pay you extra just to be there when you take the pictures. It would be such a turn-on." She put her hand on his thigh.

"Here is my number but call me only if you locate Angel's new home." She got up and left the bar. Brett was just one of a dozen individuals she had approached.

Brett typically sold his pictures through an agency and only received sixty percent of the proceeds. He could sell some photos to her and sell the balance to the agency. He would make sure each party received different pictures so they would each have original images. It was getting harder to make a living as a freelance photographer. He did not like being called a paparazzo, and there were fewer of them each year. He would put forth an even greater effort to get photos of Angel, and he looked forward to calling the lady.

Lilith rented an office across from the hospital with a view of the entrance to the employee parking garage. She used a camera with a telescopic lens to take pictures of the license plate of each vehicle entering the parking garage and a photo of the driver when the vehicles were leaving. So far, none of the drivers matched Angel's description. Lilith wondered if Angel ever left the hospital. She had run all the license plates through a lookup site. None of the vehicles were owned by Angel. After four days, no new vehicles were noted. She was wondering if Angel even owned a car.

Lilith knew she was exceptionally good at her job but wondered if someone else had collected the reward. She checked the Mortality

List, and the amount remained unclaimed. She checked with sources known only to her and received the names of other professional assassins who were in the area, hoping to claim the reward. Two of the killers worked as a team.

Angel's mother returned from her vacation and settled into her everyday work routine. She missed seeing her son, but Angel had intentionally stayed away to help keep her safe.

Martha Carpenter was driving home when a car following her turned on a flashing light. She assumed it was an unmarked police car and pulled over to the shoulder of the road. A person dressed in police clothing approached the side of her car, and she let down the window.

"I am officer Hayes. May I see your driver's license?" Martha reached into her purse and gave him the license. The person looked at the license to verify he had pulled over the right person.

"Mrs. Carpenter, please join me in my car while I run your license. It will only take a few minutes. Martha got out of her car and was escorted to the unmarked car. He opened the passenger side of his car, and she got in. She had not noticed the person in the back seat. He grabbed her around the neck, holding tight to cut off the blood flow to her brain. She passed out and slumped forward. She regained awareness but was still groggy when the man placed a damp cloth over her mouth and nose. Martha smelled an ether-like odor, and the part over her mouth had a slightly sweet taste before she lost consciousness from the chloroform.

When she regained consciousness, she was lying on a bed with her hands and feet bound with plastic zip ties. She started shouting for help. A man came into the room. "If you continue to shout, I will place a gag in your mouth. So, keep your mouth shut."

"Why have you kidnapped me? Please, let me go."

The man gagged her with a piece of dirty cloth. He felt no need to explain anything to Martha Carpenter, but he wanted her unharmed when Angel called.

Martha was afraid. She knew the kidnapping could not be for money. Wealthy individuals living in Miami could pay a large ramson, but not her or Angel. She knew it must involve Angel, but why kidnap her? She was suddenly more afraid for Angel than for herself. Martha could not believe how gullible she had been to think the man was a police officer. She thought of things she should have done differently, like not getting out of her car.

It had been a productive day and Angel was just getting ready to leave the hospital when Doctor Seneca called him.

"Mark, is there an emergency?"

"Yes, I just received a call from an unidentified party who said you needed to call them if you cared about your mother. I told them you were out of town, but they did not believe me. They said if you called the authorities, they would know about it and kill your mother. I am so sorry. What can I do to help?"

"Right now, do nothing and do not involve anyone else." Angel entered the phone number for the kidnappers into his phone.

Angel did not trust the kidnappers and believed they would kill his mother even if he met their conditions. He could not risk notifying the authorities if they had a source within the police department. Angel ran to the parking garage, located his car, and left the hospital. He forgot to put on his disguise.

Brett Farber had been staking out the hospital. He saw Angel leave the parking garage and followed him. He thought this was his lucky day. While following Angel, he called the number Lilith had given him. She answered on the third ring.

"This is Brett, I bought you a drink, and you said to call if I found out where Angel lives. I am following his car. At this time of day, I suspect he is headed to his apartment. I expect to get some excellent pictures over the next couple of days. You mentioned an additional payment for his address. I think the address should be worth a thousand dollars. However, if you get turned on as you said, we could forget about the bonus."

"Give me your location and keep me posted whenever he changes directions," Lilith said. "Leave your phone on and make sure you do not lose him. I am getting in my car now."

"You never gave me your name," Brett said.

"Joan Smith, I will be with you shortly."

Brett was excited and getting aroused just thinking about meeting Joan. Lilith never gave her real name when working. Of course, Lilith was not her real name either.

Angel thought for a moment as he was driving and made his first call. "Rick, I need you to come to my apartment. It is an emergency."

"It cannot wait until tomorrow?" Rick asked.

"No, my mother has been kidnapped, but you must not mention it to anyone. I need you to track the person I call."

"I will be there in twenty minutes."

Angel made his next call. "Judith Stephono, you told me to call you if I ever needed a favor. There is a death contract on my head, and I have successfully stayed hidden while still caring for my patients. Assassins have kidnapped my mother and plan to kill her if I do not surrender to them. I would gladly turn myself in to save my mother, but I believe they will kill her even if I comply with their request. When I call them back, I have a tech friend who will track their location. I am on my way to my new apartment. Can you help?"

"Text me your address, and I will meet you at your home."

Angel made his next call. "Joseph Adler, I need the help of the Warlocks." Angel filled him in on the situation, and Joseph agreed to help. He did not contact the Angels since he needed a gang that could meet violence with violence, and he did not want his former gang involved in such action.

Angel arrived home and notified the guard at the gate to put Rick on the visitor's list. Rick arrived at Angel's apartment and went to work on the phone. Rick had just completed the installation of the tracking app when the guard called to tell Angel he had two carloads of visitors. Judith arrived with seven family members consisting of six men and one female. They were armed and very intimidating. Angel introduced Rick to Judith and her entourage.

Angel's new furniture included a dining table with six chairs. Two of the men remained standing. Judith was direct. "Give me the short version."

"The Diocletian Knights are a well-financed group opposed to all things religious. They believe I am a threat to their goals and put out a contract on me. Several paid assassins have decided they would like to collect the fee. I have done what I could to make it difficult for them to collect the bounty. A company pays my apartment lease and all the utilities with no connection to me. The same company leases the car I use. I use burner phones when I am not at work, and Rick has installed anti-spy apps to protect my regular phone and tablet. I also wear a disguise when I leave the hospital. Doctor Seneca has my burner phone number. The kidnappers contacted him earlier today and told him to give me a message. They have my mother and will kill her if I do not surrender to them. I called my mother a dozen times, and all the calls went to voice mail. My mother always answers her phone. Rick has just installed a tracker app on my phone. It will allow us to track the phone they are using. Once I call them, I assume they will want me to go to their location. As I explained earlier, I do not believe they will release my mother even if I surrender to them."

"I agree with your assessment," Judith replied. "Tell me about the tracker."

"The tracker will give a GPS map with an exact location, and once you are close, it works like a lost phone app with a few upgrades," Rick said. "It is based on the same type of software parents use to keep track of their children. It will take you right to the kidnappers' phone."

"Put your phone on speaker and place the call," Judith said

Angel called the number, and it was answered on the second ring. "Is this Angel Carpenter?"

"Yes, it is. I want to talk to my mother."

"All in good time," the kidnapper said.

"Put her on the phone now, or I will hang up."

It was only a moment before Angel heard his mother. "Angel, I am so sorry. No matter what, don't do anything they say."

Angel heard a slap followed by a moan from his mother. It took all of his willpower not to scream over the phone.

"That was unnecessary. I am prepared to do whatever you ask if you promise not to hurt my mother."

"Your mother is in good health and will be fine if you do exactly what you are told. If you contact the authorities or fail to follow our directions, I will kill your mother." The kidnapper provided a location, and Angel wrote it down.

After they hung up, Angel turned to Rick and asked: "Do you have the location?"

"Yes, and it differs from the address you were given."

Judith made several calls.

Brett was sitting in his car when Lilith pulled up behind him. Lilith got out of her car and took the passenger seat in Brett's car.

"Are you sure it is Angel?" Lilith asked.

"Absolutely, here are the pictures." He showed her a dozen pictures he had taken as Angel left the hospital. The quality of the electronic photos was grainy, but it was clearly Angel.

"I suppose you want your prize," she said in a seductive voice. Lilith was leaning in to kiss him while simultaneously reaching inside her purse for her gun. He had outlived his usefulness. After killing Brett, she would go to the back of the development, climb over the concrete wall, knock on Angel's door, and kill him when he answered. Then, she would go back to the hotel, get a good night's sleep, and catch a flight the following morning.

"A strange thing happened right before you arrived." Then he saw her lips.

"I will tell you about that later." He leaned forward just as she pulled back.

"What strange thing?" Lilith asked as she released her grip on the pistol.

"First, a small car arrived, and a young guy entered Angel's apartment. Then, two full-size SUVs arrived, carrying eight people. There are currently nine people visiting Angel."

"What did they look like?"

"I can show you." Brett showed her the pictures he had taken of the people who entered Angel's apartment. She knew the people from the SUVs were professionals. Looking closely at the pictures, she saw the outlines of the concealed guns in the middle of their backs under their loose-fitting shirts. She also knew at least two of them had backup guns in ankle holsters from the way the pant cuffs were hanging. Now she needed a new plan. This job was proving to be highly frustrating.

Lilith looked back at the apartment just in time to see Angel and nine individuals leave the unit.

"Stay here or go home. Here is a thousand dollars. I will see you tomorrow."

Lilith jumped out of Brett's car and got back in her vehicle. She watched the young man in an older Ford EcoSport leave the complex, followed by one of the SUVs. She saw what looked like

Angel saying goodbye as he got in a third vehicle. The first two vehicles were out of sight. When Angel left, the remaining SUV was still in front of the apartment. She pulled out to follow Angel. Then, she swore as she saw Brett following her. She was looking forward to killing him.

Angel headed to the rendezvous site. They all knew where the kidnapper was waiting, so they did not need to follow each other. Judith was in the front SUV about a mile ahead of Angel when she received a call from the second SUV. "Judith, there are two cars following Angel. What would you like us to do?"

"Just follow for now. Call me immediately if they stop following or try to stop Angel. I will get us some additional backup." Judith made another call.

The first SUV arrived at the site, which was a RaceTrac gas station. They pulled up next to a gas pump, and the male driver proceeded to get gas. Judith was in the front passenger seat, and two of the men were in the middle row. Judith got out of the vehicle and entered the store. She grabbed a handbasket and randomly placed items in the basket. She watched as Angel arrived and parked in front of the store.

Angel's phone rang, and he answered it on the first ring. "I am in the blue Malibu," said the kidnapper. "If you want your mother to stay healthy, then do exactly what I tell you to do. Come to my car and get in on the passenger side."

Angel was walking toward the Malibu when Judith crashed into him, dropping her groceries. Angel bent down to help as Judith shouted at him for being so clumsy. The kidnapper was watching Angel and Judith when his car door was jerked open, and a gun was shoved against his ribs. They removed the kidnapper's gun and secured his hands behind his back. The kidnaper was small compared to his assailants. He was shoved over the consul into the passenger's seat. One of Judith's assistants took the driver's seat while another got in the backseat. Judith dumped the groceries in a trash receptacle and told Angel to leave his car. Judith and Angel got into the SUV and followed the Malibu.

Lilith arrived just as Angel and Judith got into the SUV. She continued following Angel as the SUV left the RaceTrac station. She was dismayed Brett was still following her and failed to see the second SUV following Brett.

The additional backup Judith called, consisted of two vehicles and four men. They arrived at the location where Martha Carpenter was being held. They had followed Judith's orders to wear vests and attach silencers to their guns. They parked at the far end of the parking area. They scouted the two-story building. There was only a single light upstairs, and only part of the ground floor had light. The ground floor had a front counter with empty metal shelving that were blocking visibility. There were offices on the second floor. Two men stayed in the shadows at the front door and found the front door was locked. The other two men went to the back entrance, which was in complete darkness. They used a flashlight and found the backdoor was locked but there was an additional deadbolt. They could hear a television playing on the ground floor. The two men at the back, decided it would be easier to enter through a window on the back wall. The room with the window was dark, and they saw the room door was closed. They broke a glass panel and unlocked the window. The window opened with minimum noise, and they silently entered the empty room. The room had trash on the floor with a thick layer of dust. Once they were in position, they sent a text message to their two counterparts at the front door. The two men at the front kicked in the door and ran past the shelving. They saw the kidnapper grab a gun and turn towards them, but he fell to the floor when he was shot multiple times by the men who had rushed in from the back room. They shot him through the back of the head to make sure he was dead. The guns with the silencers were muffled by the television and would not have been heard outside the building. They checked throughout the ground floor without finding anyone. The men carefully proceeded to the second floor and checked out each room. They found Martha gagged in the furthest room from the staircase. She was on a twin mattress that was lying on the floor. Martha's eyes opened wide when she saw the two men enter the room with drawn guns.

"Mrs. Carpenter, you are safe. We are here to help you," a man said as he put away his gun and gently removed her gag. "Please hold still while I cut the restraints."

She massaged her wrists. "Is my son okay?"

"Yes, your son is fine, and he will be joining us."

"Thank you so much, but right now, I need to go to the bathroom."

Angel was worried but relaxed when Judith told him his mother was safe. They drove until they reached an old industrial park. They followed the apt directly to the building. When Angel got out of the SUV, his mother rushed out of the building. They hugged tightly.

Angel stepped back. "Do you need medical attention?"

"No, I am not injured. I am so happy you are okay. At first, I was scared for myself. Then it was worst when I overheard them talking about killing you."

"Judith, can you have someone take my mother home?"

"I will wait until you can come with me," his mother said. Angel took his mother a short distance away from the group so they could talk in private.

"Mother, please leave. The longer you stay, the longer it will take before I can leave. The police will not be involved. I need you to leave here now, for your safety and mine." Angel's mother gave him a final hug and left with the same man who had removed her restraints.

Lilith and Brett were at the other end of the lot when four vehicles raced toward them with their lights on high beam. Eight men jumped out of the vehicles and pointed AR15 rifles at them. Lilith and Brett were pulled out of their cars and shoved face down onto the pavement. The men roughly searched them and bound their hands. They searched the vehicles and found Lilith's gun with the attached silencer. They forced marched Lilith and Brett to the building. Judith told Angel to wait outside. One of the men stayed with Angel, but they did not speak. After about an hour, Judith came out of the buildings and approached Angel.

"Two assassins worked together to kidnap your mother," Judith said. "They have worked as a team for a long time. There were no other accomplices. The one guarding your mother was killed during the rescue. The female who followed you is also an assassin but was not working with the other two. The male who followed you is a paparazzo. The female assassin hired him to help locate you. I will have one of my men drive you back to the RaceTrac so you can get your car."

"What are you going to do with the two assassins and the photographer?" Angel asked.

"It is better if you do not know," Judith replied.

Angel understood and nodded his head in understanding. "Thank you."

"You are welcome. You saved my life, and this helps to balance the scales. Now that we know about the contract on your life, we will keep an eye on you and try to keep you safe."

Angel was directed to an SUV and got in on the passenger side. He was driven to his vehicle and breathed a sigh of relief as he drove to his mother's home.

Judith reentered the building. They had tied up the three prisoners in separate chairs and blindfolded them. Brett, the paparazzo, had wet himself during the interrogation. The prisoners were about ten feet apart. Judith decided to take care of Brett first.

"Brett, you were working for a contract killer, and she was planning to kill you once she had murdered Angel," Judith said. "We will have to kill you since we cannot have any loose ends."

"Please do not kill me. I did not know she was an assassin. I am just a photographer. I promise I will not say anything, and I will never bother Angel again. Please, please, please, do not kill me. I will do anything, just do not kill me." Brett was openly crying.

"What do you guys think?" Judith asked.

They all took turns saying to kill him, except for the female. "He is not worth a bullet. Just slice his throat."

Judith motioned to the camera sitting on the table. "Do any of you know how to use this?" One of the men stepped forward, picked up the camera, removed the telescopic lens, and made a few adjustments. He took a picture of the male assassin.

"Brett, I will give you one chance and only one chance to save your life," Judith said. "As you heard from the screams, a man is tied up next to you. He kidnapped Angel's mother and was going to kill her after they murdered Angel. The other kidnapper is dead. There is a gun on the table right in front of you. It belongs to your girlfriend. She was going to use it to kill you. There is a single bullet in the gun, and it is chambered. All you have to do is pull the trigger. Once I release you, you will pick up the gun and shoot the guy in the chair next to you."

Judith removed the blindfold from the kidnapper. She walked behind Brett and pressed her pistol against the back of his head. She cut his bonds and removed his blindfold.

"Brett, get up, go over to the table, and pick up the gun," Judith said. Everyone had their guns pointed at Brett. Brett stopped at the table and looked down at the gun. His hands were shaking as he picked up the gun. With Judith's pistol still pressed against the back of Brett's head, she walked him over to the bound kidnapper.

"Point the gun at his head." Brett was shaking so bad he was having difficulty holding the gun.

"Get closer, so you do not miss." The gun was only a few inches from the guy's head.

"I am going to count to three. If you fail to shoot him before the count of three, I will shoot you. I want to be sure you understand. Tell me what I just told you."

"I have to shoot him, or you will shoot me."

"Very good. You have until the count of three. One, two." The assassin's head jerked back and then fell forward. The sound of the gun was dampened by the silencer.

The man with the camera had switched the setting to video and nodded. Judith held out a small garbage bag and told Brett to drop the gun. The man with the camera put it in video replay. He played the video with Brett watching himself shoot the kidnapper. He removed the SanDisk and put it in the bag with the gun. He held out the camera to Brett, but Brett was too shocked to take it, so he just put the camera strap around Brett's head.

"Brett, you just murdered a man in cold blood," Judith said. "We have your fingerprints on the murder weapon and a video of you pulling the trigger. Also, no gun was pointed at you when you pulled the trigger." She had backed out of the picture when she started counting. She placed the blindfold back over Brett's eyes and secured his hands behind him.

"If you ever mention this to anyone, we will kill you. You need to leave Miami. Even better, I would recommend you consider leaving Florida. If you do not leave, this gun and a video of you murdering this guy will be turned over to the authorities. As a minimum, you will be sentenced to life in prison, but you will not live long in prison. However, I suspect you will die while waiting for your trial. One of my men is going to take you to your car. You have twenty-four hours before we come looking for you."

After several hours, Judith approached the female assassin. She had remained quiet throughout. She had answered their questions without being tortured. It showed she had some intelligence.

"We used your key card to collect your luggage from your hotel room," Judith said. "You seem to have many names. Lilith Talon appears to be your legal name, but you have multiple passports using other names. However, the oldest passport has the name Edah bat Carel. You are Jewish by birth which is why I am curious why you would try to claim an assassination fee from a group responsible for the death of so many Jews."

"What are you talking about?"

"The Diocletian Knights is the organization offering the fee for Angel's death." Judith had just learned about the organization from Angel.

"I am not familiar with this group," Lilith said. "In the assassin guild, the Okuri posts the rewards on the Mortality List, and the employer remains anonymous while the Motojime manages the transaction. The money is deposited in advance, so payment is assured."

"Is there any reason I should spare your life?" Judith asked.

"If you let me go, I promise to leave without trying to collect the fee for Angel's death."

"You are not offering anything. I already have that by killing you. What else can you offer? Please do not insult me by offering money."

"I am not the only assassin or hunter looking to collect the fee for terminating Angel Carpenter. I have a list of the primary hunters, including their pictures, aliases, and most recent locations."

"Why would you go to the trouble of maintaining a file on these individuals?"

"When I first started, I was lucky to have an excellent mentor. He had three primary rules. Stay current on technology, keep your identity completely secret, and keep track of all the other individuals in our line of work. Technology allows me to be good at my job. I have a Bachelor of Science Degree in Information Technology and a Master of Science in Cybersecurity. I attend seminars and conferences each year to network with the best technology nerds. Technology Consultant is my primary occupation. Most people you assassinate will have friends or family. If the family becomes aware of the killer, then they are likely to put out a contract on the killer. That is the reason for secrecy. Some assassins brag about their exploits. Bragging is a good way to die since the person likely to kill an assassin is another assassin. Until today, no one knew of my second occupation. There are at least five other assassins in Miami. Two are good, while the other three are average. Killing me will not save Angel's life. You need to eliminate these other assassins and send a message to any future assassins who may think Angel is an easy payday."

Judith was thoughtful. "I have a proposition. You will stay away from Angel and assist us in eliminating the other assassins who are here. Once completed, you will send messages to all other assassins telling them to stay out of Miami unless they want to die. I will hold on to your passports and other identification documents. If you help us, I will return all your documents. However, I will distribute your documentation to all the social media sites if you double-cross us or leave before the other assassins are eliminated. Also, people who double-cross my family do not live long. Do you wish to accept my terms?"

"I do not have a choice. Yes, I agree to your terms."

Over the next two weeks, they distributed copies showing the assassins' pictures, names, and aliases to their mafia family. They used their considerable number of operatives to check hotels and motels in Miami. It usually only took a few dollars for a night attendant to give access to a hotel registry and the outside videos. Even the smallest motels had video surveillance. They showed pictures of the assassins and asked about anyone with an accent. It took time, but the mafia employed thousands of people. Lilith used her tech skills to locate people who were searching for Angel on the internet. Each time they found an assassin, Lilith would spend several days reconnoitering the location.

The first assassin brought a prostitute to his room. Lilith accosted the prostitute who used the name Josephine as her working name. Lilith paid her for the information concerning her client. The next night Lilith called him. She introduced herself as a friend of Josephine. He asked to look at her. She switched the call to video, and he liked what he saw. A little later, she knocked on his door. She shot him through the heart as soon as he opened the door. A silencer was attached to the gun, and the sound was not noticeable. He fell backward and landed hard on the carpeted floor. She shot him twice more through the heart and once through the head. She used her phone to take several pictures of his dead body. She took his cellphone and removed the SIM card. Lilith searched the room. She found a portable computer and took it with her. She was wearing gloves and left no fingerprints. Lilith had worn one of her disguises but was still careful to avoid showing her face at the security cameras.

Lilith followed the next assassin down a street at night. She shot him twice in the back as she walked past him. She was carrying some loose clothes she had purchased, which completely hid the gun. The two hollow point bullets expanded as they pierced his heart.

The third assassin stayed at an upscale hotel and had dinner at the same time each night. Lilith asked Judith to join her, and they paid the hostess extra for a table close to the assassin. The assassin was well dressed but nondescript. They discussed how Judith had been cured of cancer by Doctor Angel Carpenter. Judith then talked about spending the night with Angel at his apartment.

The assassin interrupted them. "I know about Doctor Carpenter. I want to meet him since I have cancer. Unfortunately, I could not get an appointment to see him at the hospital. Would you mind telling me where he lives? Without his help, I will die. Please, I am desperate. I will even pay you for the address. I just need to see Doctor Carpenter for five minutes."

Judith gave him an innocent look. "I do not think it would hurt to give his address to a potential patient." She gave him an address in the boondocks, away from other homes. Lilith used her rifle with its scope and shot the assassin the following night just as he stepped out of his car.

Like Lilith, several of the assassins watched the court trial of Angel which was available for viewing on various online media sites. They misinterpreted the testimony of Joseph Adler and thought he would help them locate Angel Carpenter. Most of the gang members in Miami had watched the court trial and now considered Angel to be a true gang hero. The Warlocks under Joseph Adler contacted other gangs in Miami. They were to let him know if anyone was asking about Angel. Joseph wanted it passed around that he knew where Angel lived and would disclose the address for the right price.

Joseph received a call from the Demons gang. The Warlocks had no issues with the Demons.

"Joseph, this is Luke. I am calling on behalf of the Demons. We have a guy here who is looking for Angel. I told him you knew were Angel lives. He paid me a thousand dollars to setup a meeting, but he wants it in a public place."

"Tell him to come to the Roadhouse Grill tomorrow afternoon at three o'clock." Joseph said. He immediately held a meeting with his senior members.

"The meeting is setup for tomorrow at the Roadhouse Grill," Luke said to Lotte which he assumed was a bogus name.

"Would you like to make some additional money?" Lotte asked.

"Even though the meeting is in a public restaurant, I would like to hire some backup who are not afraid of a little wet action if necessary. The meeting should only take a few minutes. I want two men to accompany me. I will pay them a thousand dollars each."

"Make it three men at a thousand dollars each, and I will join you," Luke said.

"Fine, but I will pay you after the meeting."

The following afternoon, Luke, Lotte, and two other members of the Demons arrived at the Roadhouse Grill. It was somewhat isolated. It was essentially a bar that served food. A bouncer stood outside the establishment. His job for the day was to turn away any normal customers. The only customers inside were Warlocks and employees. Few people knew that Joseph owned the restaurant even though it was not in his name. The Warlocks were spread out. Most were eating at various tables, but several sat at the bar having a beer.

As they entered the restaurant, Lotte noticed the two bouncers standing on either side of the door and knew they were armed. They proceeded to Joseph who was sitting alone at the furthest table with his back to the wall. Joseph motioned to the chairs facing him. Lotte and two of the men sat down on either side of him.

"I am looking for Angel Carpenter and heard you might know where he lives," Lotte said. A server came over to the table and set beers in front of Lotte and his guests.

"Yes, I do, but it will cost you," Joseph replied. "Before I give you the location, I am curious. What do you want with Angel?"

Lotte was beginning to feel uncomfortable. He had pulled his gun when he sat down, and it was hidden from view under the table in his right hand. He took a sip of the beer with his left hand.

"I am under the impression you do not like Mr. Carpenter. Is that correct?"

Joseph gave a tight-lipped smile and said: "You are correct."

"Then my visit with Mr. Carpenter should not concern you. I am willing to pay you five thousand dollars for the address, but it needs to be his current address. I have already visited his former apartment, and it has been vacant for several months."

Joseph turned towards Luke. "You have done us a service," Joseph said. "Finish the job." Luke had previously asked to kill Lotte to gain favor with the Warlocks. He reached for his gun.

Lotte realized he had been setup. He stood up while flipping the table over. Joseph fell over backwards behind the table. The two men on either side of him were going for their guns. Lotte shot the person on his right and used the person on his left as a shield while pumping several rounds into his body. Luke dove behind the table when he saw Lotte moving the gun in his direction. Lotte turned and ran towards the entrance door. He shot the two men standing on either side of the door. He was only halfway there when his body was struck by a dozen rounds.

Joseph was up and saw the bullets were having little effect on Lotte. He lowered his aim and started firing his 9mm Ruger at Lotte's legs. Lotte rolled on his back as he crashed to the floor and continued firing until his gun was empty. He ejected the empty magazine and attempted to reload when a dozen Warlocks emptied their guns into his body. No one stopped firing until they were certain he was dead. Joseph walked over and ripped open Lotte's shirt. Lotte was wearing a custom-made bullet-proof vest. Joseph

checked the Warlocks and his employees. Two Warlocks and two
Demons were dead. Four Warlocks and two employees were
wounded. It should not have occurred, and he knew this was his
fault. He had underestimated his opponent and his gang paid the
price for his incompetents. He took credit for the good and accepted
responsibility for the bad. He saw Lotte was wearing a money belt.
Joseph removed it and handed it to Luke.

"Divide this equally between the Warlocks and the Demons,"
Joseph said to Luke.

"Greg, call the Swartz Funeral Home," Joseph said. "Tell Miguel
we need to have some deceased members cremated. We will pick up
the ashes later for a private Warlock funeral. Luke, would you like to
have your two members cremated?"

"Yes," Luke responded. "I would like that."

"Howard, collect all the guns that were fired," Joseph said. "I
want them soaked in bleached to destroy the DNA and then
dumped in the ocean and not all in one place."

"Listen up everyone. Bring all the wounded against the far wall. I
want everyone to clean this place until it shines. Greg, have someone
remove Lotte's vest, then dump his body where it will be found.
Make sure no one sees the body being dumped and anyone touching
the body is to wear gloves." Everyone went to work.

Joseph dialed a number and waited for it to be answered. Angel
was making his rounds at the hospital when his regular phone
vibrated. He recognized the caller ID and answered the call.

"Hello Joseph. I assume this is not a social call."

"No, it is not. I need your help again. I have six wounded
Warlocks who require medical attention. Before you state the
obvious. We cannot call for an ambulance or take them to the
hospital."

"The Warlocks have a fierce reputation, and I cannot believe
another gang attacked you."

"It was not another gang. It was one person," Joseph said and paused. "And Angel, he was looking for you."

Angel knew it had to be an assassin looking to earn the reward for his death. "I will be there shortly." Angel went to his office and transferred the text message to one of his burner phones. He grabbed a duffle bag and when to the supply room.

Angle saw that someone had ordered additional cases of trauma kits. He loaded six kits into his bag along with a surgical kit, several bottles of Chlorhexidine to clean the wounds, a box of needles, Lidocaine and six bags of IV solution. Angel wrote down of list of what he had taken and went to the nurses' station.

"Michelle, here is a list of items I took from the supply room. I will replace these personally at my expense." Michelle read the list and immediately knew Angel was going to be treating gun wounds off the grid. She shook her head.

"I am going with you and do not even thing about saying no. You are going to need a nurse assistant and how do you plan to get off site. We can use my van and if you lay down in the middle row no one will see you." Michelle called admin and told them she had to leave the hospital to take care of a personal emergency.

Michelle grabbed her purse and said: "Let's go."

Angel gave Michelle the address, and she entered it into the van's GPS. Once they were a safe distance from the hospital, Angel moved into the front passenger's seat.

As she was driving, Michelle chuckled. "Angel, you are the only doctor I know who is crazy enough and stupid enough to do this."

They arrived at the scene. Angel grabbed the duffle bag, and they hurried into the restaurant. Joseph greeted them and gave a brief introduction to the patients who were either sitting or lying on the floor. Angel with Michelle assisting, quickly examined each victim. Two would need surgery, but he was thankful none of the patients were in a life-threatening condition. They set up an IV drip for the two patients who would need surgery.

They proceeded to handle the four non-surgical patients first. In each case, the bullets had gone completely through the victims. The area around the entry and exit wounds were injected with Lidocaine, a local anesthetic. They cleaned the wounds with Chlorhexidine, an antiseptic antibacterial agent. The wounds were packed with hemostatic dressing. The blood clotted and the bleeding stopped. They then applied wound seal bandages to the wounds. They worked together with precision and anyone watching would assume they had been working together for years. None of the four patients had lost enough blood to require IV fluids.

One of the patients had a large gash in his back from how he fell after being shot. Michelle agreed to take care of suturing the laceration while Angel examined the two patients who would need surgery to remove the bullets.

A young female girl approach Michelle and asked if she could help. Michelle saw the desire in the girl's eyes.

"Yes, you may assist, but you will need to listen carefully and follow my instructions. What is your name."

"Donna," she replied. "I have always wanted to be a nurse. I am saving my money for nursing school, but it is going to take me a long time."

"How did you do in high school?" Michelle asked.

"I graduated last year and was an honor roll student. My mom was very happy, but I have been unable to find a good job. I work here as a server, but the tips are not very good."

Michelle had Donna put on medical gloves. She instantly liked the young girl and Donna was helpful. She finished suturing the wound and let Donna applied Polysporin ointment over the sutures. Michelle allowed Donna to apply the wound seal bandages under her direction.

"Donna, how would you like to work at a hospital? I suspect it will pay a lot more than you are making here and it will help with your admittance when you apply to a nursing college. Call me if you are interested and I will help you with the application."

"I definitely want the job," Donna said with enthusiasm. "Can I come by tomorrow?"

"Yes, you may. Give me your cellphone." Michelle entered the name of their hospital, the address, and her personal phone number.

"Come see me tomorrow," Michelle said.

"I will," shouted Donna with excitement. The patient thanked them, and Michelle went to assist Angel.

"I want to take care of this patient first. The bullet will be easy to remove. It is not very deep, and it is against his right clavicle." Michelle injected the Lidocaine into the area around the wound. Angel was correct. It only took him a few minutes to remove the bullet. They patched the wound.

Angel examined the last patient. He was fully conscious and was joking with one of the other patients. Angel removed the IV from both patients and told one of the Warlocks that he needed to see Joseph. It was only a few minutes before Joseph arrived.

"This patient needs to go to a hospital," Angel said. "An x-ray is needed to locate the bullet. I have done all I can do without causing more harm than good. Fortunately, these other patients were not as serious. Also, I have prepared prescriptions for each patient. Make sure the prescriptions are filled and see that they take all the medication. I need to see them in three days for a follow-up. I will see them at the end of my shift. Make sure they show up."

"Greg, take Cole to the emergency room and stay with him," Joseph said. "You know how to answer any questions if the police show up." Greg had another member assist him.

"Thank you, Angel," Joseph said. "Taking one person to the emergency room will not generate the same attention as six. You need to keep your head down. This gunman was looking for you and he was not seeking a social meeting."

"I know and thank you. I am sorry for the two Warlocks who died." Angle nodded to Michelle, and they left. Michelle returned Angel to the hospital before heading home. She had heard enough of the conversations to know that Angel was in danger.

The meeting with the second assassin was in an alley on a side street. This time the Warlocks did not socialize. They shot the assassin full of holes when he identified himself. The Warlocks had a private funeral for the two Warlocks who were killed. A representative from the Demons attended. Even after dividing the money from the first assassin with the Demons, they still recovered over thirty thousand dollars from the bodies. The majority of the money came from the money belt from the first assassin. It contained gold coins in addition to the cash. Angel managed to replace the supplies he had borrowed before the monthly inventory.

The police were surprised when some of the recent murder victims were listed with Interpol as known assassins. They could not determine why so many European killers were found dead in Miami.

Judith identified the two assassins killed by the Warlocks from the mug shots posted by the Miami Sheriff's Department. Lilith used her hacking skills to post pictures of seven dead assassins under Angel Carpenter's name on the Mortality List. After careful thought, she added her own pseudonym, which increased the list to eight. She used a male body burned beyond recognition for her posting.

Below the pictures, Lilith posted a notice. "These eight assassins tried to collect the funeral fee for Angel Carpenter, but they are the ones who are dead. Any future assassins coming to Miami will be dealt with in a similar fashion. We have the identities of everyone who has ever accessed the Mortality List, and you will be killed if you come to Florida." Lilith did not have all the identities, but the assassins would believe the posting.

Judith returned all of Lilith's passports and other identifications. She also gave her a copy of the information on the Diocletian Knights she had received from Angel. They dropped Lilith at the airport and made sure she was on the departing flight.

Lilith arrived back at her residence in France and continued her work as a technology consultant. Her home had a soundproof basement where she practiced her death skills. She had a local health club membership and used it to stay physically fit.

The computer file Lilith received from Judith piqued her curiosity. She spent considerable time researching the Diocletian Knights and their location in the Bailiwick of Jersey. She was fluent in Hebrew, English, French, Spanish, Italian, and Portuguese. This allowed her to extend her research using various languages.

Lilith sent an encrypted email to Hannah, her mother, in Tel Aviv, where she worked at the Civil Service Commission. Edah bat Carel, otherwise known as Lilith, asked her mother to find whatever information she could about the Diocletian Knights. She also attached a photo of a painting by Amedeo Modigliani. Many paintings were in the digital file she had received, but Modigliani was a great Jewish painter. She told her mother the painting might be an original and asked her to check with the Antiquities Authority to see if they had any relevant information.

Lilith had left Israel after having a bitter fight with her father but stayed in touch with her mother via email. She received a reply wherein her mother would attempt to collect the information. Then she asked too many personal questions. The following day, Hannah contacted friends at several agencies requesting their help. She freely told them she was gathering the data for her daughter.

Several days later, two agents from Mossad visited Hannah at her office and asked her to go with them to their headquarters. When she arrived, her husband was there. She was surprised because he worked for Aman, the military intelligence agency. Mossad wanted to talk to them about their daughter, the Diocletian Knights, and the Modigliani painting.

Judith was satisfied with the outcome of working with Lilith. She had grown to like the female assassin. Also, her husband was supportive of her helping Angel. He loved his wife and knew he would have lost her without Angel's help.

The oldest person working for Judith said: "You differ from your father. He would have killed Lilith and the paparazzo on the same night we rescued Angel's mother."

"You prefer my father's way of handling business?" Judith asked.

"No, I did not say that. I am just pointing out the difference. Actually, I liked the way you handled everything. You were very thorough, and the results were excellent. Your father is direct and does not think about other alternatives. Over the years, I think he wasted a lot of potential assets. However, he is proud of you. He enjoyed it when I told him how you handled the paparazzo and had Lilith kill of the other assassins. It accomplished our goal and kept our hands relatively clean."

"It worked out well," said Judith. "I am glad we could help Angel. I will always be in his debt. Plus, Doctor Angel is willing to break the rules and work outside the law when needed. We may need such a doctor in the future. However, I cannot understand how a doctor could get into so much trouble. I do not believe this will be the end of Doctor Carpenter's difficulties. We will continue to protect Angel, but secretly, in the shadows."

Angel was unaware of the actions of Judith and the additional actions of Joseph. However, he had his suspicions when he read the online articles of the recent killings in Miami of known assassins. The reports said the police had no suspects. One article said it was unlikely the killers would be brought to justice, but maybe justice had already been served. The police had posted a notice asking anyone who might have information concerning the murders to contact the police department, but no one came forward. The murders were destined to be closed as unsolved cases.

Angel returned to his regular work routine but continued to be concerned about his mother. They made a point of getting together often for lunch or dinner. Sometimes, his mother would meet him at the hospital for lunch, and they would eat in the hospital cafeteria. At other times, he would wear his disguise, and they would have dinner together at a restaurant. It was a risk, but they wanted to spend more time together after facing death. Angel knew his mother missed his father and the time they spent together reduced her loneliness. She had recently become friends with a lady in a similar situation, and he was hopeful their friendship would grow.

Angel worried about his mother, his patients, and the hospital. His patients were learning how to eliminate their stress, but his stress was increasing. His meditation techniques for handling stress were no longer working. He kept wishing everything would return to normal, but he doubted he would get his wish. He prayed and hoped it would not get any worse. After praying, he felt better but also embarrassed. People were dying of cancer, and he was feeling sorry for himself. He followed his own advice and thought about all the positive things in his life. Then, he pulled up his patient files and went back to work.

CHAPTER 14 MASS MEDIA

Harrieta Connor and her producer continued to be excited as the ratings kept growing. Having Doctor Angel Carpenter on the show had moved them into the top position for their time slot. The cost of producing their talk show was low, resulting in excellent profits. Incorporating angels and specifically Doctor Angel Carpenter, into the show was driving the current ratings.

Therefore, they continued to add an angel segment at the end of each show as their ratings went up and stayed up. During the first four-week segment, each night of the show ended with a person or group all supporting the existence of angels while claiming Doctor Angel Carpenter was an actual angel. During the following four weeks, they ended their show with science fiction celebrities declaring Doctor Angel Carpenter was one of many aliens living among us. Their third four-week segment consisted of individuals who insisted Doctor Angel Carpenter was both an angel and an alien. They highlighted the hostage situation with interviews spotlighting Doctor Angel Carpenter as a fearless hero who single-handedly rescued the hostages. The show had unprecedented ratings across all demographics, with everyone glued to the show each night. The Angel segments were going so well, they made it a permanent part of the show.

Unfortunately, it was creating major problems at the hospital. The number of spectators surrounding the hospital continued to increase every day. The crowd consisted of those wanting to see the angel, those hoping to see the alien, and those wanting access to the cancer drugs. The hospital hired off-duty police officers to supplement their security guards.

Angel received a call from Doctor Stanford letting him know the two prior guests from the Vatican wished to meet with him again in the same conference room. Lorenzo and Domenico were sitting at the conference table when Angel entered, and he motioned for them to remain seated. Angel joined them and sat down.

"The situation has changed," Lorenzo said. "The Diocletian Knights originally put out a kill order for your death on the assassins' Mortality List in the amount of one million euros. The amount has just been increased to five million euros. It seems eight assassins were killed in Miami, and a higher fee was demanded. The first part of our mission is to warn you. The second part is to repeat our offer of sanctuary within the Vatican. Plus, a medical clinic exists within the Vatican where you could continue the practice of medicine."

Angel was thoughtful for a moment. "Does the Pope know I am Protestant and not Catholic?"

"Yes, the Pope knows you are not Catholic," Lorenzo said.

"Does the Pope think I am an angel?" Angel asked.

Domenico chuckled. "No, the Pope does not think you are an angel, but he believes you are doing God's work. You cannot continue that work if you are dead. The Pope watched the trial and the Harrieta Connor's Show with great delight. Unofficially, the Pope believes you are a saint. Under Catholic Doctrine, a miracle is required for sainthood and there are few of those in the modern world."

"I do not wish to disappoint the Pope, but I have not performed any miracles. The ladies who said I healed their breast cancer, did not have cancer. The hype over none of my patients dying is also not true. Mary Baker was one of my patients and she died, but she intentionally switched to Doctor Andrew just prior to her death."

Domenico had a knowing smile. "Do you pray over each of your patients?"

"Yes," Angel answered.

"Is it not a miracle each time a terminal patient survives?" Domenico asked.

Angel did not have an answer. He appreciated the church's effort in sending Domenico and Lorenzo to meet with him.

"Thank you for the warning. I am not prepared to accept your continued kind offer of sanctuary at this time, but I may change my mind if the situation does not improve. I appreciate the information you have provided. Also, please tell the Pope I am profoundly grateful for the offer of sanctuary and the information you have provided."

"You have our number," Lorenzo said. "Call us if you change your mind or if you need our help." Lorenzo doubted Doctor Carpenter understood the seriousness of the kill order contract and was hopeful Angel would change his mind. Lorenzo was surprised Doctor Carpenter still lived but did not think he would be alive much longer. He was a soldier for the church and wished he could act. He gave Angel additional digital files on the Diocletian Knights.

Angel thanked them again as they were leaving the conference room. Angel wondered if he should accept the offer of sanctuary for a short time until his notoriety died down.

The situation was getting worse. With so many people crowded together, it would not take much for the crowd to become violent. Judge Terrell was now one of his patients and was responding positively to the cancer drug. He wondered if she could help. Angel entered Judge Terrell's hospital room.

"You are responding well to the treatment."

"I do not remember ever feeling this great," Judge Terrell replied. "Besides losing weight, I am full of energy and mentally relaxed thanks to being free from the daily work-related stress."

"Your cancer cells are decreasing each day. By the end of your treatment, I expect you will be completely cured with no cancer remaining."

"Great, I knew you would cure me. After all, you are an angel. I will hate checking out and leaving the hospital. This lifestyle is excellent. The food, exercise routine, and yoga classes are wonderful. I have never felt so relaxed and physically fit."

"Are you aware of what is taking place outside?" Angel asked.

"Yes, my husband has been visiting me regularly and has informed me of the large numbers of people surrounding the hospital."

"It cannot continue," Angel said. "The Board of Directors for the hospital has continued to support me, but the support is decreasing each day. Hopefully, the crowd will dissipate if I leave, and the hospital can return to some form of normalcy. Also, there is a sizable reward for my death, and I barely survived a recent attempt on my life. I was wondering if it would be possible for me to enter the federal witness protection program and get a new identity?"

"I am sorry," Judge Terrell said. "You would not qualify for witness protection since you are not a witness, and the program under the United States Marshals Service does not allow for any variation. However, let me contact someone who may be able to provide you with a new identity. No promises, but I will do my best to help you."

Angel thanked the Judge and went back to doing follow-up examinations with his patients. He continued to be impressed with Doctor Fredrick. She and Doctor Seneca were a great team. Angel believed they would do an excellent job if they had to finish the drug trial without him.

The media had located his new apartment location, and while they could not get past the guard station, hundreds of vehicles parked outside the enclosed area. Angel was sleeping at the hospital on a permanent basis since social media showed his rental car on multiple sites. He needed to get additional clothing, suitcases, and other items from his apartment.

Angel decided it was time to visit his apartment, but he would have to get help. The day shift was nearly up. He grabbed a folded clean sheet from a linen cart before going to the front desk. Angel told the staff he lived in Wynwood and asked if they knew anyone who lived in the same area who could drop him off at his apartment.

Two of the ladies grinned at each other and said they knew someone who would be happy to give him a ride home. A young nurse was in love with Angel, and he was all she talked about.

It was only a few minutes before an attractive nurse in her early twenties showed up. "Hi, I am Jackie. I hear you need a ride."

"I would be extremely grateful. I need to leave without anyone seeing me. I will hide on the floor of your vehicle until we get past the crowd." Jackie grinned at her friends at the desk.

"I will be back in a few minutes. I drive a silver-gray Chevrolet Traverse."

Angel spotted the Traverse as Jackie drove the vehicle close to the entrance, leaned over, and pushed open the passenger side door. Angel walked out behind a couple who were leaving. He jumped into the Traverse, got on the floor, and covered himself with the sheet.

Jackie drove for several miles. "It is safe for you to get up now. We are over two miles from the hospital, and the windows are tented."

Angel maneuvered into the passenger seat and buckled the seatbelt. He gave Jackie the directions to his apartment.

"Thanks again for your help," Angel said. "Where do you live?"

"Cutler Bay," she answered.

"Cutler Bay is in the opposite direction. This is way out of your way."

"It is all right," Jackie replied. "I was happy to give you a ride."

Angel called the gate guard at his apartment complex and had Jackie placed on the visitor's list. They reached Angel's apartment without incident as he hid on the floor once again. "Would you mind if I came in for a cup of coffee, so I do not fall asleep on the way home?" Jackie asked.

"Sure, I have not been home in a while, but I have plenty of coffee."

Angel stopped, opened his mailbox, and pulled out a double handful of junk mail. Part of the mail was addressed to the company, while the balance was to the Current Tenant without specifying a name. He threw it in the nearby trash container. He unlocked the door to his apartment and held it open for Jackie.

"Make yourself at home, and I will make the coffee."

Angel put coffee in the coffee pot and turned it on. He reached into the cabinet and took out a mug. He turned around, and Jackie was standing within a few inches of him.

"I have always wanted to kiss an angel," Jackie said as she leaned into him.

She was breathless when they separated. "You will need a ride to the hospital tomorrow morning, and I am already here. Forget the coffee. I am going to take a quick shower, and you can join me in the bedroom after I am done, or you can join me in the shower if you like."

She removed her clothes and took a quick shower. She dried off and got into bed naked underneath the sheets. She called Angel, and he came into the bedroom. However, he surprised her. He opened the closet door and took out a spare pillow along with a blanket.

"Angel, are you gay?" She asked as he turned to leave.

"No, I am a heterosexual male. Before you ask, I find you attractive and desirable."

"I flirted with you several times at the hospital, but you never noticed."

"I noticed," Angel said as he chuckled. Jackie tried a different tack.

"I used to attend church, and we had a preacher who said the thought was as bad as the deed. Since we have both had the thought, completing the deed will not be any worse."

Angel chuckled again. "Your preacher was wrong. Do you really want a one-night stand?"

Jackie displayed a mischievous grin. "If it is all I can get, but I would also be receptive to a two-night stand or more."

"I am leaving Miami in a couple of days, and any involvement would not be fair to either of us," Angel said. Jackie tried another approach.

"You do not have to sleep on the sofa. We can share the bed without having sex."

Angel did not say anything, he just laughed, and she grinned shamelessly. Angel asked: "Have you tried that before?"

"Yes, a guy told me that once and convinced me to spend the night. I guess it did not work too well. We had sex before falling asleep and again the next morning." She decided to change the subject.

"Why are you leaving?" She grinned again. "I mean, why are you leaving the hospital?"

"The hospital cannot function properly with the enormous crowd, and there is the concern the crowd could become violent at some point. Over a dozen people have passed out from dehydration and exposure. It needs to end, and my leaving should help get rid of the crowd. What is not common knowledge is that my life is in danger. Also, anyone close to me could be in danger. My mother was recently kidnapped, and friends of mine helped to rescue her or she would have been killed. There is a large reward for my death. I have to leave to allow the hospital to function properly, but I also have to leave if I wish to stay alive."

Jackie was despondent. "I was aware of the problems with the crowds but did not know you were in danger of losing your life. I understand why you need to leave. Thanks for being honest with me. I will miss you."

"I will miss working at the hospital," Angel said with sadness. "I will miss the staff and helping the patients. I will miss you too."

Jackie sat up, exposing her well-formed perky breasts, of which she was quite proud.

"Angel, am I going to hell for trying to seduce an angel?"

Angel laughed again and shook his head. "No, I think any act of seduction will be overlooked when compared to all the people you help each day at the hospital. The alarm goes off at five o'clock. Hit the top to shut it off."

Jackie was not currently dating anyone. Despite appearances, she was very selective in who she shared her bed. Jackie had not dated in a while, and now she was sexually frustrated. Several men at the hospital asked her for a date, but she had turned them down because she did not want any complications at work. However, she had decided to make an exception for Angel. She had fallen in love with him from watching him interact with patients and staff.

Angel knew he needed to avoid any complications with Jackie since it could become dangerous for her if they became involved. He was concerned about the safety of anyone close to him. He was so thankful his mother had survived the kidnapping. He did not want anyone else to face kidnapping or possibly death because of him. The representatives from the Vatican were quite convincing when warning him of the threat to his life. However, he was concerned about the danger to those around him. For five million euros, an assassin would not hesitate to kill witnesses or anyone who got in the line of fire. Also, people might harm individuals close to him to gain access to the cancer drug. The recent shooting at the hospital showed how ordinary people could do unbelievable things when they were desperate.

Jackie tried one more approach. "Angel, can we forget about the future? I do not want to be alone tonight. Stay with me." Then she made her final appeal that should convince even an angel. "Pleaseee."

The following morning, they took turns taking a shower. Jackie used some of Angel's deodorant and borrowed his toothbrush. She had tried on one of his shirts, and it was just long enough to cover her private parts. However, she took it off since she figured the religious hospital was not ready for a sexy nurse. Jackie frowned as she dressed in the clothes she wore the previous day.

Angel dressed in street clothes. He filled two suitcases and four garbage bags with clothes and personal items since he did not know when or if he would return. He threw out everything in the refrigerator. They enjoyed a cup of coffee and put the cups in the sink after rinsing them out.

They put the suitcases in the Traverse, and Angel gave Jackie directions to a nearby restaurant. Angel hid on the floor until they were several miles from the apartment. They would be late to work, but they had both worked a lot of overtime and knew the shift would be covered until they arrived. After calling the hospital to report their expected arrival time, they enjoyed breakfast and talked about everything except work.

Angel again hid on the floor of Jackie's car, covered by the sheet, as they made it past the crowd outside the hospital. Angel removed his suitcases and the garbage bags from the Traverse and thanked Jackie again for her help.

Jackie reported for her shift, and it was not long before one of her friends found her and asked for the details of her time with Angel.

"He was a perfect angel," Jackie said.

"What does that mean?" Her friend asked as Jackie was walking away.

Jackie smiled as she thought about the previous night with Angel.

George Martinez was in his office when a currier arrived with a delivery requiring his signature. He was not expecting a delivery as he set the box on his desk and used a pair of scissors to open it. George started examining the contents when a cold chill went through his body. Next, he reviewed the enclosed flash drive. George had a client he was trying to get into witness protection. The client had agreed to testify against the mafia in return for no jail time. However, his client was found dead before he was able to enter witness protection. George assumed his client had shipped him the box before his death.

George called Samuel Davis at the State Attorney's office. Samuel answered the phone, and the caller identification let him know who was on the line.

"Hi George, you have some nerve calling me," Samuel said in a formal voice. "Do not even try to ask me for a favor for one of your clients."

"No, I do not need a favor, but I think it is time for you to forgive me for embarrassing your department in court."

"You were just doing your job, but why should I forgive you?" Samuel asked.

"Because I have some evidence that will allow you to bring down two mafia organizations. I believe we should meet behind closed doors to review the information and decide how you want to proceed. This is so hot I burned my hands while examining the documents."

Samuel had known George for a long time, and while they were on opposite sides in court, he respected George. He did not think George would waste his time, and George's comment had piqued his curiosity.

"I am just doing paperwork. You can come over now if you wish."

George quickly responded. "I am on my way."

George called Domino's Pizza and used the drive-through to pick up a large pepperoni pizza. When George arrived, he was carrying the pizza on top of the evidence box. They went into a conference room and shut the door. Samuel asked one of his clerks to bring them two bottles of water. Samuel and George were already eating a slice of pizza when the clerk entered with the water.

She was staring at the pizza. "Go ahead," Samuel said. "You can have a slice."

She grinned as she grabbed a slice of the pizza and left the room. She closed the door on her way out. It did not take long for them to devour the pizza.

"Thanks for the pizza." Samuel said. "Now, show me the documents."

George took the documents out of the box and separated them into two piles.

Samuel skimmed through the first pile and looked at George with a shocked expression before starting on the second pile of documents.

Samuel finished reviewing the documents and skimmed the flash drive. The flash drive contained videos of criminal activities. "Who gave you these documents?" He asked.

George knew the documents likely came from his dead client, but he had a brainstorm of an idea.

"Angel," George said. "Angel Carpenter was responsible for getting me these documents, but you must not tell anyone."

Samuel had a puzzled look on his face before it changed to one of understanding. "My god, Angel is undercover. It must be deep cover for him to get this type of evidence. You should have told me he was undercover, and we would have dropped the case."

Samuel thought some more. "Angel did not want to break cover, and you could not risk it. I wondered why Angel met with the Judge after the trial was over. She was in on it. Even if we had won, the Judge would have dismissed the case in the end. Also, I reviewed the evidence for the traffic case you won for Angel and could not understand how you had all those videos. I remember thinking only a secret agent could have such videos. He has the perfect cover. He is a medical doctor and would have complete access to the mafia while treating them as his patients. No one would suspect him because he is a doctor, and the police hate him. Tell me, which agency is he working for?"

George shrugged his shoulders. "You absolutely must not talk about Angel having anything to do with this evidence. If anyone asks, you got the information from me, and I received the box anonymously. Also, you need to move on the locations identified in those documents as soon as possible." George knew the top level of law enforcement would discuss Angel's involvement. If Angel had any criminal matters in the future, it would hopefully be dismissed at the top. It would serve as an insurance policy, but George hoped Angel would not have any more issues with law enforcement.

Samuel took his cellphone and called Luke Abbott, the State Attorney for Miami-Dade.

The clerk took the call. "I have an emergency and need to meet with State Attorney Abbott immediately," Samuel said.

"I am sorry, but State Attorney Abbott is busy and has a full schedule," the clerk said.

"Tell Luke I must see him immediately, and he should reschedule his other appointments."

A few minutes later, she came back on the line. "State Attorney Abbott will see you now."

Samuel and George went to see the State Attorney. They took the elevator to the top floor and walked down the hallway. They entered the office and remained standing until State Attorney Luke Abbott finished his call. Luke motioned for them to take a seat.

When Luke finished the call, he put down the phone. "Tell me about this emergency and why it could not wait until tomorrow?"

Samuel placed the two sets of files on the State Attorney's desk. State Attorney Luke Abbott took his time reviewing the documents. "How reliable is this information?"

"I believe it is extremely reliable as of today," Samuel replied. "However, the mafia can change their operations at any time."

"You need to tell me who provided you with this information," Luke said. "It goes to reliability."

Samuel looked at George. "I am sorry, but he needs to know."

Samuel turned back to Luke. "These documents came from Angel Carpenter, but his involvement must remain secret."

Luke was thoughtful, and it only took a second for him to reach the same conclusion as Samuel. "Damn, Angel is undercover. He takes care of their medical issues, which gives him complete access to their entire operation. Also, he is a former gang leader, which places him beyond reproach. Plus, everyone in law enforcement hates him. It is the perfect cover."

Samuel called the FBI Miami Field Office and asked to speak to Special Agent Darnell. It was only a moment before Darnell was on the line.

"I have documents, along with videos, showing the locations for all the local addresses for two mafia operations along with names, bank accounts, emails, and details for various crimes committed by these two groups," Luke said.

"How quickly can you bring the documents to my office?"

"We can be there in an hour, but I need to call the State Attorney General first," Luke said.

After they hung up, Luke called the State Attorney General. She was out of the office, so he called her cellphone. He provided her with the information but did not mention Angel. He also asked her not to discuss it with anyone else. She promptly let him know she was aware of the need for confidentiality without being told. She then thanked him for keeping her informed.

Luke, Samuel, and George traveled to the main Miami Field Office. Miami also had four FBI satellite offices known as resident agencies. After reviewing the documents and asking George several questions, they no longer needed him. Fortunately, George had driven his car to the meeting since he expected to be dismissed. Special Agent Darnell called the Special Agents at the FBI Field Offices in Jacksonville and Tampa. They left a skeleton crew at the remote offices and brought all their Florida field agents to Miami. A federal judge issued search warrants for all the locations.

Three days later, they got the local SWAT teams, K-9 Units, and the local police as support but did not tell them where to go until the last minute. They hit all the locations simultaneously and made over two hundred arrests. Gunfire erupted at several of the sites, but it ended quickly. Several officers were injured, but only one seriously. Whereas the officers killed seven mafia members during the raids and two died later from gunshot wounds. The raids at each location were expertly handled, with the criminals being completely surprised. Several locations were involved in human trafficking. Other sites included cybercrime, credit card scams, extortion, arms smuggling, and illegal gambling. They recovered large quantities of arms, drugs, and cash.

There was enough publicity to go around with everyone taking a bow. Fortunately, no one mentioned Angel in the press releases. Even though it was classified confidential, it eventually became common knowledge among high-ranking officers and detectives that an angel had provided the information.

The five original mafia families celebrated behind the scenes since the competition had been reduced. They were also thankful to see the two most violent groups eliminated or at least severely diminished. The traditional mafia families did not want the publicity associated with the other groups and preferred to keep a low profile. Everyone wondered how the FBI had obtained so much data on the two mafia families they raided. The families wondered if the FBI was collecting similar information on their operations. They universally decided to be extra diligent.

CHAPTER 15 CROWD CONTROL

A few days later, an FBI agent showed up at the hospital and asked to speak privately with Angel. They went to Angel's office and shut the door.

"We have been monitoring the crowd situation here with some concern," Special Agent Darnell said. "Judge Terrell contacted the FBI Deputy Director, and he contacted our field office. We have experience creating identities for our undercover agents and are willing to create a new identity for you." He did not mention that he thought the Director's decision to help was reinforced by the success of the mafia raids.

He did not ask Angel about the information he provided on the mafia operations, since it would be top secret on a need-to-know basis. The FBI did not casually discuss top secret matters. However, he figured Angel worked within an FBI department since it was unusual to prepare a new identification based solely upon a judge's request.

"Has there been any additional progress on the poison vials?" Angel asked.

"I cannot comment other than to say I am no longer working on the case." He did not want to say the case was moved to the inactive file and would likely never be solved.

"I understand," Angel said. "What is the procedure for creating a new identity?"

"Preparing a new identity for a person to continue in a medical profession is quite involved since it requires creating a new social security card, driver's license, birth certificate, diplomas, certificates, and other items. These must be created as authentic documents so you can pass a background check, whether from an employer or someone in law enforcement. Do you still want to practice medicine?"

"Absolutely," Angel replied.

"Then we will need to provide you with a medical license under your new name, but first, you will need to change your appearance. You will need to dye your hair and use colored eye lenses. Brown hair would help. Also, you will need a spray tan. I will need an electronic photo of you after we alter your appearance."

"Once you have the photo, how long will it take to prepare the new identity?" Angel asked.

"To do a thorough job, two to three weeks. We have a safe house you can use until the new identity is ready."

"I need to be seen in a live televised disappearance to get rid of the crowd," Angel said. "I want to do the disappearing act on the air. Do you know of a good magician?"

"No but let me do a little research."

A few days later, a different FBI agent visited Angel. He told Angel he was on loan from a field office in California. His grandfather was a magician. He helped with his grandfather's act until he when to college. Angel learned there were multiple ways to make a person disappear. They spent nearly a week preparing the props and rehearsing the act. The hospital had agreed to cover the costs of the props.

Harrieta had left several messages asking Angel to call her. Angel took a different approach and called his attorney. Angel asked George to work out a deal where he would appear on the Harrieta Connor's Show from the hospital. Also, he asked George to arrange a fee for the appearance. Angel told George he could keep one hundred percent of the fee since he represented him in the criminal trial on a pro bono basis without pay. Angel further explained they could only bring one camera into the hospital, but they should bring an infrared lens. He told George to arrange for Harrieta to meet with him in private before the show. The show was scheduled one week in advance. Every night on her series, Harrieta promoted the night Angel would be on the show. George called him back and announced he was thrilled with the fee the network had agreed to pay after some serious negotiations.

Harrieta showed up at their pre-show meeting. "As you can see, the crowd outside is continuing to disrupt the hospital," Angel said. "Dozens of people in the crowd have required medical treatment in the emergency room. It will worsen unless we get the crowd to disburse peacefully. There is a growing threat the crowd could become violent. Also, I have been living at the hospital since I can no longer go out in public. As a result, I have submitted my resignation."

"Are you blaming me and my show for these problems?"

Angel leaned forward. "You are responsible!" Angel said with no attempt at diplomacy. "Also, if the crowd outside develops into a riot, your network could face lawsuits for injuries and property damages along with potential criminal charges for inciting a riot."

"I did not anticipate needing an attorney for this meeting," Harrieta said.

"You do not need an attorney for our conversation. I have no intention of bringing any legal action against you or the network. I asked you to meet with me so we can avoid any potential unpleasantness and help your show avoid potential third-party lawsuits. I need to disappear, and I need your help. I have a magician who will help me disappear on your show. You may present it however you want. I hate to mislead the people watching the show. However, trained psychologists have been interviewing people in the crowd. They say it would only take a spark for the crowd to turn violent. We must prevent the crowd from getting out of control and possibly rioting. Will you help end this potentially volatile situation?"

Harrieta thought for a moment. "Yes, I will help. I understand the need for secrecy, but I have to inform the producer."

Angel stayed extra busy preparing for his exit from the hospital. He called a meeting with Doctor Seneca, Doctor Fredrick, and the two interns. They met in Angel's office after borrowing a couple of chairs from Doctor Seneca's office.

"First, I would like to congratulate our two interns. You are now officially resident doctors," Angel said.

Both former interns thanked all three doctors who had helped with their internship training. They especially thanked Angel. They both knew having interned under such a famous doctor would permanently enhance their careers.

Angel continued after everyone settled down. "Harrieta Connor is going to conduct a live show here at the hospital. On the day of the show, my employment at the hospital will end."

"No, you cannot leave the hospital," Doctor Seneca said. "We need you here. They cannot fire you. You are responsible for the success of this drug trial."

Angel spoke with a subdued voice. "I voluntarily resigned to keep the hospital from being forced to terminate my employment. It is the only way to get rid of the crowd surrounding the hospital. I will miss working with all of you, but you no longer need me to continue to cure our patients. Mark, the Board of Directors has already approved you as my replacement to be in charge of this center. I know you will continue to do a fantastic job. The hospital has approved the addition of two new interns. I think our new resident physicians will enjoy challenging them the same way we challenged them." Both of the new residents grinned and nodded their heads.

"I have good news," Angel said and waited until he had their full attention. "I received notification from Tyzugmod that the FDA has approved the cancer drug, and I will make the announcement on the show to help spread the word."

"Finally," Doctor Seneca said.

Angel turned to Doctor Fredrick. "Tyzugmod has asked if you would like your job back with a promotion. It seems their other researchers are not having the same success as when you were there."

Doctor Fredrick shook her head. "I will send them my thanks, but I like working here too much to return to my old job, even with a promotion."

"I am glad you are staying," Angel said. "You four make a great team."

Doctor Benita Fredrick did not tell Angel how she and Mark had become much more than friends. At the hospital they used their last names, but after work it was Mark and Benita. She did not know if she was in love with Mark, but it was getting close. Regardless, she enjoyed working with patients and would not be happy returning to pure research. Here, she applied her research methods to real-life situations each day. Benita knew the real breakthrough improvements for the cancer drug were occurring at this hospital with actual patients and not in a lab. She was curing terminal patients, and testing mice did not provide the same satisfaction. Doctor Carpenter's positive attitude was affecting her belief in the holistic approach. She now believed the process might make it possible to improve the efficacy of other drugs. Without realizing it, she had accepted Angel's belief that most patients could eliminate their reliance on medicines if they lived a healthier lifestyle. However, there was little hope that people would change their lifestyles. The trillion-dollar drug industry would continue to grow, and she would always have a job.

Angel met briefly with Doctor Stanford and thanked the Chairperson for his support. Angel assured him the cancer drug trial would continue to do well without him.

"You have accomplished so much during your time with us," Doctor Stanford said sorrowfully. "This hospital is world famous because of your efforts. However, right now, it is a little too famous. Please keep in touch, and if you ever need a reference, just ask. You will always receive my highest recommendation."

Angel had one last goodbye. He located Jackie.

"Tomorrow will be my last day. I wanted to say goodbye."

"Come with me." She grabbed his hand and pulled him down the hallway and into one of the patient's rooms. There was an older lady asleep in the bed.

"I want a goodbye kiss."

Jackie put her arms behind his head and pressed her lips against his. He responded by putting his arms around her waist. Their bodies merged, and Jackie felt the same excitement she had during their first kiss. Her passion flamed, and she felt the heat of his body. After a moment, they pulled their lips apart with their bodies still pressed firmly against each other.

"I wish you were not going."

"I have the same wish, but there are no other options."

"We could stay in touch with email and the occasional phone call," Jackie said with complete seriousness. "I could use my vacation time to visit you, or maybe you could take me with you."

Angel lowered his voice. "You do not understand. I am going into hiding. I do not know where I will be from one day to the next. I may have to move about a lot. It will be difficult for one but impossible for two."

"If you are ever back in the area, you have an open invitation to stay at my place. You have my number."

"Thank you. I may just do that." Angel did not want to be cruel and say it was highly unlikely they would meet again.

They released their embrace, and Angel left the room. "Was the kiss as good as it looked?" Jackie was startled by the older lady, who was now awake.

Jackie walked over and sat in a guest chair to catch her breath. "No one can kiss like an angel. I hope he does not forget me."

"I think he will remember. He also seemed to enjoy the kiss."

"I had better get back to work," Jackie said with a sigh.

"If you ever need to kiss another angel, use my room. It is more entertaining than these reality shows."

Angel had ordered two additional large suitcases online, which had arrived several days earlier. He placed his personal Healthcare Pocket Ultrasound Dual Probe in the suitcase along with a doctor's medical kit, a doctor's trauma kit, two cases of antibiotics, a case of the cancer drug sufficient for eight patients, multiple bottles of the twenty most prescribed medications, an ultra-small portable defibrillator, a portable ultrasound, a Ri-Scope LED Otoscope and Ophthalmoscope Set, a urine analyzer, and a blood analyzer. The medical supplies filled two large suitcases and five wooden shipping boxes. He had purchased most of the items online and had received permission from Doctor Stanford to take whatever he wanted from the hospital's inventory. Each item from the hospital was separately approved and documented. All the equipment he ordered was the best currently available with the latest technology. The prices for medical equipment were technology-driven, and the costs were relatively inexpensive compared to historical prices. He wanted to be equipped to practice medicine wherever he went, and he would purchase other items as needed. Also, he needed to spend down his current bank accounts. He could not transfer funds from his old bank account into his new account since such transfers could be traced.

Angel purchased a new computer tablet with extra memory and a large drive for personal use. He downloaded the complete physician's library with a voice search smart app and the entire drug trial holistic files.

Angel purchased eight computer tablets and health watches since he had enough cancer drugs for eight patients. To these tablets, he downloaded the daily schedules for the cancer patients, the videos from the live class lessons, the daily menus, and all the holistic programs set up for the patients. Angel got the extra drugs even though production was still limited. The FDA was no longer involved in the distribution of the drug and Angel hoped to obtain additional drugs as needed.

Angel called his landlord and explained how he needed to break the lease, but all the furniture would be left behind in the apartment. She called him back two days later and said the unit had already been leased at double what Angel had been paying. She had listed it on eBay with bids starting at what Angel was paying or rent it now at double the amount. The apartment was leased ten minutes after the listing. She joked how she should have asked for three times the amount Angel paid. It seems people will pay a premium to live in an apartment formerly leased to an angel.

The landlord called Angel back a few days later. "You will not believe what the new tenant is doing at your apartment. He went on eBay and Amazon. He listed each item in your apartment for sale as owned by an angel. He is making a fortune. I am a complete idiot. Do you have anything else you do not want?"

"No, I left about everything I own at the apartment," Angel said. The landlord sighed and said goodbye.

The day arrived for the show. Harrieta interviewed dozens of preselected people outside the hospital earlier in the day. They then selected the best interviews and edited the final selections. They decided the show's interviews would have two-thirds saying Angel was an angel and one-third believing Angel was an alien. They added one interviewer who accused the drug company, the FDA, and the hospital of withholding a cancer cure and letting people die. They started with an aerial view showing the thousands of people surrounding the hospital. The interviews aired right before Angel's meeting but with a commercial break in between.

The stage was an empty conference room with two chairs. Angel and Harrieta were sitting at a slight angle to each other while facing the camera. Harrieta started the interview.

"There is a massive crowd outside. They all want to see you. Do you have any words for them?"

Angel looked straight at the camera with a solemn expression. "I wish everyone would return to their homes. It is dangerous to have so many people crowding around the hospital."

"I understand there was a recent shooter inside the hospital, and you were instrumental in getting him to surrender," Harrieta said.

"You are correct," Angel replied.

Harrieta hoped for more dialog from Angel. "I understand the gunman shot three people, and one died. What else can you tell us about the incident."

"Let us forget about the incident with the shooter," Angel said. "I agreed to meet with you to let the crowd outside know they are disrupting the hospital's operations and the cancer drug trial. However, tonight I have some good news. The FDA has approved the cancer drug. Cancer treatment centers throughout the United States will have access to the new drug. However, any center receiving the medication will need to be pre-approved and verify it will incorporate the holistic approach so they can achieve the expected results."

Angel paused for effect and then continued. "Further, as I have previously explained, the drug used alone is only around forty percent effective. That is why only pre-approved centers will be eligible to receive the drug. Treatment using the cancer drug with the holistic approach at Christian Health Hospital has resulted in a cure rate above ninety percent. The holistic approach has been posted on the hospital's website and is accessible to whoever wishes to download it. Also, the cancer drug with our holistic approach will continue to be offered at the Christian Health Hospital. That is the good news."

Angel paused for effect. "Now for the bad news. Unfortunately, the drug is difficult to manufacture, and the supplies will be limited until the Tyzugmod Corporation can increase production. Also, health insurance will only cover the cancer drug cost and routine medical care. Christian Health Hospital is a non-profit institution. The hospital will provide the meals and other parts of the holistic approach at cost, but the patients will have to cover these costs. However, many patients cannot pay for the costs not covered by insurance. The hospital depends on your donations, and your donations are desperately needed. The methods for making your contribution will be shown during the next commercial break and is also available on the hospital's website."

The producer motioned with his hand, indicating a commercial break. "I wish we had another camera and more room, but it still looks good," he said. The commercial break lasted four minutes, and they were back live.

"Everyone should be extremely excited with the FDA approval of the cancer drug," Harrieta said. "Again, we ask everyone surrounding the hospital to return to their homes. The continued crowd has created a hardship for Angel and the hospital. Angel, would you like to provide some additional information to our audience?"

Angel had prepared an additional announcement he had reviewed with George to avoid subjecting the hospital or the network to a lawsuit.

Angel looked straight at the camera again. "A different matter has come to my attention. I need to say the following are allegations and may be false. There is an organization operating out of the Bailiwick of Jersey that manages a billion-dollar Trust. It is my understanding they have complied with all the laws on the island. However, there is an allegation of a group within this organization who allegedly call themselves the Diocletian Knights. It appears they may have inadvertently supported Hitler during the war and may unknowingly possess artwork taken from France, Italy, and the Jewish community. Hopefully, the organization's top executives, who are serving as Trustees, will discuss the matter with the authorities to resolve any misunderstandings or show how these allegations are false. These are the current Trustees."

Photos of the five Trustees with their names were shown for several seconds before switching back to Angel.

"The following are a few of the paintings in possession of these individuals. These paintings appear to be originals."

They showed several paintings from each country describing each masterpiece before switching back to Angel.

Angel continued. "Further, it saddens me, but I want everyone to know that I can no longer continue my work at Christian Health Hospital. I have submitted my resignation to the hospital. My final act at the hospital and my purpose for agreeing to be on the show tonight is so I could say goodbye."

Harrieta used her acting skills to act surprised. "What exactly do you mean?"

Angel got out of his chair. He walked to the back wall and turned to face her.

"You may wish to switch your camera to infrared," Angel said.

The camera operator nodded to indicate he had switched the lens.

Angel looked directly at the camera. "My desire is for all of you to have a long, healthy, and faithful life."

Angel paused. "Goodbye."

There was a bright flash of both heat and bright light, which blinded everyone. There was a loud bang. It was a few seconds before they could see again, but Angel was gone. Harrieta looked around. There was only one door into the room, and it was behind the camera operator.

Harrieta did her best to look in the direction of the camera while her eyes were adjusting after the flash. "Angel has left us."

As planned, they switched to a commercial break. The commercial break ended, and they were back live. Harrieta stepped over to the wall and pulled down the white curtain they used as a backdrop for the camera. There was a solid wall with no exit behind the curtain. Harrieta examined the wall and banged her hand on it several times to show it was solid.

Harrieta faced the camera. "It appears Angel has disappeared from an enclosed room. He said goodbye, so it appears he has left us. I am not sure if Angel accomplished his disappearance using angel powers, advanced alien technology, or a magic act. However, I have received confirmation from the hospital that Doctor Angel Carpenter is no longer an employee. I would ask the crowd outside this hospital to honor Doctor Carpenter's request to disburse and return to your homes."

Harrieta saw the signal from the producer. "This is Harrieta Connor saying goodnight."

The camera operator turned off the camera. Harrieta methodically examined all the walls as she searched for a hidden door.

She looked at the camera operator and her producer. "That was some magic act. Does anyone have any idea how he did it?"

The producer and camera operator both shrugged their shoulders. They gathered up the equipment and left the hospital.

The FBI magician had watched from a monitor. The disappearance had been accomplished magically. His grandfather would have been proud of the act. He proceeded to the conference room to pick up his equipment. When he entered the room, there was a meeting in progress. They told him it was necessary to move the Harrieta Conner Show to a smaller room. The Agent went to the alternate room and saw his equipment was set up correctly. He wondered what technique Angel used to perform the disappearance since the rehearsed act relied on an exit door behind the curtain in the larger conference room. He nodded his head since they had discussed multiple ways to disappear.

Elsewhere in the hospital, Angel changed clothes, and the FBI agents escorted him through empty corridors to an emergency exit. The door alarm had been disconnected. A van was parked next to the door. Angel stepped into the van, and the door was closed. The agents had previously collected his personal property, including all the suitcases and boxes.

They drove Angel to an eye care facility that had agreed to stay open for a late visit. There was only one vehicle in the parking lot. They entered through a side door for employees only. An optometrist was waiting and took Angel to an examination room. The optometrist measured the curvature of Angel's eyes with a keratometer to determine the dimensions for the contact lenses. The examination did not take long since the optometrist only needed enough information to order custom color lenses and not corrective lenses. The complete process took about twenty minutes. The agents checked the parking lot before allowing Angel to return to the van. They drove for another hour before reaching the safe house.

The optometrist had expedited the order. A local lens manufacturer received a premium payment for an early morning delivery the following day.

Angel thanked all the agents for their help. The safe house had four bedrooms and three bathrooms. At least one agent would remain with Angel at all times. They had informed Angel that, unlike the Federal Witness Protection Program, they only provided the new identification. They would assist in locating potential employment and transport him to a destination he selected, but then he would be on his own.

The Trustees of the funds for the Diocletian Knights in the Bailiwick of Jersey had an emergency meeting. They dedicated the entire session to the old business of Doctor Angel Carpenter. They loudly expressed their displeasure with Doctor Carpenter. They were outraged he had the temerity to disclose their operation and show photos of them on a network talk show. Also, with his disappearance, it would be the perfect time to dispose of the doctor without drawing worldwide attention. They were concerned he would show up at a future date and continue to affect religion positively. They were unanimous in their desire to seek revenge for Angel's disclosure of their operation. A motion was made and approved to increase the amount to ten million euros for the assassination of Angel Carpenter. It would be a general offer open to anyone who could make the kill. The price would be over twelve million dollars at the present exchange rate. They knew such an offer was generous enough to interest the top assassins. Still, the amount would also attract lower-level assassins hoping for a big score and the chance to be taken seriously for future high-priced hits. They did not care who killed Angel. They just wanted him dead.

Lorenzo was unable to reach Angel. He called the attorney, George Martinez, provided the increased amount offered for Angel's death, and sent him an email with the attached documentation. Angel had informed George of his plans to change identities and move to a different location. George would miss seeing his longtime friend and hoped Angel's new identity would protect him. George's association with Angel had brought him priceless advertising, and he had hired two attorneys and four additional paralegals to handle the increased business.

Clients were retaining George for high-profile criminal cases, including very lucrative white-collar criminals. The district attorneys offered attractive plea agreements to George's clients because of the reputation George earned from defending Angel. Plus, the district and state attorneys were still understaffed and did not want to spend time in court with prolonged court trials. His clients similarly provided free advertising by telling everyone how the severe charges with long prison sentences were dropped by pleading to a minor charge. In some instances, all charges were dropped when George's preliminary evidence provided reasonable doubt. George's competitors did not receive the same generous plea agreements, and knowledgeable non-criminal attorneys started referring clients to George as their first choice for anyone needing a criminal trial attorney.

George paid off the mortgage on his condominium, paid off the balance of his student loans, bought a new car with cash, and was starting to build a nice nest egg for the future. His staff was doing an excellent job, and they were getting better each day.

CHAPTER 16 HIDING OUT

An agent brought Angel's suitcases and boxes to the safe house. The FBI had assigned Special Agent Ruiz to the safe house for the duration. Angel left his old tablet with Mark and canceled service on the old cellphone. Agent Ruiz had destroyed Angel's old cellphone before bringing him to the safe house.

Angel was given brown hair coloring, which he used to dye his hair before turning in for the night. It looked dyed. The next morning, he woke up at his usual time of five o'clock. After taking a shower and shampooing his hair, he noticed his hair had a more natural look. Angel dressed in jeans, a navy polo shirt, and white sneakers trimmed in blue.

Angel went into the kitchen and prepared a pot of coffee. He could not remember the last time he had nothing to do. He made breakfast for himself and the agent. Angel was on his second cup of coffee and had just started eating when Agent Ruiz entered the kitchen.

"Your breakfast is on the stove," Angel said and pointed to the food.

Agent Ruiz made himself a cup of coffee and grabbed a plate. He loaded his plate with scrambled eggs, bacon, and pancakes.

"Thank you for breakfast. How long have you been up?"

"I have been getting up every morning at five o'clock for so long that I just wake up automatically."

After breakfast, they stacked the dishes in the dishwasher. It was not long until they heard the garage door open and close. The door into the garage had been locked. There was a knock on the door.

Agent Ruiz knew never to assume anything. With his hand on his gun, he stood to one side of the door. "Who is there?"

"Darnell."

Agent Ruiz relaxed and unlocked the door. Agent Darnell gave Angel a small bag containing his brown contact lenses. It took Angel several minutes to put the lenses in his eyes since he had no experience using contacts. He did not like the feel of the lenses but figured he would get used to it in time. Angel had perfect vision and had never needed glasses. He looked in the mirror. The brown contacts and hair dye had significantly changed his appearance.

"We are going to a spray tanning salon, so you need to change into loose-fitting clothes," Agent Darnell said.

Angel returned to the bedroom, changed into shorts, and removed his socks. When Angel was ready, the three of them went into the garage. Agent Darnell took the driver's seat. Agent Ruiz slid into the front passenger seat, which left the backseat for Angel. The early morning Miami traffic was always bad. It was only a little after nine when they arrived at an upscale spray tanning salon. A reservation had been made, and Angel was their first customer. The Agents checked out the entire facility before allowing a salon employee to take Angel into one of the back rooms.

An employee told Angel to undress down to his underwear. Then, the employee helped him apply a moisturizer to his entire body.

"The special moisturizer will make the tan last longer," she said. "Our tanning salon is unique because we use both a tanning bed and a spray tan. For a Floridian, you have almost no tan. Therefore, you will only spend five minutes in the tanning bed before we spray you.

The spray tan will last about two weeks, while the tan from the bed will last from four to six weeks.

She painted his fingernails and toenails with an ointment. She explained how the ointment would wash off but would prevent his nails from discoloring. The sales pitch was to show how their salon provided all the little extras not available at the cheaper spray tanning salons. The alarm in the tanning bed sounded after five minutes. After being sprayed, he remained in a waiting room for about thirty minutes before the spray was dry enough to get dressed. The written instructions said to wait twenty-four hours before taking a shower. They drove back to the safe house. Agent Ruiz remained with Angel.

The following morning Angel shampooed his hair for the second time. After showering, he got dressed and looked at himself in the mirror. The medium tan and brown hair appeared natural. Putting in his colored contact lenses proved easier, but the lenses were still uncomfortable. Angel conducted a search on wearing contacts and read how it would take several days to get accustomed to the lenses.

Shortly after breakfast, a photographer came to the safe house and took a dozen digital pictures of Angel. "For your identification photos, I will lighten your skin color to about halfway between your current tan and your normal skin color. People will forget about Angel Carpenter in a month, and your tan will not be an issue. However, your hair color and contacts must be maintained indefinitely."

Agent Darnell sat down with Angel. "Do you have a preference for your new name?" He asked.

"Raphael Smith," Angel said. He still wanted angel as a first name and healing angel was as close as he could get. If someone said Raphael, he would automatically respond by turning his head and it would help maintain his new identity.

"The last name is not very original, but we will use it for your new identity."

Later in the week, Agent Darnell returned and gave Angel a driver's license, a new social security card, a passport, a medical license, an undergraduate degree, and a medical degree. All of his documents showed his new name with a Los Angeles address. Agent Darnell assisted him in opening a bank account online using his new identity.

"We will need to cash out all your existing bank accounts and savings accounts," Agent Darnell said. "The cash can then be redeposited or used for expenses."

"I only have one checking account in my old name. It has a little over four thousand dollars remaining in the account."

Angel did not say that Tyzugmod provided a cash advance while cashing out his first stock option for ten thousand shares. Angel had used the cash advance to pay off his student loans and the balance he owed Rob for the bail. Plus, he paid for the medical equipment and supplies he had purchased. Angel currently had no debt. Tyzugmod had announced the approval by the FDA, which had gotten some publicity, but when Angel announced the FDA approval on the Harrieta Connor Show, it went viral. Everyone wanted to own stock in the company. The company would make billions of dollars every year for the life of the patent, which was twenty years.

"Write me a check payable to cash for the exact amount in the old account," Agent Darnell said. "I will close the account and bring you the cash." Angel wrote out the check and gave it to Agent Darnell.

George had an estate attorney prepare new documents for Angel, including a will and a trust using the new name of Raphael Smith. At Angel's request, Agent Darnell had one of his assistants pick up the documents from George's office. Angel wanted to make sure everything would go to his mother in the event of his death. Angel signed the Documents in front of two witnesses and a notary. The agents served as the witnesses, and they brought a notary from their office.

George had included two personal notes with the documents. The first note told him to call Lorenzo asap. The second note was about Donald Bailey. George had worked out a plea deal for Mr. Bailey and it was precisely as he had previously explained to Angel. Mr. Bailey pleaded guilty to involuntary manslaughter and received the minimum sentence under Florida law. The judge sentenced Bailey to nine years and four months. If they had gone to trial and Bailey had been found guilty of manslaughter with a firearm, he would have faced 30 years in prison. Also, they could have added three additional years for each non-lethal shooting, bringing the total to 36 years.

Angel still felt partially responsible for one person being dead and another serving over nine years in prison. Still, it was not a complete tragedy since ten-year-old Thomas Bailey was responding to the cancer drug and would live a full life. Mrs. Bailey sent a letter to Angel thanking him for saving their son. In the letter, she explained how her husband was also thankful. He gave up nine years to save his son. He considered it a bargain since he would have given his life. However, he was genuinely sorry his actions resulted in the death of another human being.

Later in the day, Angel opened a brokerage account in the name of the trust with his new name as Trustee of the Trust. He then called Tyzugmod and transferred the proceeds from the sale of options to the brokerage account less the advanced payments he had previously received. The net proceeds were slightly over one million, two hundred thousand dollars. He transferred the amount above one million dollars to his new checking account. At Agent Darnell's prompting, he had already canceled all the utilities and other services at his apartment. He deleted everything under his old name, including the electronic subscriptions.

Agent Darnell sat down with Angel. "There is a medical clinic about a hundred miles south of Fairbanks, Alaska, which needs a doctor. They have been without a doctor for over a year. The clinic is in Etzuta with approximately two thousand people, but there are another three thousand people in the surrounding area. I suggest you go there for two years. By then, everyone will have forgotten about you. You can then keep your new identity and move wherever you want."

Angel was shaking his head no but said: "Okay."

Agent Darnell continued. "An FBI jet will take you to Fairbanks. Our main office in Alaska is in Anchorage, but we have a satellite office in Fairbanks. One of our agents will assist you upon your arrival."

"There is one more thing I would like you to do for me," Angel said. "I want to pay off the mortgage on my mother's home, and I want to buy her a new car, but I cannot do it directly. I want your help to pay the money from my account so it cannot be traced back to Raphael Smith."

"We can prepare the transfer through our wire services that cannot be traced."

"Can someone from your office explain to my mother the circumstances of my disappearance?" Angel asked. Agent Darnell nodded.

"I will provide her with enough of an explanation to put her mind at ease without providing information that could jeopardize your new identity. I will set up a method for her to send letters to you through our office, and you can do the same in reverse. We will provide you and your mother with a secure email account on our server, which the two of you can use. Regardless, you must not contact each other directly. I will help her with the car purchase and the satisfaction of her home mortgage."

The following morning Angel boarded an FBI jet at the Miami Opa Locka Executive Airport for his flight to Alaska.

AUTHOR'S COMMENTS - SEQUEL

THE THRILLS CONTINUE
IN
ANGEL IN HIDING

Thank you for reading Hospital Angel. If you liked it, please tell your friends, and consider writing a review.

I am currently working on the sequel. The next book in the series is *Angel In Hiding*. The FBI gave Angel a new identity. They helped him find a job as a doctor at a small town in central Alaska between Fairbanks and Anchorage. The FBI flew him to Fairbanks and dropped him off at a hotel. At that point, they were no longer responsible for him. The small town between Fairbanks and Anchorage welcomed him since they had been without a doctor for over a year. Angel expands the clinic and starts a secret cancer center using the cancer drug. Unfortunately, his enemies find him. He flees into the Alaska wilderness while being chased by paid assassins from Miami. First, he must survive the wilderness. Even if he stays ahead of the assassins and survives a deadly blizzard, another group of expert killers from Europe is patiently waiting for him. The second book in the series contains suspense, adventure, intrigue, violence, humor, and romance.

ABOUT THE AUTHOR

JESS LEVINS grew up on a farm in Plant City, Florida before obtaining degrees from five universities including two doctorates. He is an attorney, engineer, and financial analyst. Over the years he has worked as a waiter, bartender, engineer, attorney, and corporate executive. At an early age, he participated in extreme sports. He has traveled extensively throughout North America, South America, and Europe. He believes in the holistic lifestyle as presented in Hospital Angel. He currently lives in Fort Myers, Florida.

Visit www.JessLevins.com[1] to find out about future novels.

Don't miss out!

Visit the website below and you can sign up to receive emails whenever Jess Levins publishes a new book. There's no charge and no obligation.

https://books2read.com/r/B-A-XSXT-HPFAC

BOOKS 2 READ

Connecting independent readers to independent writers.

www.ingramcontent.com/pod-product-compliance
Lightning Source LLC
Chambersburg PA
CBHW020911200626
46814CB00001BA/279